Lene Aurousseau

Claire François

Rae Taylor

Misha Jur

I'm in LOVE with the VILLAINESS

NOVEL

3

WRITTEN BY

Inori

ILLUSTRATED BY

Hanagata

Airship

Seven Seas Entertainment

WATASHI NO OSHI WA AKUYAKU REIJOU 3

© INORI 2020
Illustrated by Hanagata

This edition originally published in Japan in 2020 by
AINAKA SHUPPAN, INC. Shizuoka.
English translation rights arranged with
AINAKA SHUPPAN, INC. Shizuoka.

Seven Seas press and purchase enquiries can be sent to
Marketing Manager Lianne Sentar at press@gomanga.com.
Information regarding the distribution and purchase of
digital editions is available from Digital Manager CK Russell
at digital@gomanga.com.

Follow Seven Seas Entertainment online at
sevenseasentertainment.com.

TRANSLATION: Kevin Ishizaka
ADAPTATION: Nibedita Sen
COVER DESIGN: Nicky Lim
LOGO DESIGN: George Panella
INTERIOR LAYOUT & DESIGN: Clay Gardner
PROOFREADER: Meg van Huygen, Jade Gardner
LIGHT NOVEL EDITOR: E.M. Candon
PREPRESS TECHNICIAN: Rhiannon Rasmussen-Silverstein
PRODUCTION MANAGER: Lissa Pattillo
MANAGING EDITOR: Julie Davis
ASSOCIATE PUBLISHER: Adam Arnold
PUBLISHER: Jason DeAngelis

ISBN: 978-1-64827-557-9
Printed in China
First Printing: July 2021
10 9 8 7 6 5 4 3 2

Table of Contents

CHAPTER 9
Our New Life
7

CHAPTER 10
The Imperial Academy
93

CHAPTER 11
The Assassination of the Pope
187

Bonus Stories
267

BONUS CHAPTER
The Lady Who Leapt Through Time
333

Afterword
451

9

Our New Life

"**D**ON'T JUST SIT THERE! Out with it already! What are your thoughts on my cooking?"

When the young lady with golden curls spat those words at me, I didn't really understand what was happening. She looked at me as if the very sight of my face infuriated her. I told myself to stay calm and assess the situation. Nothing good could come of panic.

I was seated in an average-sized house—well, I say average, but it was really quite spacious compared to the house I'd grown up in. I was with the young lady with golden curls and two adorable little girls, all seated around a table. The problem: no one I could see, including the young lady, looked even remotely Japanese.

Putting the young lady aside for the time being, I racked my memory to retrace the steps I'd taken to get here. Ohh—I remembered now. I'd been transported to this world resembling medieval Europe (with strange touches of Japanese influence), where I'd met her.

"Ahh," I said. "Miss Claire?"

"Well, I never! You're back to using 'Miss' again! How many times have I told you to just call me 'Claire'?!"

That shrill voice was unmistakable. The girl with the golden curls was Claire François, a character in one of my favorite dating sims, *Revolution*. She was also my beloved wife.

"Miss Claire."

"That's better," Claire huffed. "I much prefer it when you're not so formal—wait, you haven't changed a thing!"

"Do you remember my name?"

"Whatever is the matter with you, Rae Taylor?"

I was beginning to understand what had happened. On the table in front of me sat a plate piled high with food—if you could call it that. Based on the circumstances, my guess was I'd suffered something akin to an out-of-body experience after eating Claire's cooking.

My original name was Rei Ohashi, but Rae Taylor was the name I had in this world. As of this moment, I lived a life of domestic bliss with Claire and our sweet twin daughters, little May and Aleah.

"Yahoo!" I cheered.

"Wh-what? Are you feeling all right? And don't use vulgar expressions like 'yahoo.' You're setting a bad example for May and Aleah." Claire began to spout complaints, but I paid her no mind. For a moment, I'd almost thought the past year had all been a dream—that meeting Claire, the bond we nurtured, the friends that supported us, the near-insurmountable wall known as revolution, and even the days of peace after it were all over.

But it hadn't been a dream.

"Miss Claire."

"What is it? And don't you think it's about time you dropped the 'Miss'?"

"I like you."

"Huh?" Claire looked puzzled.

"Miss Claire, I love you."

"Wh...wh-wh-what...?!" As my words sank in, Claire rapidly grew flustered. She was too cute. Undoubtedly, the person I loved most in this world.

My favorite character in *Revolution* wasn't one of the boys the game set you up to choose from. It was Claire. Claire François, the villainess who bullies the heroine, becomes her rival, and finally loses to her. The daughter of an aristocratic family, with a wicked personality to boot, who always caused the main character trouble. But that was all in the past, of course.

This was Claire. This was the villainess, and I was completely smitten.

She held on to her pride to the bitter end, and her beautiful voice rang like a bell. Her mean streak, however, had been absent as of late. Even though she was sitting right there, I couldn't help but grin as I remembered our time together. Claire always behaved so cruelly to the protagonist, but I loved her so much that I welcomed the disdain. Each and every aspect of her was dear to me. Claire was a saint, and I her follower, helplessly in love. I had a bad case of Claire fever, and there was no cure.

"What in the world are you saying, Rae?! And in front of the children, too!"

"Is it bad if we're here?" May asked.

"Why?" Aleah questioned.

"Ah, no, don't worry about it, my dears. You'll understand when you're older. Honestly, Rae... There's a time and place for these things!"

"What's the matter?" I asked. "I'm just saying 'I love you,' that's all."

"H-hmph! You think saying that will get you on my good side? Well, it's pointless. My affection for you is already as high as it can be!" Claire turned away in a huff.

"You're so cute..." Oops. The words fell out of my mouth before I could stop them.

"Wh...wh-wha...!" Claire looked even more upset. "You... Are you...horny?!"

"No, I'm—well, that's irrelevant to cuteness, because, Miss Claire, you are cute."

She went silent as her face turned crimson. How perfect— such an innocent reaction.

"Does Miss Claire love me?"

"O-of course!"

"Then everything's fine. Please keep loving me as much as you can."

"Wh-what in the world is with you today, Rae?" Claire began to look at me with worry.

"Now, let's get this super fun dinner started, Miss Claire! We're going to have a great time!"

"What is this sense of déjà vu?"

With the revolution over, I could now spend my days doting on my beloved Claire to my heart's content. It was safe to say I'd earned it.

"Anyway, are you all right?" Claire pressed. "It seemed you weren't with us for a moment there."

"I was so overcome with awe at Miss Claire's cooking that I blacked out."

"Oh, please."

"No, really. I saw a million-dollar view from atop the highest floor of a skyscraper!"

"A million dolls? Sky staple?"

Oops. I'd absentmindedly described the sights that had flashed before my eyes during my out-of-body experience, confusing Claire. I didn't understand the scene I'd seen either, to be fair. I'd never actually laid eyes on such a vista in my past life.

"Never mind, it's nothing. I'm okay now."

"Really? If you say so..."

I was living the dream. To think a day would come when Claire would be genuinely concerned for my well-being! Now all that was left was for her to open those cherry-pink lips of hers and scold me!

"Rae?"

"Yes, yes, yes?" If I had a tail, it definitely would have been wagging. However—

"Are you really...okay? You sure you're not just stressed because I was asked to go to the empire?"

Oh. That was right... The second act of my life in another world was looking bright—or at least, it had been. In truth, the months of peace we'd enjoyed were about to come to an end.

Let's rewind a month.

It had been a little over a year since the revolution.

"Miss Claire, do you have everything?" I called out to Claire as she put her shoes on at the entrance to our house, about to head to work.

"Rae, just how old do you think I am?" She shot me a glare.

Even that glare of yours is wonderful, Miss Claire!

"I believe you're turning seventeen soon." It would be unthinkable for me to forget her age. In fact, I'd long been fantasizing about all the things I would do for her approaching birthday.

"That's right, seventeen. The two of us are already adults raising children, are we not?"

"I'm well aware. Regardless, do you have your handkerchief?" I asked, also well aware of how overbearing I was being.

"Of course," Claire curtly replied.

"And some tissues?"

"Of course."

"And your lunch box?"

"Of course."

"I spiked it with something special this time."

"Of cour—you did what?!"

"Relax, I'm obviously joking!"

"It doesn't sound like a joke when you say it." Claire sighed, seeming exhausted all of a sudden.

"What's with the long face, Miss Claire? You can't go in looking like that."

"And whose fault do you think it is?!"

It was mine, of course. All intentional, too. Tee hee.

"Mama Claire, you still haven't gone to work?"

"Won't you be late?"

Teasing Claire had run longer than I realized. May and Aleah approached, finished with their breakfast.

"Did you two clean up?" Claire asked.

"Uh-huh!"

"Yes, Mother."

"Very good. I'll be off, then. I leave them to you, Rae."

"Of course. Have a nice day."

"Have a nice day!" the twins called together.

We all waved goodbye to Claire's bouncing curls. This was our routine. Claire and I now taught at the Royal Academy, meaning we usually both left for work together, but occasionally, one of us could stay home. Today was such a day.

"Shall we brush our teeth, then?" I asked the girls.

"Yeah!"

"Yes, Mother!"

May and Aleah generally obeyed directions, but they had grown more willful of late. Despite the added trouble this caused, I was glad they'd come to a place where they could both state their own desires, considering the difficult lives they'd led. I found myself smiling as I watched them brush their teeth.

"Mother Rae, check me, please!"

"Me too! Me too!"

"All right, one at a time now."

Aleah climbed onto me right after I sat on the carpet. She opened her mouth wide, allowing me to brush her cute, neat little rows of baby teeth.

"All done. Next up, May."

"Thank you very much, Mother."

"Move, Aleah! It's my turn!"

May—the rowdier of the two—practically pushed Aleah aside as she climbed into my lap. I gave her teeth a thorough brushing, like I'd done with Aleah's. "All done! Make sure you gargle now."

"Okay!"

May ran off to the washroom, her feet making adorable pitter-patter sounds as she went. In my former life, those of my friends who had children always described parenthood as an uphill battle, which made me thankful that May and Aleah were so easy to deal with. Claire and I lacked experience as caregivers, but the girls had yet to give us any real trouble. We occasionally struggled to calm them down when they cried, but I had a feeling that didn't compare to the ordeals my friends had faced.

Soon, it would be a full year since we'd adopted May and Aleah. They'd changed so much in that time. It was hard to imagine now, given their current happiness, but their eyes had once been devoid of life, just like a doll's.

Then again, perhaps the battles my friends had described were merely yet to come.

"Ah! Mother Rae, May spilled water!"

"Aleah! Why'd you tattle? I was going to wipe it! Meanie!"

This kerfuffle interrupted my thoughts. I picked up a couple of cleaning cloths and headed to the washroom, where May sheepishly met my eyes as she tried to wipe up the spill with a small towel.

"May, thank you for cleaning up your mistake," I said.

"He he!"

"But let's make sure we use a cleaning cloth, not the towels."

"Sorry..."

"It's okay, you didn't know. Now then, shall we clean up together?" I handed one of the cloths to May and watched as she furiously got to wiping.

"That's not fair! Only May got praised!"

"Do you want to help too, Aleah? I have another cloth here."

"Yes, please! May, it's a contest! Let's see who can wipe more!"

"I won't lose!"

I couldn't help but smile as I watched the twins. Aleah was as stubborn as Claire, constantly challenging her sister at every turn. I guess children took after their parents, even if they didn't share blood.

"We're finished, Mother!"

"Done!"

"Spick-and-span. Good job, you two."

I stroked the top of their soft heads. The girls smiled happily back at me, and we all lived happily ever after. The end.

Well, that was what I'd like to say. But—

"Who did better, Mother?"

"Yeah, who?"

"Umm..."

They inched closer to me. I thought they might be joking for a moment, but their serious eyes said otherwise.

"Can't we just say you both did well?"

"Unacceptable! Please choose one of us!"

"Who won?!"

"U-umm..."

Children tended to get hung up on the strangest things. I couldn't just play it off for now either; just a year of being a parent had taught me I'd regret that down the line.

"Do you know how we tell good cleaning from bad?" I tried changing the focus a bit.

"I don't know."

"How?"

"The first factor is thoroughness. We can say Aleah is a winner because she wiped the most vigorously."

"So I'm the winner!" Aleah proudly declared.

In contrast, May furrowed her lips and began to pout. "Aww..."

"But cleaning a wide area is also important," I continued. "In that sense, May is a winner."

"Yay!"

"Huh?" This time, Aleah pouted as May celebrated.

"So it's a tie."

"Huh?!" And now they both looked displeased.

Good grief. "Is something wrong?"

"Yes, something's wrong!"

"I don't like it!"

"Would you prefer it if I chose one of you randomly?"

"I wouldn't like that..."

"Yeah..."

"That's why it's a draw. You both did your best." I stroked their heads again, but they still looked grumpy. "Why don't you go play in the yard? I still have some cleaning to do. Ralaire, can you come here?"

A semi-transparent, amorphous creature came creeping forth at my call. This was Ralaire, my water slime familiar. These days, she was the size of a large dog, which was normal for adult water slimes. I missed the days when I could carry her in my school bag and feed her treats.

"Ralaire, can I have a piggyback ride?" Aleah asked. Ralaire extended her arms—or whatever you'd call her amorphous tendrils—and heaved Aleah onto her back. "May, you too!"

It seemed the competition was over. Perhaps Aleah wanted to make amends by inviting May to join her?

"Yeah! Ralaire, me too, please!"

Ralaire easily scooped May up as well before heading out the front door to the yard.

"Faster, Ralaire, faster!"

"Right! Go right!"

Ralaire was May and Aleah's best friend. Other children their age also lived in the neighborhood, but our girls spent all their time playing with Ralaire. I didn't know how to feel about that. I had to discuss it with Claire later.

"Well... I'm sure it'll turn out all right."

Parenting was about trial and error. Sometimes, that meant you had to let go and allow nature to take its course. No parent was omniscient, after all.

I never once regretted coming to this world. But after raising my own children, I wished I'd had a chance to thank my real parents for raising me. There were just some things you couldn't appreciate until you had children of your own.

"Waaah!"

"Mama Rae! Aleah fell down!"

"Coming!"

Goodness. No time for being sentimental, it seemed. But strangely enough, I didn't mind being kept busy one bit.

"Um, Mother Rae?"

"There's something we want to ask."

Just past noon on a holiday, May and Aleah approached me while I was reading a book at the table out on our terrace. They didn't come to me like this very often—they usually went to Claire, who was currently working on her embroidery in the living room.

"What is it?"

"Um, what does—"

"What does Mama Rae like about Mama Claire?"

"Aleah!" May frowned. "I was asking first!"

How shocking. They were only six; had they already taken an interest in romance? While I knew girls tended to develop interest in such topics earlier than boys, this still seemed early. My, what precocious children.

"No fighting, you two," I chided. "Hmm... That's a tough question. I can only say I love everything about her."

They squealed in unison, placing their hands on their cheeks. The reaction felt just a touch too mature for them. They couldn't have been transported from another world like me, could they?

"Oh, but Miss Claire was pretty different when I first met her," I said.

"How so?"

"Tell us, tell us!"

The two of them looked at me expectantly. They adored Claire. Of course, I considered myself second to none when it came to loving her—not even them.

"Well, she was a lot more high-strung when we first met. Of course, Claire's great as she is now, but I'll never forget how wonderful she was when her pride was stacked high as the ceiling." *Ahh, how I wish she'd scold me again...* But those days were long gone.

"High...strung?"

"Stacked...pride?"

They seemed confused as to what I meant.

"Yes." I thought back to when I had just met Miss Claire. "If I had to put it simply...she was the very embodiment of those confident aristocrats who put their hand over their mouth and laugh 'Oh ho ho!' She always bullied me directly rather than use her underlings to do her dirty work for her. She'd insult me to my face, telling me how she couldn't stand the sight of me, but being the kind of person who acted first and thought second, she never anticipated that her insults would only make me happier—backfiring on her to the point where she'd break down in tears. Her voice is also just perfect: it's energetic like a young puppy's, but cute and high-pitched like a cat's, so you're covered irrespective of which you prefer, and—"

"M-Mother Rae, please stop!"

"Please, calm down!"

Oops—I'd gotten carried away. My daughters began to pat me, saying "there, there," which I sometimes did to calm *them* down. I didn't know how to feel about that.

"Do you understand now?" I asked.

"Not one bit!" they said in unison.

"Oh. Well, the main thing is that Miss Claire is cute."

"I can understand that!"

"Mother Claire is always cute!"

"Very good! All together now, ready? Oh ho ho ho!"

"Oh ho ho ho!" we chorused together.

That was the end of that conversation. I was so happy May and Aleah had come to talk to me—so happy, in fact, that I never noticed Claire listening in.

For some reason, Claire stepped on my foot.

"O-oh, pardon me!" she stammered. "I-I-I...thought you were an insect!"

"Is something the matter, Miss Claire?"

"Huh? Umm...a-ah! You've been cheeky, Rae!"

"Hmm?"

I've been cheeky? Huh...

"I apologize if I offended you in any way, but I don't recall doing anything."

"Th-that's not what I meant!"

"It's not?"

"F-forget about it!" Claire stormed off.

What was that all about?

A while later, Claire hid one of my books. "What's wrong? Is your measly salary not enough to buy books?"

"Our salaries are the same, though."

"O-oh, right..."

"Actually, I'm pretty sure I have more savings than you." I frowned. *Why is she bringing up salary? Unless...* "I'll try my best to make more money!"

"N-no, you're fine as you are! That's not what I'm getting at!"

"It's not?"

"N-ngh! Rae, you meanie!" Claire stormed off once again.

Huh? What in the world's going on?

And now, I was being left out.

"He he. May and Aleah only want to play with me now! How's that?"

"Oh..." A tear welled up in my eye.

"Y-you're actually crying?!"

"It's fine. I'm happy as long as you three are happy. I'll just settle for watching from a distance..."

"Go comfort Rae, you two."

"Okay!"

"There, there, Mother Rae."

I was consoled by my daughters. Ahhh, bliss.

Later that night, Claire doused me with hot water—which didn't feel out of place at all, since we were both in the bath.

"Oh, dear," she started. "You were just so dirty, I th—"

"Oh, thank you very much. I was just about to wash my hair."

"H-huh?"

I grabbed the soap bottle and began to wash Claire's hair. "Your hair is beautiful, Miss Claire."

"Th-thank you very much... Wait, that's not it!"

"Is this too rough?"

"No, it feels wonderful."

My talents had been recognized. I could die happy now.

After the bath, there were flowers waiting for me on the table.

"How about that?!" Claire declared.

"Oh, what lovely flowers. They've been arranged wonderfully, too."

Claire was silent.

"Miss Claire?" Surprised, I looked over at her. She looked put out for some reason. "What's the matter?"

"I'm fed up with this..."

"You've been acting odd today."

"And whose fault do you think that is?!" Claire howled. Even her angry face was lovely.

"Miss Claire."

"What do you want?"

"Thank you for showing me your villainess side again."

"So you did notice?!"

Of course. It was obvious she'd been trying to replicate what she first did to me at the Academy. "I loved watching you try to play the villainess."

"Of course you did. You were teasing me the whole time!"

"Yep! Thank you very much!"

"Oh! Well, you're so very welcome! I'm going to bed!" Claire rushed to the bedroom. I stopped her by grabbing her arm.

"Miss Claire, won't you try saying you hate me?"

"Huh? What for?"

"To put the finishing touch on your villainess routine."

"Honestly..." Claire sighed. While she sounded like she dreaded the idea, she still turned around and faced me with a determined look on her face. "Very well then. I—"

"Yes?"

"L-L-Lo—no, I mean—h-h-haa...h-h-haa—"

"You're almost there, Miss Claire! Don't give up!" I cheered her on as her face turned red as a beet.

"—aaate you!"

"It's over, Miss Claire! You did it! You really did it!" I praised Miss Claire as if she were a hero who'd just won an epic battle.

"It was difficult...so unbelievably difficult..."

"You've done well."

"It seems I can no longer curse you as I once could."

"He he. You must love me lots, then."

"I do. You better take responsibility."

"Of course."

Claire smiled. She linked her arm with mine and rested her head on my shoulder. Together, we disappeared into the bedroom.

Meanwhile, our daughters were talking in their room.

"What was Mama Claire doing today?" May asked.

"I know! Sister Lene told me! It's something called 'S and M play.'"

Of course, Claire and I were oblivious to their conversation.

We stood on the Royal Academy's athletic field as a tender

sun befitting of early spring shone down on us, the chill of winter almost entirely gone.

"Good morning, everyone!"

"Good morning!" Twenty or so students cheerfully returned my greeting, all wearing Academy uniforms and radiating motivation. Today was the start of the spring semester, making this our first meeting.

My first year of teaching had taught me the importance of making a good first impression. If your students thought you weak, they'd walk all over you. It wasn't as bad as when the student body had been mostly nobles, but even commoners could be ruthless if they smelled blood in the water. That said, you didn't want to come across as too strict either. You had to strike a balance.

"Nice to meet you, everyone. I'm Rae Taylor, and I'll be teaching you practical magic. Let's have a good semester. Oh, please also be kind to Miss François, who'll be teaching you magic theory."

Practical magic and magic theory were new subjects established last year. As their names suggested, they covered practical implementation of magic and academic approaches to the same, respectively, and had previously been lumped together with general magic classes. I was better at practical magic, while Claire had a better grasp of theory. Combined with our high magic aptitude, this made us the best candidates to teach the new classes.

"Seeing as it's only the first day and no one's measured their magic aptitude yet, let's start off by introducing ourselves and then going over what the class will cover."

But first—

"As I explained earlier, my name is Rae Taylor. Please call me Miss Taylor." Personally, I had no problem being called Miss Rae, but as a teacher, I had to set some boundaries. "Some of you are older than me, but please understand that I ask this not as a matter of age, but one of respect."

The Academy differed from modern-day Japanese schools in that students of different ages could be put in the same class. It had been the same way back when I was a student.

"But of course!" a student exclaimed. "Miss Taylor, you're the legend who achieved the highest test score in the history of the academy, all while in your first year!"

Oh, no... Not this again.

"Aren't you also a hero of the revolution, Miss Taylor?!"

"It's an honor to be taught by you!"

"Please show us your ultra-high aptitude magic!"

The students all began speaking at once. Jeez.

For better or worse, I had made a bit of a name for myself in the Bauer Kingdom. I hadn't done much—a bit of this, a bit of that—and somehow, I still wound up being considered one of the key figures of the revolution. But I mean, really? The entire time, I'd had nothing on my mind but stopping Claire's execution.

At any rate, I had to do something about this situation. Maybe I could try that thing I did last year again?

"Is anyone here afraid of heights?" I asked.

"Nope!"

"Not a problem!"

"More importantly, show us your ultra-high apt—"

No one? Up they go, then!

"Uplift!" The earth rose from underneath my students' feet, lifting them thirty feet or so into the air. It was the opposite version of the pitfall magic I used to toy with Claire.

"Wh-whoa!"

"S-so high!"

"Eek!"

Psychologically speaking, thirty feet felt higher than it actually was. Furthermore, I lifted them each individually instead of as one big group, giving them frighteningly little space to stand on. Naturally, I was ready to catch any student who fell—but they didn't know that.

"Please don't interrupt me while I'm talking," I called up to them. "If you do, I might have to punish you like this. *Are we clear?*"

The students furiously nodded.

"Very good. I'll lower you all down now."

The students breathed a sigh of relief as they returned to level ground.

"Let's have you introduce yourselves, then. Starting from the right."

The students gave me no further problems. Sometimes you had to show you meant business to make them listen to you. Of course, as I mentioned earlier, that didn't mean you should be a tyrant. You needed to earn their attention by proving you had something real to teach them—hence the earth magic. While students of the Academy tended to be gifted or privileged, they still hadn't received any training in the practical application of magic. Many students hadn't so much as *seen* magic before.

But just showing off wouldn't earn me their respect. That's why I lifted them into the air—to show I was serious while also driving home how terrifying magic could be when handled correctly.

I listened to the students introduce themselves while observing their expressions. Most of them were still reeling from the shock of being lifted. Occasionally, a student would introduce themself with a shout, but that wasn't anything more than false bravado. Charming in its own way, though, I had to say.

"Hey, guys! Nice to meetcha! I'm Lana Lahna and I come from Euclid, just like Miss Rae!" This girl seemed a bit of an oddball. Her brown eyes sparkled with life, apparently undeterred by my earlier demonstration, and a white headband adorned her red hair. She was about the same height as me, if not slightly taller.

Her carefree smile, combined with the way she talked, reminded me of the gyaru girls I used to see in Japan.

"I'm, like, *suuuper* bad at studying, but magic looks *so* fun! I hope to be like Miss Rae one day!" Lana finished her self-introduction in one breath and started to wave at me. It seemed I had another fan. Well, given how weird I was, she should be disillusioned in no time. My condolences.

"My name's Eve Nuhn... Same hometown as Lana. Nice to meet you." An incredibly gloomy-looking girl introduced herself after Lana. She didn't seem perturbed by my display of magic either, but her personality was the polar opposite of Lana's. She had long, black hair shaped into a braid and wore glasses—a rarity in this world that hinted she came from a reasonably affluent family.

None of that bothered me. Everyone had their quirks; her gloomy demeanor didn't faze me a bit. But those eyes...

She had a death glare trained on me, like I had personally killed her parents. I racked my brain but couldn't summon any memory of her.

"I'm Joel. Joel Santana. I'm from the kingdom."

The next to introduce themselves was a tall boy with blue hair and brown eyes. The image of a lean wolf came to mind when I looked at him. Not a shred of excess fat on his body. Possibly from training?

"I come from a family of soldiers, so I can fight," Joel finished up, keeping his introduction short, to the point, and almost mechanical. "I like studying but am not very good at it. Nice to meet you."

The rest of the introductions were nothing to write home about. I finished the class by going over the warm-up exercises we would do daily at the start of each session.

"That'll be all for today."

"Thank you very much!"

Class ended and everyone dispersed. I started to make for the staff room when Lana called out to me.

"Miss Rae! There was a part I didn't understand!"

"But I haven't taught you anything yet."

"The warm-up exercises! I need help on this one—look!" Or so Lana claimed, but I couldn't see any problems in her form. I guess she simply wanted to talk to me. I didn't mind having a fan, but I already had Claire. I needed to come up with a way to let her down easy.

Then I felt a sharp, sudden gaze pierce my back and turned to see Eve glaring at me. I didn't know her deal, but if I could help it, I didn't want to start the year on bad terms with a student. I smiled and waved to her, trying to invite her to approach me, but she just scowled before spinning on her heel and walking away.

"Yikes. What's up with Eve today?" Lana said.

"I recall you and Eve both came from Euclid?"

"Ah! Miss Rae, you remembered!"

"I'm also from Euclid. Have we met each other before?"

"Nope! But we totes know about you! If anything, we're fans!"

Her enthusiasm gave me an intense feeling of déjà vu... Just my imagination, right? Right.

"Oh, but Eve has, like, a bone to pick with you or somethin'."

"Huh? Why's that."

"Something about you snatchin' her lover or whatever."

"I'm sorry, what? I'm pretty sure I've never done something like that." My heart belonged solely to Miss Claire, after all.

"That's enough about Eve," said Lana. "Why don't you ask about me now?"

"I'm sorry, but I have to leave for my next class."

"Aww! Meanie! But I like that part of you, too!"

I somehow managed to give Lana the slip and made my way to the staff room. I couldn't help but think about Eve along the way. *I snatched her lover?*

It was certainly a misunderstanding; the problem would be figuring out why such a misunderstanding happened in the first place. I need to make sure I talk to Eve later.

"Looks like this year's students will be a handful." I sighed. I watched as the vapor faded into the spring haze of the sky.

"We're all ready, Miss Claire."

"Good. Let us be off, then."

At eight in the morning, the sun still hung low in the sky. It was hard to believe it could be so cold at this time when it was already the fourth month.

"We're going on an outing!"

"Yay! Outing! Outing!"

May and Aleah wore warm jackets hand-sewn by Claire. A testament to her skill, the jackets were so high-quality that one could mistake them for products of the tailors' guild. May held Claire's hand and Aleah held mine as we walked along the path to the Bauer Cathedral.

"I can't wait to use magic!" Aleah grinned from ear to ear.

"I want the same, umm...aptitude as Mama Claire!" May smiled at Claire.

The four of us were on our way to get May and Aleah's aptitude measured. In the years post-revolution, the Bauer Kingdom had come to value magic even more highly than before. This led to compulsory magic aptitude evaluations for all citizens when they turned six. Magic aptitude could fluctuate in early childhood. Some people were born with low aptitude that increased as they aged, but even then, generally speaking, aptitude stabilized around the age of six.

May and Aleah's birthday was the thirteenth day of the twelfth month, meaning they had just turned six about four months ago. The two of them often watched as Claire and I used magic and were eager to try it for themselves. We could have started teaching them without first measuring their aptitudes, but that came with its own risks, so we'd decided to hold off until their evaluation.

"Mother Claire can use fire, right?" Aleah asked.

"That's correct. I have high aptitude in fire."

"What magic do you think I'll have?"

"Hmm, I have a feeling you'll have the wind attribute, because you're so clever," Claire answered without needing to think about it. It was true—Aleah was very clever. Perhaps it was because of her young age, but she was always a fast learner. Lilly had mentioned she learned reading and mathematics faster than May.

"What about me?" May asked, shaking Claire's hand. "What magic do you think I'll have?"

I couldn't help but notice they both asked Claire. Which was fine. I wasn't hurt at all. *Sniffle.*

"I think May will have the fire attribute. Because you're always so lively."

"Yay! I'm the same as Mother Claire!" May began hopping about like a rabbit, even though Claire's prediction was no guarantee. While Aleah couldn't be called by any means shy, May was undeniably the livelier twin. Aleah often tried to imitate adults by doing things such as standing on tiptoe to look taller, while May embraced her childish impulses.

"Aww, I wanted the same as Mother Claire..." Aleah whined.

"Well, we still don't know your aptitudes, Aleah," I said. "But even if your attribute is wind, you'll still match Lady Manaria, whom Lady Claire respects."

"I can be the same as Sister Manaria?!" Aleah's dejected face lit up as she looked at me. "Then can I be a quad-caster, too?"

"Well, I don't know about that one. The only known quad-caster in the world is Lady Manaria, after all."

"But there's a chance?"

"That's... I suppose." I didn't want to get her expectations up too high, but I just couldn't say no to that face. Children really were my weakness.

"We're here," Claire announced. Sure enough, a majestic cathedral came into view. Many families were already lined up, all with high hopes glimmering in their eyes. "Let's get in line."

"Okay!"

"Yeah!"

We joined the end of the line, which moved at a decent rate. Perhaps we wouldn't have to wait long at all.

"May, let's play the word chain game!"

"Okay!"

"You lose if you end a word with N! I'll start: 'dress.'"

"Squirrel!"

"Mmm, lizard."

"D... D... Donkey!"

"Yard."

"D... D... Dragon!"

"You lose!"

"Ah! Wait, that didn't count!"

We had only just lined up and they were already playing games—but that was children for you, I guess. This word chain game helped with their vocabulary, so Claire and I often played it with them.

"Okay, May, one more time! Starting from D."

"D... Umm, doom!"

"M? Hmm. How about mini?"

"Umm, intimate!"

"That's not a word!"

"Yeah, it is! Mama Claire and Mama Rae are always intimate with each other in their bedroom!"

Wait just a moment—did I hear that right? I broke out in a cold sweat. "M-May? What do you think that word means?"

"Huh? It means you're super nice to each other!"

"Oh... R-right..."

In my previous life, intimate could also have *that* kind of meaning. I looked over at Claire and saw a bead of sweat drip down her brow. Children could be frightening at times.

The line progressed quickly. Before we knew it, it was May and Aleah's turn. A familiar face conducted the assessment.

"It's good to see you, Miss Claire, Miss Rae."

"Oh! It's been a while," I said. This was the priest who'd taught us to perform the ceremonial dance alongside Lilly a while before the revolution. She was strict—I still bitterly remembered her training—but a trustworthy woman.

"Good morning, Miss Priest!"

"Good morning!"

"Ah. Yes... Yes, good morning, children." The priest stumbled over her words for a moment, taken by surprise as she recognized the twins. "I'm shocked. You've both become so expressive."

Oh, that was right. No wonder she was shocked—May and Aleah had still been so closed off to the world when the priest last saw them.

After losing their family in the events surrounding the revolution, the girls had wound up living in the slums, selling magic stones to survive. You see, their blood was cursed. Anything their blood touched would turn into a magic stone. Thankfully, people with strong magic of their own could resist the curse. This had led Claire and I to adopt them—but I won't get into that now. Suffice to say that before we met them, May and Aleah had been under the church's care.

"I'm so glad you both found a home." The strict priest gave us a rare smile. She must have been worried about the girls. Lilly often criticized the church for its many real problems, but people like this priest gave it meaning. "Now then, shall we begin measuring you two? Please put your hands on these crystals."

"Okay."

"Like this?"

The twins each put their hand on a spherical magic tool made of crystal. Dazzling light began to shine—but only from May's crystal.

"Oh, dear." The priest seemed troubled. She replaced the crystal under Aleah's hand in case the tool was faulty, but the second one didn't shine either. "Hmm..."

"Is there a problem?" Claire worriedly asked.

"No. At least, not from what I can currently tell. We will confirm the results and send them to you soon." It seemed the results arrived by mail at a later date. "That concludes the assessment. Thank you for coming."

Claire and I both had a bad feeling about this. Still, we decided the best we could do was to go home for now. As we headed back, May and Aleah began talking.

"I wonder what I'll get."

"Well, I just know I'll get the wind attribute. Mother Claire said so!" Aleah proudly declared.

They were so innocent and excited. My heart sank as I imagined those smiles fading.

"Picnic, picnic!"

"We're going on a picnic!"

May and Aleah held hands as they skipped before us. The trees rustled in the wind, their leaves just beginning to grow in anticipation of the coming summer.

"May, Aleah, you can skip, but you'll fall if you don't watch your step," Claire warned the twins, her casual picnic dress fluttering.

"We'll be fine!"

"Yeah! We'll be—ah!"

May fell, despite Claire's warning, bringing Aleah down with her because of their linked hands. Ralaire, oozing along by their side, tried to catch them but didn't make it in time.

"Ah... I told you so. Are you two all right?" Claire and I ran to them at once, checking them for injuries.

As I mentioned earlier, the girls had a curse in their blood. We were safe for now; Ralaire used one of her abilities to nullify the curse. Still, that didn't mean I could just go and let them sustain so much as a scratch. No girl would have her skin marred on my watch!

"Aleah, you seem all right. Good job stopping your fall. May, I see you've got a little scrape. I'm so proud of you for not crying." I praised the twins and began healing them with my water magic.

"Thank you, Mama Rae."

"Thank you, Mother."

They immediately returned to skipping while holding hands despite their fall moments before.

"Oh, those two..."

"You've really grown accustomed to motherhood, Rae." Claire smiled at me, basket swinging in her grasp.

"Not at all. Those two still run circles around me. More importantly, Miss Claire..."

"Yes?"

"Allow me to hold that basket!"

We'd brought a picnic blanket, boxed lunches, and drinks—

quite the load. Ralaire held the heaviest basket, but Claire carried the rest.

"Absolutely not. You woke up early to make this lunch for us. I can't make you carry it as well." Claire grinned. My wife was so adorable, it hurt.

"Mama Rae, what's for lunch?" May asked.

"I bet it's rice balls!"

They must have overheard the word *lunch* because they both curiously approached us now.

"We'll be having sandwiches today."

"Yay! Sandwiches! Did you make ham ones?" May adored ham sandwiches.

"Of course."

"I trust you made sure to leave the green pepper out, right, Mother Rae?" Aleah primly asked.

"Of course not."

"Bleh..."

Aleah had acquired her distaste for green pepper from Claire. While it was cute how she mimicked Claire's speech and mannerisms, I really wished she wouldn't take after her to the extent of picky eating.

"Why'd you put green pepper in?" she asked.

"Because it's very nutritious."

"But aren't there other nutritious things?"

"Well, yes..."

"Then why do I have to eat green pepper?"

"Because one day there might not be any other foods."

"I'll be a good girl and eat green pepper if that's all that's left! But is there a good reason why I have to eat it now?"

"Well..." Oh, no. Was I seriously losing an argument to a six-year-old?

"That's not the issue, Aleah," Claire began. "You mustn't be picky with your food."

"But why?"

"All food is a blessing from our God, the Great Spirit. Thus, it is rude to play favorites on your plate."

"I don't get it..."

"We must show gratitude to all the food we receive. Green peppers are living things, too."

"Really? Then green peppers are the same as me?"

"That's right."

Aleah thought for a bit. I was sure Claire's explanation had won her over, but—

"Then I won't eat them, because I'd feel bad for them."

"I see..."

We could take the easy way out and say, "That's just how things are," or "Them's the breaks," but Claire and I always did our best to explain our reasoning to the girls. A difficult task, as the current situation proved. A child's mind worked very differently from an adult's. Sometimes, when an adult explained something to a child, the adult ended up with way more to think about.

But we enjoyed it. Kids gave you a new perspective on ordinary things.

"Will you stop eating meat, then?" Claire said.

"Huh? No! I want to eat meat!"

"But meat comes from chicken, pigs, cows, and many other animals. Everything we eat comes from something living."

"Hmm..."

"All the animals and even the green peppers gave their precious lives for you, Aleah. That's why you need to show them proper gratitude."

"Hmm..." Aleah appeared deep in thought again. Surely, she was convinced this time, I thought. But: "Then why do you make a funny face whenever you eat green pepper?"

Children were formidable opponents.

We continued to talk back and forth until we arrived at a hill some ways from the house. It lay only a quick walk past the woods and was lush with short grass.

"Watch your step, you two!"

"Okay!"

"Yes, Mother!"

We had a bird's-eye view of the Bauer Kingdom from atop the hill—everything from the towering palace and cathedral to the bustling markets and residences below.

"Where's home?" May asked.

"I know! It's that one!"

"Ah, you're right. Whoa... It's so small!"

"Around here seems good." Claire placed her basket down. "Thank you for carrying that, Ralaire. Go ahead and set it down here."

Ralaire obediently plopped her basket down, and Claire and I got to work laying out the picnic sheet.

"May, Aleah, come sit down. It's time for lunch." Claire gestured to the twins to sit with us.

"Yay!"

"Lunchtime!"

The girls, who'd been enthralled by the view, snapped to attention upon hearing the word *lunch*. They took off their shoes before hopping onto the picnic sheet, staring expectantly at the picnic basket.

"Open it, Mother Rae!" May urged.

"Quickly!"

"Okay, I'm opening it. Ready? Ta-da!" I paused to build up their anticipation before dramatically flipping off the cloth covering the basket.

"Whoa! It's so pretty!"

"Indeed!"

Today's lunch consisted of three types of sandwiches: egg and scallion with mayonnaise, ham and lettuce with basil sauce, and chicken and green pepper with sweet and sour sauce, as well as fried chicken and different vegetable and fruit smoothies. I'd put a lot of thought into the menu, adding lots of vegetables to balance out the fried chicken and provide contrasting colors and textures.

"I'm hungry! Can we eat?"

"Hurry! Let's eat!"

"All right, all right. Ready? Hands together—"

"Bon appétit!"

No sooner had we said grace than May and Aleah were

reaching for the food. May went for the ham and lettuce sandwiches, while Aleah opted for the fried chicken.

"Yummy!"

"Mmm! It's delicious!"

"Glad to hear it."

It was worth waking up early if it meant I could see these satisfied faces. Claire reached out and took a chicken and green pepper sandwich.

"Oh? I thought you used green peppers in this?"

"I did."

"But I can't taste it at all—it's usually so bitter."

"Ah. That's because I chopped them up finely and made the sweet and sour sauce a bit stronger than usual."

"Very clever. Aleah, why don't you try some of this?" Noticing Aleah hadn't eaten anything but fried chicken, Claire offered her a sandwich.

"But isn't there green pepper in that?" Aleah grimaced.

"Trust me. It's delicious."

"Really?"

Reluctantly, Aleah put the sandwich into her mouth, gingerly chewing it. Her expression slowly brightened. "Ooh. It's delicious!"

Those few words sent me over the moon.

"There's no icky green pepper taste, and the sauce is yummy."

"Ha ha, thank you, dear. Make sure you eat lots, then," I said.

"Ah! Me too!" May said.

Walking must have made them hungry, as the sandwiches were gone in no time.

"That was yummy!"

"Yeah!"

"Truly. Thank you for another wonderful meal, Rae."

"Anything for you three."

Just seeing them eat so happily made all my efforts worthwhile. I chatted with the other ladies in the neighborhood every so often, and apparently their husbands didn't so much as say a word of thanks after eating—even when they made croquettes! And making croquettes was far from easy. Incidentally, the one who distributed the recipe for croquettes after Mt. Sassal's eruption was yours truly.

"Should we relax a little before heading back?" I suggested.

"Sounds good."

"Can we go play?"

"I want to pick flowers!"

"Go ahead. But don't go too far, okay? And take Ralaire with you."

"Okay!" They dashed off to a flowery area with Ralaire in tow.

"It's been a while since we've been able to relax as a family like this." I spoke to no one in particular as the gentle breeze brushed my cheeks.

"Indeed. It's not often we both have a day off that isn't spent on shopping or housework."

"Taking care of them doesn't leave much time for rest either."

"I'm glad we came today. Thank you, Rae." Claire kissed me softly. It had been my idea to have a picnic.

"I know we're both worried about the aptitude assessment, so I thought we could go out for a change of pace."

"And it was a good idea. Just look how happy May and Aleah are."

There was a decent chance the aptitude assessment result wouldn't be great. That was why I'd suggested we go out. Perhaps for our sakes more than the children's...

"I'm hoping for the best, but reality can be harsh." Claire frowned.

"There's no point worrying about it now. The results should arrive soon. Until then, let's enjoy ourselves as much as we can."

"Yes. Yes, you're right." Claire shook her head in an attempt to dispel her negative thoughts and then smiled. "We overcame that mess of a revolution together. I'm sure we can both overcome whatever lies ahead as well."

"No, Claire. That's wrong."

"Hmm?" Claire tilted her head in confusion.

I couldn't help but grin at her. "It's the four of us from here on out."

"Ah. He he, that's right." Her face seemed to say *you got me there*. I couldn't resist her cuteness. This time, it was my turn to give her a kiss.

I held Claire in my arms as we enjoyed the quiet spring afternoon.

"How were they?" Claire asked.

"I managed to get them to sleep, but Aleah was acting strange."

"I see..." Claire furrowed her brows with worry. It was 8:00 p.m., and she was already in her pajamas. but instead of moving to the bedroom like usual, we sat down across from each other at the living room table to talk. I'd brewed some tea, as I had a feeling it would be a long discussion.

"I still can't believe Aleah has no aptitude."

The assessment results had arrived, and it was just as we feared.

"She was looking forward to using magic so much." Claire looked pained.

Both girls had been excited about using magic, but it was clear Aleah longed for it more than her sister. Aleah adored Claire and wanted to be like her in every regard, to the point where she mimicked her speech patterns. Naturally, this meant she wanted to use magic like Claire as well. Fire magic had to look astounding to a child's eyes, even more so when Claire so elegantly controlled it.

"How should we tell them?" Claire asked. We hadn't broken the news to them yet. The children, possibly sensing our unease, hadn't asked us either.

"I almost wish they *both* had no aptitude—as cruel as it is to say." The problem was the disparity. If May had no aptitude as well, then we wouldn't have been so worried. They'd both be disappointed, of course, but they'd bounce back quickly and find new goals to pursue.

"Indeed. But May is a quad-caster. It's practically her *duty* to learn to use magic."

Indeed—May was now the second confirmed quad-caster in the world. As Claire said, this left her no choice but to pursue a magical path. Aptitude was immutable and inherent; neither hard work nor genetics could affect what elemental affinity you were born with. If they could, the twins wouldn't have such drastically differing abilities.

"We can't hide it from them forever. They didn't say anything today on our account, but it's only a matter of time before they ask." Claire let out a deep sigh. Smart as she was, she clearly had no idea what to do.

"Maybe it's best we tell them straight?" I suggested. "Get it over with, rather than beat around the bush."

"Only someone who's never had to worry about their capacity could say such a thing." Claire frowned at me.

"Never had to worry about their capacity... That'd be you, wouldn't it?" From my perspective, Claire was nothing if not gifted. Outside of her inability to cook, she was perfect in every regard.

"Don't forget, Rae. You're a dual-caster, with ultra-high aptitude at that. I still haven't forgotten the humiliation I suffered when we competed over the first test results."

"You're not wrong." But I was pretty sure that was as far as my notable talents went.

Claire sighed. "I'm aware I'm more gifted than most. Yet sometimes, I can't help feeling I can never compare to those who've truly mastered their craft. You know what they call people like me? Jack of all trades, master of none."

"Such a phrase doesn't do you justice, Miss Claire. I think your many talents are wonderful." I pointed at the embroidery on the wall as I spoke.

"Even so, being forced to face your own shortcomings can hurt."

"I'm made aware of that every day I spend with you."

"Don't tease me." Claire gently flicked me on the forehead.

I rubbed my temple as an idea surfaced. "Hey, Miss Claire."

"Hmph. What is it?"

"There's something bothering me about the aptitude results."

Claire straightened and positioned herself for listening. "Go on."

"Even if we chalk up Aleah's results to bad luck, aren't May's results still astronomically rare? This feels rather improbable."

"Improbable? How so?"

"Well, to start, Aleah having no aptitude at all can't be right!"

Claire wore a sad smile. "Rae... I think your bias as a parent is affecting your judgment."

"No, think about it. Their blood is cursed."

"Ah." My implication finally dawned on her.

Both girls bore a curse that made everything their blood touched turn into magical stones. Not just May—*both* girls.

"We don't understand how curses and magic aptitude might be connected," I said, "but isn't it deeply unlikely that there's *no* connection?"

"That's true. But then, why does Aleah have no aptitude?"

"Well, I have an idea, but it's nothing more than a theory."

"I'm listening," Claire urged me to continue. A glimmer of hope had returned to her eyes, as I'd been sure it would. The thought of only Aleah being deprived of magic had really been eating away at her.

"I think they were touched by something while they were in the womb," I said. "Something that determines magical aptitude. And I think that it affected them on opposite ends of some spectrum."

"Is such a thing possible?"

"We can't say it isn't."

I'd seen an American movie about twins in my previous life, starring that super macho guy, Schwarz-something or the other. It was a story about two brothers, one incredibly gifted and the other incredibly inept, who were trying to find their mother. It was pure fiction, of course, but part of the plot centered on how all of the talent had been concentrated in one twin at birth. In this strange world where magic was real, I couldn't entirely rule out the possibility of something similar happening.

"Supposing you're right," Claire said. "It still doesn't help Aleah."

"I wouldn't be so sure."

"And why's that?"

"I have another theory, although it is reliant on the previous one being true. If we suppose Aleah isn't naturally without aptitude but somehow *became* this way, then something must be causing it!"

"Even so, it doesn't change the fact she's currently stuck with no aptitude."

"Yes, but that's only within the scope of our current understanding of magic." There was a chance—however slim—that whatever was affecting Aleah went beyond what we knew.

"You're grasping at straws."

"Perhaps."

"We shouldn't tell Aleah this. Nothing good can come from getting her hopes up over a fleeting possibility."

"But—"

I tried to argue, but Claire raised her hand to stop me. "Calm down, Rae. We're both too worked up right now."

"You're right... I'm sorry. I got a little heated." I couldn't help but worry about my daughters. If I were in their stead, I'd probably be thinking more calmly.

"There's nothing to gain from arguing between ourselves."

"You're right. We need to come up with a solution together." That being said, I couldn't think of any solutions at all. Did a solution even exist?

"Let's consider the inevitable," Claire began. "We need to tell them the assessment results."

"Yeah. Either we tell them together or we tell them separately."

"As for Aleah's potential unknown factor, I don't think we should tell her."

I hesitated for a moment before finally nodding. "You're right. It'd be too cruel if nothing came of it."

"All that remains is how to break it to them. But...I really can't think of any method other than giving it to them straight." Claire brooded, deep in thought. She would do anything to soften the blow for our children, even if by a little bit.

"We could fib about the exact aptitude level," I said.

"What would that achieve? Aptitude level aside, May still

has four attributes. That fact alone makes her one of two unique quad-casters in the world."

"Then, what if we just told Aleah she had low aptitude?" I said.

"I don't think that's a good idea either. She can't *ever* use magic, Rae. Would you really be so cruel to give her false hope?"

"Yeah, no."

We were at a dead end. No matter how much we brainstormed, no solution presented itself.

"If only I could give Aleah some of my magic," Claire said defeatedly, her words barely audible as they slipped out of her mouth. I would share my magic in a heartbeat too, if I could. I wondered, did all parents harbor these kinds of worries?

A heavy silence formed between us.

"I guess there's nothing to do but tell them."

"Oh, Rae..."

"I'm afraid no matter how we go about it, Aleah will be hurt."

"Mmm..."

"All we can do is let them know we will always equally love them both."

"That's really all we can do, isn't it?" Claire hung her head.

I felt like I was giving up, but what else could we do? Some problems couldn't be solved through love alone, no matter how much you tried. And while it pained me to admit it, this was one such problem.

"I can't do a thing for her. And they called me the hero of the revolution. Some hero I am..."

"Miss Claire..." It hurt to see Claire talk about herself like that.

Claire was just as important to me as May and Aleah. For her sake, I had to be strong.

Just then—

"Mothers, are you fighting?"

"Please don't fight."

May and Aleah appeared, walking into the living room while drowsily rubbing their eyes.

"Are you fighting because of me?" Aleah gingerly asked.

"Or is it because of me?"

They looked as if they could cry at any moment. Claire and I burst into a fretful mess.

"We're not fighting, dears! We just wanted to talk a bit, that's all."

"That's right! We would never fight! We're always lovey-dovey—super-duper lovey-dovey even!"

Claire went for a serious approach while I went for a sillier one. But neither seemed to work.

"But you two were making super scary faces..."

"And were using big voices..."

The twins sniffled, a sign the floodgates were about to break. Wait—how much had they heard?

"I'm sorry. We didn't mean to scare you. Come here, you two." Claire hugged them to her as she apologized from the bottom of her heart. They wept in her arms as she whispered words of comfort in their ears and kissed their hair repeatedly.

Claire waited for the crying to die down and then looked them squarely in the eyes as she spoke in the gentlest voice she could muster. "May, Aleah, there's something we need to tell you."

They nodded before moving to their chairs.

"Before I begin, I want you two to remember that no matter what happens, Rae and I will never come to hate or abandon either of you. Okay?"

May and Aleah looked puzzled, but nodded.

"Remember when we went to the cathedral to measure your magic aptitude the other day? Well, the results have come in."

"Really?!"

"Tell us, tell us!"

Their faces lit up. My heart ached as I thought of how those bright smiles would soon cloud.

"First, May. You have aptitude with all four attributes. Congratulations."

"Like Sister Manaria?"

"That's right."

"Yay!"

May jumped off her chair in joy. Aleah eyed her enviously.

"And Aleah. I'm sorry, but you have no aptitude."

"Huh...?" Aleah looked confused, like she didn't understand the words. May abruptly stopped celebrating. "No aptitude? What does that mean?"

"You can do many things, Aleah. But magic can't be one of those things."

Aleah went silent. Claire's phrasing was measured and careful, but the shock was still great.

"Mama Claire, Aleah can't use magic?" May asked.

"Sadly, yes."

"Because she has no aptitude?"

"That's right."

"But why? Why do I have four then?"

"Only the Great Spirit knows."

May pondered a bit before breaking out into a grin. "Then I'll give Aleah half of mine!" she innocently declared.

Aleah's eyes widened in hope at the idea.

"That's very kind of you, May. But I'm sorry, magic aptitude can't be shared."

"It can't?" May said sadly.

"I'm sorry."

Aleah looked even more dejected than before. "Mother, will I really never be able to use magic?"

"No. I'm sorry."

"No matter what? Even if I'm a really good girl?"

"No... But being a good girl is a wonderful thing, so please continue to be one."

Aleah went silent again. The mood weighed down on us all.

"Aleah, it's okay even if you can't use magic," I began. "You're good at so, so many other things."

Aleah didn't respond.

"Magic is just one thing in the end, and everyone has at least one thing they can't do."

"Mother Rae, please be quiet for a bit," Aleah said.

"Okay..." I'd been shot down by a child. *Sniffle.*

Aleah appeared deep in thought. I could see her mind race as she desperately searched for a way to fight the reality that had been thrust upon her. "Mothers, will you be sad if I can't use magic?"

"No," said Claire definitively. "Even if you can't use magic, we'll be happy as long as you are."

"You won't hate me?"

"Never."

"You won't play favorites with May?"

"Of course not."

"Oh." Aleah looked relieved. "Then it's okay. I don't need magic as long as my mothers love me." She gave us an undaunted smile.

"Oh, Aleah..."

"So, Mother Rae?"

"Yes, Aleah?"

"Can you teach me how to cook?"

"Cook? Of course, I can, but why?"

"If I can do something Mother Claire can't do, then I'll have her beat even more so than if I learned magic!" Aleah giggled impishly.

"Ah! No fair! I wanna learn how to cook, too!" May exclaimed.

"Nope! You'll be busy with magic instead!"

"Aww." May puffed up her cheeks.

"Sounds good, then," I declared. "May will learn magic with Miss Claire, and Aleah will learn cooking with me."

"That sounds wonderful," Claire said. "Are you two okay with that?"

"Yes."

"Yeah!"

Things had finally calmed down to the point where we could take a moment to breathe. I'd been so worried, but it looked like everything would be all right. Our daughters chattered excitedly about what food they would cook and what magic they would use, looking more eager than anything. Had our fears been unwarranted?

"You're a very strong girl, Aleah," said Claire. "And May, thank you for not saying anything mean."

"He he!"

"Eheh!"

The girls clung to Claire, allowing themselves to be fussed over. The tension left my shoulders as I finally allowed myself to relax.

That was to say, I let my guard down.

"Have I been a good girl?" Aleah asked.

"Hm? Y-yes?" said Claire.

"I really tried my best to be strong, so..."

"Aleah?"

"So just for today...please forgive me..." Tears welled up in Aleah's eyes. "Waaah!"

She sobbed at a volume you wouldn't expect from her small frame. May followed suit, sobbing with an intensity that matched her sister's. Tears streamed down their faces as they bared their sadness to the world.

"May! Aleah!" I hugged the twins, unable to help myself. Claire joined me, and we cried together as we held them tight.

I was sure the neighbors would complain, but regardless, the four of us cried our hearts out. May and Aleah would cry themselves to sleep that night.

"Thirty-two! Thirty-three!"

Early in the afternoon on a holiday, Aleah's motivated voice rang out from the yard as she took practice swings with a wooden sword.

"Forty-nine...fifty!"

"Nice work. Go ahead and take a break now."

"Yes!" Aleah gave a spirited reply, prompting the man clad in light armor to roughly pat her head with his one arm.

"Good job, Aleah. Thank you for coming today, Master Rod," I called out to the twins as I brought tea and refreshments to the table on the terrace.

"Nah, don't worry about it."

This easygoing man was Rod Bauer, an ex-member of the royal family. A while ago, he'd abdicated his claim to the throne and instead became the commander of the army. Every now and then, he took advantage of his new status as an ordinary citizen to come visit us.

"Mother Rae, did you see me?!"

"I did. You did amazing, dear."

"I swung it fifty times today!" Aleah enthusiastically announced as she tried to catch her breath. I wiped the sweat off her face, which seemed to tickle her, but she made no effort to stop me, instead basking in the glory of her accomplishment.

"She's your daughter, all right. She's got talent." Rod dexterously scooped Aleah into the air with his one arm and began lifting her up and down, causing her to squeal in delight.

"We're not related by blood, though."

"Sure, but I still sense an innate talent for combat in her." His words gave Aleah reason to smile, and me as well.

Rod was teaching Aleah swordplay, since she couldn't use magic but still needed a way to defend herself in a world with monsters and all. Incidentally, demons were also a problem in this world—not that I was likely to ever see one here in the Bauer Kingdom.

We'd consulted Rod about teaching Aleah self-defense a while ago, and he'd offered to train her himself. It seemed that, though he relied on magic to fight in the past, he'd begun studying the sword in earnest once he became a commander. This, combined with the basics of hand-to-hand combat that had been drilled into him back when he was in line for the throne, made him a wonderful teacher.

But demons, huh? They'd only been referenced in passing in the game, but I supposed that if I continued to live in this world, I might someday happen across one. It wouldn't hurt to have a plan in place.

"Am I good at swordplay?" Aleah asked.

"Oh, yeah. You'll definitely get better than me one of these days. You keep practicing and you might even reach the level of the Sword God."

"Sword God?" Aleah asked quizzically upon hearing the unknown term.

"That's what they call the strongest swordsman. The empress of the Nur Empire."

"Is she strong?"

"Legend has it that she annihilated an entire Sousse battalion single-handedly using just a sword, though I couldn't tell you if that's true."

A battalion was a military unit denoting a troop of three hundred to a thousand soldiers. Someone single-handedly taking down that many foes armed with just a sword might seem far-fetched, but I knew it had actually happened. As for why I knew that, you'll just have to wait.

"How strong does that make the empress?" Aleah asked again.

"Hmm, I guess the strongest in the world?"

"Stronger than you?"

"Hate to say it, but yeah."

"Stronger than Mother Claire and Mother Rae?"

"If you don't count magic, then yeah."

"Stronger than Sister Manaria?!"

"Huh... Dunno. I did hear Manaria is also pretty good with a sword."

Aleah's eyes sparkled. She yearned to be like her idol Manaria, as well. "Can I become a Sword God, too?"

"Sure, you can. But you're gonna need to work hard at it."

"I will!" Aleah said as she began her practice swings again. Rod and I looked on with smiles.

"It's not fair... Only Aleah gets to have fun!" May puffed up her cheeks. She was sitting in the yard with her eyes closed.

"Isn't what you're doing training, too?" Aleah rebutted.

"But it's so *boring*!"

Claire smiled wryly as May complained. May was working on the first and hardest step in training to use magic—learning to be able to sense magic itself. To misquote a manga that I read a long time ago, "Only once you feel can you begin." Even if May was a quad-caster, she couldn't do a thing without first clearing this initial hurdle.

"Hey, focus," Claire warned.

"Hmph." May huffed before returning to meditation. Sitting still felt like torture to her, as she loved to do nothing more than move her body.

"Can you feel something warm inside you?"

"Mmm... I don't know..."

"There's no need to rush. Let's do this slowly, at your own pace."

"Okay..."

Sensing magic was an abstract concept. If May were better able to describe what she felt, then we could guide her better, but a six-year-old didn't have the vocabulary to do that. If anything, we were already asking too much of her.

"Magic feels...like what you feel inside when you're happy," Claire explained.

"When I'm happy?"

"Yes. When your body feels light, or when your heart is afloat."

"Hmm?" May didn't seem to understand.

But Claire didn't give up. Her teaching methods had improved since she became an instructor at the Academy, and she'd had a lot of practice explaining difficult concepts in the easiest ways for her pupils to digest. I had no doubt May would learn to call on her magic any day now under Claire's direction.

But it seemed that day would not be today.

"Mmm... I don't get it!" May let out one big shout before sprawling on the ground.

"That's all right. This isn't something you can learn in a single day." Claire scooped up May, now sulking, and came to join us on the terrace.

"You tried your best, May," I said. "You too, Claire."

"But I can't use magic..." May pouted.

"Not right away. We can take our time and learn, all right?"

"Ha ha ha!" Rod let out a hearty laugh. "I guess the world's second quad-caster also has some way to go!"

"I'll figure it out soon!" May pouted.

"Oh? Will you?"

"Master Rod's a meanie! You always play favorites with Aleah!"

"May," Claire warned. "We're the ones who asked him to train Aleah, remember?"

"Hmph!" May fumed.

"Ha ha ha! It seems you dislike me! Very well, then. You can come fight me first thing once you learn magic!"

"I don't wanna!"

Rod took May's ill temper in stride, simply laughing her hurtful words away.

"How are things with you lately, Master Rod?" Claire asked.

"I've been busy testing that one large-scale technique I told you about." He was referring to what was supposedly a new kind of magic he'd invented. Not even Manaria could beat him anymore, or so he claimed. "I've also been working on countermeasures for those earthquakes we've had of late. The citizens still haven't gotten over that big one a while back."

"Ah, yes. There have been quite a few of those lately..."

There hadn't been any aftershocks following the eruption in the original game, yet there had been several earthquakes in as many months. Most problematically, the earthquake caused by the eruption of Mt. Sassal had set off the revolution that was so vividly burned into the people's memory. Naturally, every time we had another earthquake, the citizens feared history would repeat itself.

Rod had his hands full dealing with that. Even modern-day Japan hadn't developed perfect earthquake countermeasures yet. I was sure our administration was having no end of trouble as well.

"Other than that, we gotta deal with a bunch of diplomatic issues," Rod grumbled.

"The army does? Oh, dear. I hope it's nothing serious." Claire looked genuinely worried. We had withdrawn from the political stage once the new government stabilized. At this point, the only things we knew about foreign affairs came from the newspapers.

"It's not going so well, if I'm being honest. We might need to ask you two for help again, although we're trying our best not to let it get to that point."

"You better. Don't get in the way of my lovey-dovey time with Claire!" I complained as I made a face at Rod.

"Rae," Claire rebuked me.

Rod grinned. "You two seem to be doing well. Good. But if things ever turn sour, Rae, I'm still free."

"No one likes an overly persistent man."

Rod casually laughed my comment off. Actually, wait—this guy still hadn't given up on me?

"Well, all jokes aside—things have changed since the revolution. We must work harder than ever to protect the happiness of the people." Rod wore a complicated expression as he took a sip of tea.

Claire and I worriedly looked at each other. Perhaps things were even worse than he admitted.

The Academy had a test this time every year, the same one Claire and I had first locked horns over. A lot of things had changed at the Royal Academy since the revolution, but this test endured.

"The culture test will begin momentarily," I told the students. I was serving as proctor, meaning I handed out sheets and made sure nobody cheated. On a scan of the room, I estimated roughly sixty percent of the students were nervous, thirty percent were normal, and ten percent felt something else entirely.

While the test remained, its contents had changed. The etiquette portion had been done away with, largely due to the abolishment of the aristocracy. Incidentally, the Academy no longer offered etiquette as a required subject. However, the Academy *was* still expected to train the next generation of the country's leaders, which meant we expected our graduates to master a certain level of cultural knowledge. That said, some questions about ancient history had been replaced with ones about more recent events—kind of similar to what had happened in modern Japan.

Meanwhile, the magic test had been split into two parts: the basic magic power test and the magic tool wielding test. To be fair, the magic test Claire and I had taken so long ago had been similarly divided. The sections hadn't changed; they were just administered as their own separate tests now.

"You have sixty minutes to complete the test. Please begin."

The students simultaneously flipped their sheets over. Following that, the only audible sound was the scratching of pencils on paper.

While the Academy only accepted exemplary students who were unlikely to need to cheat, I still had to fulfill my duties as a proctor. I double-checked the magic-hampering magic tool to ensure it was indeed working as intended. The tool mainly blocked the usage of telepathy via wind magic, an ability I'd directly experienced via Manaria in the past. There might still be ways of cheating via magic that the Academy couldn't anticipate, so we prohibited all usage of magic during the culture test.

I walked around the room, taking care not to make a sound. I recognized many familiar faces from my classes. Among them was Lana Lahna, the girl who always tried to talk to me after each class. It hadn't been that long since the start of the test, yet her answer sheet was already more than halfway filled out. She'd claimed to be bad at studying, but maybe that had just been humility?

Or so I thought, until I saw her roll her pencil. On the sides of her pencil were numbers. She continued to roll her pencil, filling out her answer sheet with the number she rolled—just like the roll of a die. I'd expected too much from her.

The next familiar face I found was Eve Nuhn, the girl from the same hometown as Lana and me. She had filled out a third of her sheet and, from what I could see, all her answers were correct. Truly brilliant.

Suddenly, Eve turned to face me with her usual look of hatred. "Tsk..."

Lana had said something about Eve hating me because I stole her lover, which had to be a misunderstanding. I wanted to talk it out with her, but I hadn't yet found a good opportunity.

The last person to catch my eye was Joel Santana. He scratched his head as he looked at his answer sheet, clearly perplexed by the questions. I snuck a peek at his answer sheet to find it mostly unanswered. The ones he had filled in were mostly incorrect, too. He'd also claimed to be bad at studying. I guess *he* wasn't being modest.

The test finished without a hitch. I collected the answer sheets and returned to the staff room. Claire was already there, holding a matching stack of sheets.

"Oh, Miss Claire."

"Hello, Rae. I see you've finished proctoring."

"I see you're done, too."

"Yes. It seems we have many outstanding students this year. You'd never imagine they were commoners with scores like these."

"No more commoners, Miss Claire. Just citizens."

"Oops. That's right. You must forgive me," she said as she laughed off her mistake with an *oh ho ho*. Even her slip-ups were so adorable.

"It's probably because your assigned class has so many advanced students. My class was about average, overall."

"Is that so?"

One of the changes to the Academy was the separation of classes based on academic ability. Despite some opposition to the idea, Mr. Torrid—the school principal—had pushed the change through. To refresh your memory: Mr. Torrid was the kingdom's only tri-caster, a man who'd made significant contributions to the kingdom's magic technology.

The opposition had come from teachers who insisted that separating students by ability would lead to preferential treatment. While the idea of treating students equally was noble in theory, the fact remained that not all of them operated on the same levels of knowledge and skill. To ignore this would be a disservice to all the students—or so Mr. Torrid claimed.

I mostly agreed. People learned better when put in a class tailored to meet them where they were at. If someone lagged behind, sending them to the next level of class would only exacerbate the problem.

Claire had differing opinions on the matter.

I handed the answer sheets to the teacher in charge of grading. "Next up is the basic magic test," I said.

"Indeed. I look forward to seeing what diamonds in the rough we find this year!" Claire looked genuinely thrilled. She took great pleasure in being the one to discover new talent. She'd told me a while ago that she might actually be well suited to teaching, and I had to agree with her. Her only flaw was that she tended to expect too much from her students, causing her classes to be a little draconian.

"Hmph. You look like you're having fun," I said with a hint of irritation.

"Hmm? Is there something wrong with that?" Claire looked puzzled.

"No, nothing's wrong with it."

"Then what?"

"Oh, nothing."

"C'mon, spit it out," Claire urged.

Hmm... Should I say it? "Can you promise not to be taken aback?"

"Is it something I'd be taken aback by?"

"You can't answer a question with another question!"

"So you say, but I'm the one who asked a question first! Just say what's on your mind already."

Hmm... Oh well. Guess I'll just say it. "I'm sad."

"What?"

"I'm happy to see you live a fulfilling life as a teacher, but I can't help feeling sad over having less you-and-me time."

"Wh-wh-what—" Claire covered my mouth in a panic. "What do you think you're saying, Rae?! We're at the Academy, and the staff room at that!"

"Mmghh!"

"Ah, sorry." Claire removed her hands.

"What's the problem? Our relationship isn't exactly a secret."

"That's not the issue!"

As I said, our relationship wasn't a secret. We didn't flaunt it, exactly, but I was pretty confident almost all of our colleagues knew. Many of the teachers had been around when we were students and had witnessed my passionate pursuit of Claire.

"You need to draw a line between our private and public lives. As marginalized individuals, we *must* project an upstanding image of *not* being obsessed with the physical side of relationships. Or would you rather reinforce those stereotypes, Rae?"

"No, but..." What Claire said was correct in every regard. But I was seriously at my limit. My body was on the verge of a critical Claire-cium deficiency.

Claire sighed. "Bear with it for today, and I'll pamper you all you want once we're home."

"Really?!"

"Aren't you happy... You know, I can't help but feel your mental age is younger than May and Aleah sometimes."

"And I can't help but feel mommy vibes from you."

"Sorry, mommy vibes...?!"

"Ah, nothing. Don't worry about it." *Oops. Watch yourself, Rae.* "It's a promise then, Miss Claire?"

"Yes, yes. Just make sure you do your work properly, okay?"

"Of course!"

I went on to magnificently proctor the remaining magic tests.

That night, I dosed up on Claire-cium to my heart's content for the first time in a long while.

The doorbell rang.

I was currently home, cooking dinner while I waited for Claire to return from work. The vegetable pork soup simmering in the pot still needed more time. I couldn't extinguish the flame like I could with a gas stove, so instead, I left it to simmer as I prioritized answering the door.

"Yes, who is—oh, Matt."

"It's been a while, Rae."

I opened the door to find Matt Monte waiting for me. I suspect most readers have forgotten him, so to refresh your memory: Matt was a former student of the Academy, the one who was severely injured during the Commoner Movement in what came to be known as the courtyard incident. Claire and I had gone to ask him for his version of events as he recuperated in the Spiritual Church's clinic. He had graduated after the revolution and become a bureaucrat in the new government.

"Something up? Actually, why don't you come inside? I have to keep an eye on the stove."

"Ah, thanks. Pardon the intrusion."

I showed Matt to the living room and returned to the stove. *Good, nothing's burnt.* "You mind if I cook and talk?"

"Not at all. It might be a long talk, though. Where's Miss Claire?" Matt had resented nobility ever since the courtyard incident, but he always addressed Claire respectfully. I thought it a little strange.

"She's still at the Academy. Did you know she became a teacher?"

"I've heard. She's amazing, you know? She was the hero of the revolution but chose not to take a position in the new government. She's nothing like the other nobles, the ones who only act in their own best interests!"

Ahh, so that was how it was. Matt respected Claire for the role she'd played in the success of the revolution, despite being a noble herself, and for willingly living the life of an ordinary citizen afterward.

"So what brings you here today?"

"Well...to tell the truth..." Matt hesitated. I turned my eyes from the stove, looking over my shoulder at him. "We want Miss Claire to go to the empire."

"So what's the meaning of this?" Claire sternly asked Matt.

She'd made it home shortly after Matt's arrival. It was dinnertime for our family, so we called the children over to eat and asked Matt to join. The children regarded Matt with curiosity, as it was their first meeting, but quickly lost interest and went to play in their room once they finished eating.

"Allow me to start by updating you on recent changes to our

international ties." Matt reached into his bag and pulled out a world map. "As I'm sure you know, the Nur Empire has aggressively invaded a number of other countries over the years. Many have been reduced to vassal states."

He pointed to a large country bordering the eastern side of the Bauer Kingdom.

"Even we weren't safe from the empire's machinations. We would have become their puppet if not for Miss Claire and Rae's efforts, and the aid from Sousse and the Alpes."

"Yes, yes. But what of now?" Claire pressed Matt to continue.

"Sousse and the Alpes have also experienced acts of aggression from the Nur Empire. That's why the three nations have decided to come together and form an allied force under the leadership of Queen Manaria of Sousse."

"An allied force... I had no idea things were so dire." Claire frowned as she muttered. We'd taken a backseat on political matters immediately after the establishment of the new government. It was hard to believe world politics had soured so much since then.

"But the Nur Empire is canny," Matt said. "Before the alliance could be made official, they proposed a peace treaty to the Bauer Kingdom."

"I see. So that's what they're aiming for." Claire nodded, understanding the implications.

I hadn't a clue what was going on. "Um, can you explain?"

"They're trying to buy time. Isn't that right, Matt?"

"It's as you say."

According to Claire's explanation, it was like this: Despite being a military superpower, the Nur Empire didn't stand much of a chance against the combined might of the Bauer Kingdom, Sousse, and the Alpes. They would need time to gather their forces—hence the peace treaty.

"The fact that they picked us to offer the treaty to is pretty telling with regard to our country's circumstances as well. Let me guess. The kingdom is tight on resources, and—despite just moving to establish an alliance with Sousse and the Alpes—wishes to avoid war if possible?"

"You saw through it all, Miss Claire," Matt said with admiration.

"What's that got to do with Miss Claire going to the empire?" I asked.

"The empire proposed an exchange student program as a sign of goodwill between the nations. Claire's name came up as a candidate."

"Me? Why?" Claire looked bewildered. She was nothing more than a mere citizen now, after all.

"Purely political reasons. The Nur Empire sent their crown prince for the exchange. The Bauer Kingdom has to send someone of similar value in return."

"Still, why me? I'm no longer even a noble."

"Yes, but you are the hero who changed the foundations of the kingdom and thwarted the plans of the empire."

"You want Miss Claire to be a hostage?!" I finally understood what was going on. They intended to sacrifice Claire. "That's enough! We refuse!"

"Please, hear me out!"

"No!" Blood rushed to my head as I grew livid. We'd finally found some peace and quiet after the revolution. Why should Claire have to suffer again?

A calm voice called out to soothe me. "Rae, calm down. Let's hear him out."

"Miss Claire?!"

I couldn't believe what she was saying, and yet those calm eyes of hers—still as the surface of a deep lake—shut me up more effectively than her scolding ever did.

"Please continue, Matt."

"Yes. Officially speaking, the kingdom will be sending Lady Yu, as she was formerly third in line for the throne. Miss Claire will be going as her attendant."

"Of course. No one would accept a former noble in exchange for a crown prince."

"I'm sure you've already realized this, but we're also choosing to send those whose absence wouldn't greatly impact the kingdom's ability to operate. We'd send government officials if we could, but the administration still lacks stability."

"Naturally. Lady Yu has abandoned her right to the throne, and I'm nothing more than a citizen. It's a splendid decision."

I couldn't keep up with the conversation. I felt like I didn't know this Claire at all—like she had become a completely different person.

But deep down, I knew that was wrong. The Claire before me was the same noble Claire who had willingly walked to her own execution.

"We're aware this request is unreasonable. Of course, we will prepare whatever compensation we can, but it likely won't match the risk you'll be undertaking."

Claire said nothing.

"The kingdom has no other choice. I ask of you: would you please accept this unreasonable request?" Matt bowed deeply.

I prayed for Claire's next words to be ones of refusal. But she simply replied, "Will you give me a week to decide?"

"Why didn't you turn him down, Miss Claire?!" I hounded Claire the moment Matt left, clinging to her chest as she stood stock-still.

"Quiet down, Rae. You'll scare the girls." She was calm, a stark contrast to my frenzied state. I hated that calmness, but I didn't want to scare the children either.

I spoke in as collected a tone as I could muster. "I'm sorry, but you should have refused him on the spot! There's no reason to accept such a request!"

"You're right. As a citizen, I have no reason to accept."

"So you understand?" I was relieved. She could overcome her pride after all. "Then there's no need to wait a week, let's just—"

"But if I were to refuse, what do you think would happen?" Claire cut me off.

I was stunned for a moment but gathered myself and thought about it. "Won't they just send someone else to go?"

"Indeed. They'll find someone else who'd satisfy the conditions."

"And what's wrong with that?" I couldn't understand what Claire was getting at, not one bit—and yet my heart drummed hard, warning me I wouldn't like the outcome awaiting ahead.

"The empire is a dangerous place to be."

"Of course it is! That's why—"

"If I were to refuse, someone else would be sent into danger in my stead." Claire looked me square in the eyes as she spoke.

Had she not changed? Had she not grown accustomed to civilian life since the revolution? Had she not wished to continue this ordinary yet happy life together with May, Aleah, and I?

No—she hadn't changed.

At her core, she was the same person she'd been before the revolution. She was still proud and honest, and she never allowed others to suffer in her place—just like the virtuous nobles of the past. And, once again, that same Claire would sacrifice herself for someone else's sake.

"Miss Claire, you're not a noble anymore... You can think about your own happiness now."

"That's not it, Rae. I made this decision with my own happiness in mind." Claire beckoned me to sit as she sat down herself. I was still unnerved but obeyed—partially to try to calm my nerves. "Nothing makes me happier than knowing you and my daughters are happy and well."

"It's the same for us. Your happiness is our happiness."

"Thank you, Rae. But this happiness can only last as long as we have peace." Claire spoke softly, as if soothing a child throwing a tantrum. "The kingdom is still unstable; it's only been a year since the revolution. Matt is right. We have no other choice."

"But that doesn't mean *you* have to be the one to sacrifice yourself!" I raised my voice.

"Don't misunderstand. I'm not sacrificing myself. I'm going so I can secure peace for the kingdom with my own two hands."

The girl making this bold declaration was unmistakably the same girl I had loved for all this time.

"If I were to refuse Matt's request," Claire continued, "I would be entrusting our future to a stranger—and I will *not* stand for that."

"Miss Claire..." This was Claire. The girl who always played the hand she was dealt and never sat idle. The villainess who was unafraid to get her hands dirty to have her way.

"I'm not one to throw my life away in vain. Trust me. I'll have the empire dancing in the palm of my hand soon enough." *Just watch me,* Claire seemed to say as she smiled. "I'm going for the sake of my family's happiness."

I saw the light of determination in Claire's eyes.

Ah...I couldn't do it.

I couldn't stop her again.

I was going to lose her again.

I had given up all hope—making Claire's next words all the more a shock.

"And you're coming too, Rae."

"Huh?"

"What do you mean, 'huh'? Of course you're coming. Where I go, you go. Did you think you had a choice in the matter?" Claire tried her best to sound haughty, but I could tell it was an act. She couldn't hide the overflowing trust and love in her words. "Did you really think I was going alone?"

"I'm sorry..."

"Actually, it's my fault, isn't it? I do have a prior offense." Claire smiled wryly as we both recalled what had happened during the revolution. "I thought that was best for everyone. But I was wrong. It finally hit me when you cried at my execution, showing me your true selfishness for the first time."

She stood from her chair and walked over to me, softly hugging my shoulders.

"I'll never leave you alone again. No matter the danger, we'll face it together." She gently touched her forehead to mine, stared into my eyes, and asked, "Will you come with me?"

"Of course I will. I'd come with you even if you begged me not to."

"He he. Good."

We giggled before exchanging a quick peck on the lips.

"But what about May and Aleah? You're not thinking of bringing them, are you?" I asked.

"While I feel bad for them, we'll have to leave them in the care of someone we trust. Maybe the cathedral priest, or Master Rod—"

"No!"

"You can't!"

Our beloved daughters ran in suddenly. I'd been wondering why it was so quiet in their room... They must have been eavesdropping.

"What are you two doing here?"

"Oh, May, Aleah..."

"I'm going wherever you two go!" May insisted.

"Me too!" Aleah insisted as well. The two rubbed their teary eyes.

"I'm sorry, but you can't. The place we're going is very dangero—"

"Nooooo!"

"We're coming, too!"

They cut Claire off again. I didn't think I'd ever seen them react to anything so strongly before.

"May, Aleah..."

"You can't abandon us!"

"I don't wanna be alone again!"

Claire looked like a deer caught in headlights. I probably wore a similar expression. How could we have forgotten?

May and Aleah had been passed on to their relatives after their parents died and then became orphans when those relatives died in turn. By the time we met them, their suffering had made them cold and blank—emotionless dolls made in the image of people. They'd recovered thanks to the love Claire and I showered them with, but the memory of those times still lived inside them. They couldn't help but react now.

"Are you going to abandon us, too? Are we going to be alone again?"

"I don't wanna be alone... I wanna be with my mothers!"

They sobbed, their small frames trembling as they pleaded with us. Claire froze up, unsure of what to do.

"Miss Claire... Let's take them with us."

"Rae, do you know what you're saying?!" Claire seemed appalled I would suggest such a thing, but I pressed my case.

"It'll be fine. I've made up my mind. We'll face the empire head-on."

"R-Rae?" Claire looked at me, nonplussed, but I smiled at her and approached May and Aleah.

"I'm sorry we worried you two. We're not going to leave you behind."

"Really...?"

"Really, really?"

"Yeah. So in exchange, can you two promise to be good girls?"

"Uh-huh!"

"Yes!"

May and Aleah leapt into my arms. It wasn't often that they did this with me. We'd really scared them.

"It's not like me to try to play things safe. I can protect my family myself."

I'd made my decision. All that remained was to prepare and take action. For the first time in what felt like an eternity, I kicked my brain into top gear.

"A spin-off?"

"That's right."

The night after we decided to go to the empire as a family,

Claire and I began discussing our plans. May and Aleah were already in bed, so the only ones in the living room were Claire and me, along with a bunch of documents I had prepared.

"As I explained to you during the revolution, I'm able to predict the events of this world to a degree."

"Right. Something about a book of prophecies."

"Correct." Although it wasn't actually a book of prophecies but a dating sim. "The name of the book of prophecies was *Revolution*, and it had a spin-off called *Revolution: Lily Side*."

Revolution: Lily Side, or *Revo-Lily* for short, was—as you might have guessed from the title—a yuri spin-off of *Revolution*. The truth was that I had actually played *Revo-Lily* before *Revolution*. I was the kind of nerd who played all kinds of games, but my sexual orientation had made me particularly fond of yuri games. Yuri games hadn't been popular back in my first turn at youth, but *Revo-Lily* had still managed to be widely regarded as a masterpiece.

"*Revolution: Lily Side*—that's a bit long, let's shorten it— *Revo-Lily* has information about the empire that we can use."

Revo-Lily was one of many spin-offs released after the success of *Revolution*. Its protagonist was the princess of the Nur Empire. You played by pursuing one of three love interests, which were the empress, a government official, and a classmate. Of course, being a yuri game, all the relevant characters were women. I eventually came to play the original *Revolution* after falling for Claire, who made a guest appearance in *Revo-Lily* as an exiled noble.

"If we guide Princess Philine down a certain route, the entire empire will fall apart."

"R-really?"

"Really."

There was a revolution route in *Revo-Lily*, too. You could opt to romance no one and instead lead a revolution to overthrow the imperial government—just like in the original *Revolution*, which was, in fact, the very same route I had taken a year prior.

"That said, bringing down the entire government of the empire would just open a whole new can of worms. It's not completely off the table, but for now, let's aim to bring down any elements agitating for conflict."

"Sounds good." It had to seem like I was pulling all this information out of thin air, but Claire agreed unhesitatingly regardless.

"I love you," I said.

"Wh-what are you saying so suddenly?"

"Just thinking how nice it is that you trust me."

"Well, why wouldn't I?"

"He he." I proceeded, having basked for a moment in Claire's love for me. "We need the support of many people to make this plan work, but the most important person will be Philine. She's extremely shy and has trouble speaking her mind."

"Can such a person really start a revolution?"

"Not now, but it's her character growth that makes her so interesting."

"Growth? In that book of prophecies?"

"Ah, sorry. Just thinking to myself."

In my experience, the protagonists of dating sims tended to be devoid of personality. I understood that this was meant to allow players to project themselves onto the character, but I still didn't love it. *Revo-Lily's* protagonist, Philine, started out as one such husk. But as the story progressed, she grew stronger and more independent. This growth was most notable in the revolution route.

Incidentally, Claire, as a guest character, always proved to be the greatest obstacle in Philine's path. She played the role of villainess, just like in the first game, but had many more cool scenes than in the original. In one, Philine condemned Claire as a criminal and had her executed, but Claire just laughed defiantly in her high-pitched voice as they lopped off her head. I watched that scene countless times...and always fell into a three-day depression afterward.

"Anyway, our plan of action is to make contact with Philine and lead her down the right route."

"Okay. What should I do then? I can't let you do all the heavy lifting, after all," Claire said, filling me with reassurance. This time, I wasn't working alone. With Claire by my side, I could do anything.

"First, let me cross-reference the events I remember against the events that have occurred. In the version of events I remember, Claire was an influential noble of the empire."

"Of the empire?! How could such a thing be possible?"

"Meh, let's skip over that for now."

"What?! Isn't something like that important?!"

"We're skipping it."

"I don't get you sometimes..."

I didn't want to explain. It would take too long. "Anyway, the Claire from my book of prophecies supported the Nur Empire, which means you're in the opposite situation now."

"I see. In that case, your knowledge might not be too helpful here."

"Compared to the revolution, yes. But that doesn't mean it's completely useless."

"I'm counting on you."

Her words made me so happy that I wanted to hug her tight right then and there. But we were talking about serious stuff, so I restrained myself.

"Actually, your current position might make things easier," I said.

"What do you mean?" Claire tilted her head. She was just the cutest.

"Philine is shy, but she's also kind. She doesn't approve of the aggressive actions taken by her government."

"Which means?"

"Which means she holds you in high regard as someone who achieved a nonviolent revolution while thwarting the empire."

"Really?" Claire asked doubtfully.

"Well, I'm sure it's not actually that simple. But she should have some interest in you that we can take advantage of."

Claire sighed. "I feel like I'm a shameless adult trying to deceive an innocent child."

"Perhaps that's not too far off. Don't worry, I'll be a shameless adult with you."

"I guess we have no other choice."

I'd managed to get Claire on board so far. I continued as she sipped her tea. "There's a good chance we'll make contact with Philine during the exchange student program. Once we do that, things can begin."

"So we're leaving it up to luck?"

"I prefer 'playing it by ear.' For the time being, could you try to memorize all this information about *Revo-Lily* I've written down here?"

"I can, but is that really all right? Didn't you say sharing the future might change it to something you can't predict?"

I was surprised she remembered. That had been quite a while back.

"I couldn't tell you back then because the matter directly concerned you. This time is different. We can work together to woo Philine."

"Could you not say 'woo'? It sounds like we're trying to court her."

"Perv."

"Oh, so you want me to burn you that badly?" Claire asked as the François family crests floated above her head.

"It was just a joke, Miss Claire! There's no need for your Magic Ray! Please, you'll burn the house down!" I cowered. "L-Let's start by discussing Philine's circumstances. There's quite a bit to cover."

"Sounds easy enough," Claire said. "Memorization is one of my strong suits."

From that day onward, we began designing our plan to manipulate the empire.

"And that's everything that happened until now."

"Um, who are you talking to, Rae?"

"Oh, sorry. Just myself."

And so, we returned to where our story started. The present day, right after Claire had given me an out-of-body experience by treating me to her wonderful home cooking.

"We've done all the planning we could. All that's left is to put it into action," I said.

"Yes. There have been a number of surprises along the way, but I have a feeling it will all work out... No, we'll *make* it work out."

"That's the spirit, Miss Claire! You're marvelous!"

"Don't make fun of me." Claire huffed, but I saw the smile on her face. She was so easy to please.

Our preparations involved many things, including having Hans—the shopkeeper from my hometown—send us information about the empire. I was confident this world was largely identical to that of the game, but I wanted to make sure the empire as it existed in this reality was faithful to its representation in *Revo-Lily*. I wouldn't have gone to such lengths if it were just me going, but Claire and our two daughters were also coming. Better safe than sorry.

Other than Hans, I also asked Rod and my father-in-law, Dole, to thoroughly investigate the situation we were walking into. I couldn't verify every minute detail from the game, but so far, it seemed the empire was as I remembered it. To say I could finally relax would have been a stretch, but at least I had something to count on now.

"In the end, how many people are traveling to the empire, Rae?" Claire had left the information gathering to me while she studied my *Revo-Lily* notes.

"About fifty."

The centerpiece of the group would be Yu, just as Matt had said. Yu had once been third in line to the throne and was now cardinal of the Spiritual Church, giving her great value as a hostage. Of course, Yu's close confidant, Misha, would also come. Some of the other participants included Lana, Eve, and Joel from my class.

We decided to enroll May and Aleah at the Imperial Academy's elementary school. I couldn't help worrying about what the empire would teach them, as I did have a rough idea of their curriculum, but we needed someone to look after them while Claire and I schemed.

"Sousse and the Alpes are also sending students. Lene will be among them."

"That's fantastic news!" Claire's face lit up upon hearing Lene's name. She loved Lene as much as ever. I made a sour face.

"Oh, my. Are you jealous?"

"Whatever. Hmph!"

"Don't be like that. Lene may be a close friend of mine, but you're my one and only lover."

"I know... But I still can't help but feel a little needy."

"He he, you're adorable." Claire smiled angelically, then kissed me.

"Ah! It's not fair Mama Rae is the only one! Me too! Me too!" May insisted.

"Me too, please!" Aleah insisted as well.

"Yes, yes, one at a time." Smiling all the while, Claire gave May and Aleah a kiss on the forehead. The two girls looked ticklish but happily accepted their kisses regardless.

"Will we make friends?" May said.

"I'm worried..." Aleah said.

We headed out for the empire tomorrow and, as shy as they were, the girls were worried about moving to a new environment.

"I'm sure you two will be fine. You're so cute, after all," Claire said.

"I'm cute?" May asked.

"That's right."

"Me too?" Aleah asked.

"Of course."

"Yay!"

"He he, Mother Claire said I'm cute!"

Claire smiled as May and Aleah kissed her on the cheeks.

"What about me?" I asked.

"Does Mother Rae want kisses, too?" May smiled.

"You have to say 'pretty please'!" Aleah insisted.

"Pretty please!"

"Okay, fine!"

"Fine, fine!"

I received strangely different treatment but was kissed nonetheless. I seized the opportunity to grab them and began raining kisses down on their marshmallow-soft cheeks.

"Ahh! Nooo!"

"Let go, please!"

It seemed they truthfully didn't like it, so I reluctantly let them go. That kind of reaction made Mommy sad...

"I think I understand the family hierarchy now," I said. Claire was at the top, May and Aleah at the middle, and I was at the very bottom.

"Ha ha, our family has no such thing. May and Aleah both respect you very much. Isn't that right, dears?" Claire tried to cheer me up.

"I really, really like the food you make!" May exclaimed.

"Now that I learn from Mother Rae, I understand just how good at cooking she is!" Aleah said.

My greatest asset was cooking, it seemed. That kind of hurt in its own way. No, I needed to be happy! I loved cooking, and it was a fine life skill... But I wouldn't mind if they had said something a little nicer, you know?

"All right, time for bed, you two. We have to get up early tomorrow," Claire said. It was almost 8:00 p.m., the children's bedtime.

"I don't wanna sleep yet!"

"I'm not sleepy!"

The girls objected, which was out of character for them.

"Oh really? You two look pretty sleepy to me," Claire said.

"N-no..."

"I'm not...sleepy..."

Was something wrong with them? They usually went to bed when we asked them to.

"I don't wanna sleep...because when we wake up, we'll have to say bye-bye to the house..." May said as she rubbed her eyes.

"I don't wanna say bye-bye..."

"Oh," Claire said, shocked.

But of course. This house had been the first place they could happily call their own home. Neither the streets of the slums nor the communal living space of the convent had the hallmarks of a place where they truly belonged, and they would part with it tomorrow.

"May, Aleah, we're not saying bye-bye to this house yet."

"Huh?"

Claire grinned at their confused, sleepy countenances as she continued. "For moments like these, we say 'be back soon.'"

"Really?"

"Are we coming back soon?"

"Yes, and this house will be here, waiting to say 'welcome back' to you." Claire scooped them up. "How about we all sleep together tonight?"

"Yay!"

"Can we?!"

"Why not? If that's okay by you, Rae."

"Of course. I'll fetch the futons."

"Thank you."

Claire carried the girls to the bedroom. I thought of the trials to come as I brought the lightweight goose-down futons over.

I'll make sure everyone comes back to this house alive.

I was sure our life in Nur wouldn't be as peaceful as our life here. Making contact with Philine and defeating the empire would likely involve difficult decisions, more difficult than the ones made for the revolution.

Even so, I'll find that happy future for my family. For their happiness.

That night, we all slept side by side, with Claire and I sandwiching May and Aleah. The two girls argued over who would sleep on Claire's side and played rock-paper-scissors, ending in May's victory. My feelings weren't hurt or anything...

The next morning, we packed our bags and left the house. A carriage waited outside, ready to take us to the empire. Claire locked the door behind us, and we were finally ready to make our journey. But before that, one last thing. We turned to the house and smiled.

"Be back soon!"

10

The Imperial Academy

THE NUR EMPIRE lay to the east of the Bauer Kingdom, Sousse to the south, the Alpes to the west, and the Loro Empire—separated from the Alpes by a desert—even farther west than that.

This meant that, of the countries participating in the proposed three-nation alliance, the Bauer Kingdom sat closest to the Nur Empire. In turn, we faced the highest risk. Of course, I didn't think for a second that Manaria—who had proposed the alliance—would hang us out to dry, but the dog-eat-dog world of diplomacy didn't allow for personal feelings. No matter what Manaria herself wanted, Sousse had its own agenda as a country.

The same went for the Bauer Kingdom. We had every right to refuse the empire's peace treaty, form the three-nation alliance, and confront Nur directly. But such a decision could not be considered sound, at least not with the kingdom's current need for resources. We had no choice but to take a stance of peace, even if only temporarily.

Shrewd Nur noticed this weakness in the three-nation alliance and took advantage.

That being said, while the empire was indeed a thorn in the kingdom's side, not many Bauer citizens actually understood anything about it. The layperson on the street would likely describe it as a dictatorship that exploited its people and only used its budget on military spending. But reality had a way of surprising you.

"The empire is...not quite what I expected." Claire gawked in surprise at the streets around her. "The city's so lively, and there's hardly a soldier to be seen."

We had arrived in Ruhm, the Imperial Capital of the Nur Empire, and were making our way to the Imperial Castle on foot after leaving the carriage.

"Well, this street runs through the central market. If the central market wasn't doing this well, I doubt the empire would have the leeway to even think about waging war," I said.

The city teemed with life no matter where you looked. Citizens thronged around us, gleefully touting their wares or shopping for goods. The lines of stalls sold not only imports from abroad but also the local specialty goods of the many countries annexed by the empire.

"Wow... I've never seen so many different people in one place. I've never even seen some of these hair colors and skin tones in Bauer. And as far as I can tell, not one person is enslaved. Everyone treats everyone else as free citizens," Claire said.

This was a new sight for me as well, who'd formerly lived in

Japan, a largely homogeneous country. Of course, the European-style Bauer Kingdom had felt foreign to me when I first arrived, but the Nur Empire felt even more so with the diversity of its populace. This diversity was largely made possible by the Nur government's policies.

"Miss Claire, do you remember the underlying beliefs of the Nur Empire's policies?"

"I believe it was meritocracy, the same ideology the late King l'Ausseil supported." As expected of an educated lady like Claire. She was well informed about neighboring countries, not just her own. But her answer lacked something.

"The empire takes meritocracy to a much higher level than our kingdom does," I said.

"Oh?"

"You know how the empire is invading and annexing countries left and right?"

"But of course."

"People from those annexed countries who show promise are given citizenship without question."

The heads of the conquered vassal states despised this policy, but those in the lower echelons of society embraced it with open arms. For people whose talents might never otherwise see the light of day, being annexed by the empire could be a heaven-sent opportunity.

Of course, not everyone saw it that way.

"The empire's minister of foreign affairs was originally from an annexed country to the north called Rasha," I said.

"You're telling me they let a non-native handle the country's foreign affairs?!"

"Indeed. It wasn't always like this, though. It took decades after the current empress came to power for these policies to become so well established."

The empire had always taken an aggressive approach to diplomacy, but it hadn't been until the current empress, Dorothea, unified it under her brand of rationalism that it achieved its current form. Dorothea Nur had been born the second daughter of the prior emperor. For generations, the eldest son had inherited the throne, with women shut out of the line of succession. But Dorothea had overcome that with her resourcefulness, willingness to use violence, and harsh rationalism. She had usurped her own father.

"This was simply the fastest way," she'd said apathetically as she killed her father. At the time, she had been a mere seven years old. Of course, she'd had adults backing her usurpation, but they hadn't been able to make her their willing puppet after the impact she'd had on the empire.

"That's quite the harrowing story."

"I can tell you for a fact that her talent is the real deal. She's not just a strong leader; she's an unparalleled warrior known as the Sword God. Master Rod mentioned her, didn't he?"

"Yes, he said the empress routed an entire battalion of Sousse soldiers single-handedly. But that had to be an exaggeration."

"Not at all. It's the truth."

The empire was a dictatorship, but it was held together by its charismatic and competent leader, Dorothea. Maybe you've heard something like this before? *Better to live in a dictatorship with a competent leader than in a democracy with an incompetent one.*

While I didn't agree with the idea, there was *some* truth to it.

"Oh, Her Majesty isn't that scary."

The Nur man guiding us flashed us a wry smile. His tone wasn't one of admonishment but rather of reassurance. He seemed used to correcting people about the empress.

"I'll admit," the guide continued, "there are a lot of unsettling tales about Her Majesty Dorothea. But everyone who meets her only has good to say. She's charming. You'll understand once you see her in person."

He spoke as if she were a close friend. I assumed he had been granted audience with her before.

"You see, I come from a country to the south called Xixi. Back when it was annexed, I participated in protests against the empire. But those protests soon died down when it became apparent that life under Empress Dorothea's rule was far better than life under the Xixi aristocracy."

"I take it you don't resent the empire?" Claire delicately asked.

"Of course not. If anything, I'm thankful." The guide smiled at Claire. I didn't think most people agreed with his point of view, but it still spoke to how much trust the people had in Dorothea. "We've about arrived at the castle."

We looked in the direction the guide pointed and found ourselves faced with an enormous building.

"That's...a castle?" Claire voiced the same thoughts I had.

It resembled a fortress more than anything. Bauer's royal palace was regal and imposing, but the imperial castle of Nur was completely utilitarian in design. Clearly, its only apparent function was to resist invaders. Its forbidding facade was perhaps a reflection of the empress who lived within.

"Oh, I forgot to say one thing," The guide came to a halt before turning to face us. "Welcome to the Nur Empire."

In contrast to its spartan exterior, the inside of the castle was well furbished. Not in terms of fancy fixtures or artwork—I saw none of either—but it had evidently been constructed of the highest-quality materials, making it regal in a different way from the royal palace or Bauer Cathedral in the kingdom's capital.

After arriving at the castle, we were seated in a waiting room until we could be granted an audience. Obviously, the entire group of fifty wasn't going to be allowed to see the empress. Only the representatives—Yu, Misha, Claire, and I—would be permitted. The four of us had changed into formal attire and double-checked our gifts. All that remained was to wait.

"We're finally going to see the empress. I wonder if she'll live up to the rumors?" Lady Yu sat snugly on a sofa, which was positioned at the head of the table. With her hair grown out, wearing makeup that Misha had carefully applied, it was hard to believe people had once thought she was a boy. She moved with dainty grace, tilting her head slightly to the side as she mused.

She'd always been rather androgynous, but finally being able to live openly and freely as a woman had brought her natural beauty shining forth.

"Lady Yu, I trust I needn't remind you that we are not here for fun? Don't neglect your duty as a representative of the kingdom." The woman situated by Yu's side, wearing a habit and warning Yu for the umpteenth time to take her role seriously, was Misha, of course. She'd taken rather well to life as a nun. Maybe it was simply meant to be, considering how humorless she'd always been.

"Me? A representative? Don't you mean sacrifice?" Yu joked.

"Please don't say such things. We're here on legitimate diplomatic business. If anything were to happen to you, hostilities would resume immediately."

"I know, but I feel like you only care about the politics. Aren't you at all worried about me?"

"Please consider the time and place before making such remarks, Lady Yu."

"So cold." Yu shrugged at Misha's curt reply.

Get a room, you two, I thought.

Yu turned to us. "Anyhow, it's been a while since we last met, Rae and Claire. How have May and Aleah been?"

"They've been well. Thank you for your help last time." Claire bowed her head.

"Not at all. I'm sorry we couldn't be of more help. How's their curse been?"

"We've tried many things, but to no avail," I replied, to which Yu knit her brows.

Half a year ago, Claire and I had asked to use the Tears of the Moon to remove May's and Aleah's curse. The Tears of the Moon was a secret relic of the Spiritual Church, the kind we'd normally never have access to, but Yu and the church owed us a favor. While the higher ranks of the clergy were reluctant, Yu's support and the pope's final word got our request granted.

Yet the curse in May's and Aleah's blood remained. The Tears of the Moon was a magic tool that removed negative status effects, but its strength was proportional to the amount of time it spent absorbing moonlight. It had been used on Yu just half a year ago at the time, so perhaps it needed more time to recharge before it could dispel the curse. Regardless, the fact remained that we had yet to find a cure.

"What manner of curse is this? Most curses would be dispelled with half a year's worth of moonlight," Yu said.

"I don't know, but we *must* find a way to dispel it. I don't want those girls to suffer any more than they already have." Claire's expression was grim but determined. Of course, I felt the same way.

"Misha's doing her best to find some information that can help," Yu said. "She's been poring through the old tomes stored in the church archives."

"Thank you for all your help, Misha," Claire said.

"Not at all. I'm sorry I can't do more."

"We'll let you know if we find anything once we're allowed to review the specific use history of the Tears of the Moon." Yu said.

"Please do." Claire bowed. I followed suit.

"Still, I'm surprised how much you two have changed. It feels like just yesterday you two were bickering with each other at the Academy, and now you're together with kids." Yu giggled as Claire blushed beet red.

"There's no one more surprised than me, you know?" Claire sighed. "I feel like I haven't had a moment's rest since I met this girl."

"Do you hate it?" Yu asked teasingly.

"Th-that's, well..." Claire wavered.

"Lucky you, Rae. Your efforts paid off."

"It's an honor! I'm the luckiest girl in the world!" I proudly declared.

"Rae!" Claire stepped on my foot. It hurt, but pain was a reward in itself when you were in as deep as me.

Claire sighed heavily. "We both have it rough, don't we, Misha?"

"We do indeed, Miss Claire."

They seemed to have found common ground. Huh? What was so wrong with Yu and me wanting to show our lovers some love?

"Backtracking a bit: How much do you two know about the empress?" Yu asked.

"I only know the bare minimum," answered Claire.

"I've only heard that she's a dictator, but also a strong, fair, charismatic leader," I said.

"I see. That's about all I know, too. The problem is that everyone who meets her says the same thing. 'She's charming,' ad infinitum."

Come to think of it, our guide had said the same thing.

"I have a feeling there's some magic at work," Yu continued.

Claire frowned. "You're suggesting she maintains her rule through mind control?"

"It's not improbable. This is the same woman who usurped the throne at the age of seven. Even if we assume she was an early bloomer, there's no way she could secure that many supporters at so young an age."

"H-hold on, aren't we in for it, then?" I said. "If you're right, we'll be brainwashed as soon as we meet her. And if they control all four of us, they'll control the entire exchange student group."

"Ah..." Claire's eyes widened in understanding.

We four were the key members of the exchange group. Some officials were accompanying us for administrative purposes, of course, as well as some actual students, but we mattered more than anyone. If we got brainwashed, Bauer's fate was sealed. Mind control hadn't been in the plot of *Revo-Lily*, but Yu's allegation had troubling logical weight.

"Indeed," said Yu. "That's why I brought this. Misha?"

"Yes." Misha extended her right hand. Her palm cradled a small ring.

"What is this?" Claire asked.

"The Tears of the Moon," Yu replied.

"What?!" Claire stared, astonished. "But...the relic used on May and Aleah was quite a bit larger..."

"That's a decoy. This small ring is the real deal."

In other words, the large ritual item they'd brought out for us back then was a fake.

"Then...the reason May and Aleah weren't cured was because—"

"The church didn't trick us, Claire," I cut in to pacify her; she'd begun eyeing Yu and Misha with distrust.

"So you noticed, Rae?" Yu asked.

"Yes. I saw the real ring on your finger when the decoy was brought out."

"I take it you don't want us to ask how you know the true form of the Tears of the Moon?"

"That would be nice."

"Very well, then." Yu smiled bitterly. She was likely dying to know. "Moving along—this ring can keep at least one of us from being brainwashed. I think our strongest fighter, Rae, should wear it."

"I'm fine with that, but are you sure you want to put your faith in me?"

"I know very well what kind of person you are. Just don't tell the church or the kingdom. They wanted me to wear it." Yu gave me a wink.

"Misha, aren't you going to stop her?"

"Considering my position, I should. But I think Lady Yu is right this time. In terms of raw combat strength, Miss Claire would also be a wise choice, but she can't use water magic to potentially dispel mind control effects. You're our best option," Misha said with a sigh.

There was a knock at the door. "Thank you for waiting. Her Majesty Dorothea is ready to see you."

It was time.

Yu stood. "Now then, shall we go meet Her Majesty?"

A woman with long hair of deep crimson and eyes red as flame sat silently atop her throne. Her body was clad in pitch-black armor, draped in an equally black mantle. By her hip hung two swords. Her elbows listlessly rested on her armrests as her idle gaze trained on us.

"You have done well to come all this way. I am Dorothea, the Empress of Nur." A surprisingly deep alto rang out. Her husky voice and masculine manner of speech were still simultaneously, unmistakably those of a woman. It was a voice of profound and regal power; one that compelled you to unconditionally obey.

"It is an honor to meet you. I am the representative of Bauer Kingdom's exchange student group, Yu Bauer. Thank you f—"

"Enough. I have no interest in greetings smothered in meaningless diplomatic courtesy." Dorothea looked annoyed as she cut off Yu, someone who always kept her true feelings hidden behind many veils.

Yu faltered, taken by surprise.

Dorothea continued, undaunted. "You've seen the Imperial Capital. Give me your thoughts."

"The capital is marvelous. Its people are spirited, and—"

"I have no use for your empty flattery. That's twice I've had to warn you, Yu Bauer. I won't forgive you for wasting my time again." Dorothea rested her head on one hand as her other hand tapped her armrest in irritation. "I'm getting nowhere with you. You, Rae Taylor, answer instead."

"Huh?"

"Don't dally. I asked for your impression of the capital."

I was dumbstruck. I couldn't just say nothing, so I simply said what was truly on my mind. "I don't have much to say about the capital when we only just got here, Your Majesty. If you're really going to squeeze me for an answer, then I guess 'lively' sounds about right?"

"Rae!" Claire scolded, even though I was tailoring my tone based on my knowledge of Dorothea's personality from *Revo-Lily*.

"Do you mean to say my city was not enough to impress you?"

"It wasn't too different from the Bauer Kingdom."

"What of the myriad races my people represent? Surely that can't be found in your kingdom."

"Oh, yeah. That was a little impressive. Like, 'Oh, wowzers, it's really a meritocracy,' you know?"

Claire stared at me, mouth agape. I was speaking to the monarch of a massive empire with an unimaginable degree of rudeness. But I had a feeling this was the correct way to proceed.

"Hmm...I see. So my empire was not enough to impress you. The Bauer Kingdom must be a more noteworthy nation than I first thought."

"Oh, but I was impressed by how much the citizens adored Your Majesty. I figured they'd fear you."

"There is logic to ruling through fear, but it can't compare to adoration and respect. And I'm a devout believer in rationality."

"You don't say? I think it's a pretty good way of going about things. By the way, can Your Majesty use mind control magic?"

"Rae?!"

"Wha—Rae!"

This time, it was Yu and Misha's turn to be appalled.

Maybe that was a little too direct? I thought as I waited for Dorothea's answer.

"Pfft... Ha ha..." Dorothea's shoulders trembled as she hung her head. "Ha ha ha ha! You seem to have full knowledge of my nature, Rae Taylor! You're as mysterious as they say."

"Sure."

"Brainwashing, you said? Did you bring that *trinket* from your house of worship because you suspected such a thing?" Dorothea scoffed.

Yu's eyes went wide in shock. Dorothea knew. And about the true form of the Tears of the Moon at that!

Yu quickly lowered her head. "Forgive our rudeness... We..."

"Enough. Your actions are logically sound. Well then, I sit before you now. Do you feel some sort of artificial adoration for me?"

"No, not particularly. What about you, Miss Claire? Are you head over heels for Her Majesty yet?"

"Rae!"

"It's fine. Speak your mind, Claire François. You're Rae's lover, are you not? Do you find yourself mesmerized by me?" Dorothea seemed to be enjoying herself now. So she even knew about our relationship?

"I think Her Majesty is a very interesting person, but I feel no artificial attraction toward you."

"Of course not. Miss Claire is smitten with me, after all," I added.

"Rae!"

"Ha ha ha ha! I see, I see! So I'm not even a threat? I find that slightly vexing."

Dorothea stood up and walked toward us, her mantle billowing, before stopping in front of Claire and me. Her intensity from up close was searing. She was beautiful. I'd heard she was in her late thirties, but she didn't look a day older than her mid-twenties.

"You two were doubtlessly the heart of the Bauer revolution." Dorothea smiled confidently.

"Not at all, Your Majesty," Claire replied. "The revolution was brought about through the power of the people. Rae and I played a very small role."

"I don't need your modesty. I regard you two quite highly. You managed to crush the plan I spent years preparing."

Wait—had she just openly admitted she'd been plotting against the Bauer Kingdom? Here, on our first step toward peace?

"Won't you two be mine?"

"Huh...?"

"Don't make me repeat myself. Come serve me as my subjects. You've proven your capabilities. I can assure you you'll be well compensated. How about it?"

Claire looked bewildered, and understandably so. We'd come

here on a formal diplomatic mission, and now suddenly, we were being headhunted?

"Do you jest?" Claire asked.

"Claire's already spoken for, so I'd appreciate it if you didn't try to woo her," I stated.

"R-Rae!"

"Ha ha ha! The rumors were true—you really do like to play the fool, Rae Taylor. I'll allow your transgressions to slide, so long as you continue to entertain me."

"I didn't come here for Your Majesty's entertainment," I said, which prompted Dorothea to clap.

"Oh! That's right. This meeting was part of the plan to placate the Bauer Kingdom."

"Your true thoughts are leaking through. This meeting was to formally greet the exchange students, Your Majesty."

"Oh, I do remember something like that. Forgive me, I don't see any merit in remembering such dull falsehoods."

Was it really okay for the empress to say such things?

"Your Majesty!" A man beside the throne who looked like an advisor was growing panicked.

"Silence, old man. I'll entertain your grumblings later."

The advisor, who looked older than Dole, held his tongue. I felt for him, having to advise an empress like this.

"Well, this should be good enough for greetings. Do you have any further business?"

Yu returned to formalities. "We've come bearing gifts from our kingdom. Please accept them."

Dorothea waved her hand disinterestedly. "Just leave those wherever. I'll send something suitable to your country in return. Anything else?"

"That'll be—"

"May I ask something?" Claire abruptly cut Yu off. "Does Her Majesty have no intention of ceasing her invasion of other countries?"

"Claire?!" Yu said, alarmed. Even I, who never really felt perturbed, was a little taken aback by the frankness of Claire's question.

"Hmph... You're bold to ask such a thing, Claire François."

"I apologize for my rudeness. May I have your answer?"

I was certain we had crossed the line, but the empress just stood there, thinking. "Invasion... I suppose that's how it must seem to your people."

"Are we wrong?"

"No, not at all. No matter my true intent, from your perspective, it is but invasion. I think that logical."

"Then what is your true intent?"

"I cannot tell you that yet. Unless you'd be willing to serve me."

"Then it seems we have nothing further to discuss."

"I see. That's too bad." Dorothea looked somewhat dejected. She was acting...right? "Any further business?"

"That'll be all from us," said Yu. This time, nobody interrupted her.

"Very well. Enjoy your stay in my empire. You may leave."

And so our first audience with Dorothea came to an end.

"So that was Empress Dorothea. She's a tyrant, all right," Yu reflected as Misha helped her change.

We were currently inside a dormitory assigned to the Bauer exchange students. Well, I say dormitory, but it was actually an inn that had been remodeled to accommodate us. Each room was bigger than those in the Royal Academy's dorms, a show of the empire's wealth.

The four of us had gathered in the lounge after our audience with Dorothea. We wanted to reflect on what happened as we shed our formal outer layers.

"I didn't expect her to entirely eschew diplomatic courtesy," I said.

"That's probably what seems logical to her. She's the worst kind of opponent for someone like me, who uses words as weapons." Yu sighed as Misha removed her coat. Dorothea had largely ignored her even as we left. "Rae is a better match for Dorothea. I'll let you handle things next time we meet."

"Don't say that, Yu. Rae was only able to act without restraint because you showed the bare minimum of required formalities." Misha was trying to cheer her up. They really were a good match.

"Miss Claire, cheer me up, too!"

"Why? You seem chipper enough to me." Claire curtly denied my request, much to my dismay.

"Let's hear everyone's impression of Dorothea, starting with Misha," Yu said.

Misha fell into thought for a moment. "She seemed to act without consideration of others. But...perhaps that's more a quality of a ruler in itself."

"What do you mean?"

"She doesn't seem the type of person to let herself be swayed by those beneath her. That kind of single-minded focus might be necessary to unite people in pursuit of your goals." Misha seemed to think Dorothea was the polar opposite of a less strident leader like the late King l'Ausseil or Thane.

"I see. She doesn't have to weigh the opinions of her retainers, which would otherwise force her to perform an impossible juggling act. She can act without hesitation."

"That's it," Misha affirmed.

"She's a tyrant, no doubt. But she isn't conceited, and she doesn't ignore the needs of her people. Misha's right—that's leadership in its own way. What do you think, Claire?"

Claire frowned. "I don't think I can ever see eye to eye with her."

"Why is that?"

"Our values are too different. I don't see any respect in the way Dorothea treats others, and I simply don't like those who so thoroughly disregard decorum."

I thought back to when Claire had taught May and Aleah the basics of etiquette. "To be without etiquette is to be unclothed," she'd said. Claire valued the traditions of the bygone noble world. People like Dorothea, who spoke and acted without such mindfulness, offended her sensibilities.

"But I do understand why one might say she's charismatic. She seems the type of person people want to follow, the type to never lose sight of her goal."

You could see Dorothea's beliefs reflected in her empire. Nur had a clear goal that all citizens jointly strove for. In pursuit of that goal, they sought out talent regardless of origin or creed, and they explicitly outlawed discrimination for the same reason.

"Yeah. To tell the truth, as someone who lacks that strength of purpose, I can't help but admire people like her. Of my siblings, I'd say she's most like my brother Rod," Yu said.

I thought Rod and Dorothea were similar, too. They were both leaders who could act without hesitation and inspire people to their cause.

"How about you, Rae?"

"I think...she's childish."

"Hmm?" Yu looked confused. Misha and Claire also gave me puzzled frowns.

"She does whatever she wants and doesn't listen to what other people say, but despite that, she still needs other people to help her. She's basically a child."

"I...hadn't considered that." Yu smiled as she nodded, realizing the truth of my words.

Dorothea was an adult, and a frightful one at that. It was easy to be intimidated by her. Yet my first impression was that she was childish. She stood at the head of the empire and was glorified by many, but at heart, she was immature. What she called "logic" and "rationality" were just excuses to do only as she pleased.

"Well, even if she is a little eccentric, she's still the ruler of this empire," I continued. "She's clearly incomparable to a normal child. Just like my children."

"Is that parental bias I hear?" Yu said teasingly.

It's true, I swear! I moved on. "Seems there was no mind control involved in the end either."

"Yes. It was just her natural charisma at work. That charisma wasn't enough to win over Rae, though." Yu fiddled with the box containing the Tears of the Moon. "I guess we brought this ring with us for nothing."

"No, this is still an enemy country. You never know when we might need it," Misha warned. She was right. We couldn't let our guard down.

"Anyway, good work, everyone. We'll be starting at the Imperial Academy tomorrow, so make sure to rest well tonight." Yu's words signaled the end of our meeting.

"Are you feeling tired, Miss Claire?" I worriedly asked as we walked back to our room. While she had more stamina than most people, our long journey from the kingdom, immediately followed by that audience with the empress, had to have been mentally draining.

"I'm all right. Thank you."

"Are you sure? You're not just putting on a brave front?"

"And what would that do for me? I'm fine, really. More importantly, I wonder if our luggage has been delivered to our room yet."

"It should have been. I hope May and Aleah haven't been up to any mischief."

I opened the door to a wide room. Our luggage was there, but I saw no sign of the girls. The four of us were to lodge together—Yu had considerately traded rooms with us so we could have the largest one. It wasn't the same as our beloved home in the kingdom, but for now, it would have to do.

"May? Aleah?"

"Mama!"

"We're here!"

I called for the twins and immediately saw two small figures run toward us from the back of the room and straight into Claire's arms.

"Boom!"

"Welcome back!"

"Thank you, May, Aleah. Were you two good girls?"

"Uh-huh!"

"Yes, Mother!"

We had kept them waiting alone for quite a long time, but the twins didn't seem particularly put off. Come to think of it, back in Bauer, Claire and I had had to leave them home alone a lot. Maybe this wasn't out of the ordinary for them.

"Shall we eat, then? Rae, could you prepare something for us?" Claire asked.

"Leave it to me."

That overly formal, pain-in-the-neck audience with the empress was finally done. Claire, and even the children for that matter, had to be tired.

I'll whip up something special, I thought as I headed to the attached kitchenette.

"Y-you'd dare oppose the empire?!"

"Oh, dear, whatever are you saying? Are we not both merely students? Your name wouldn't happen to be 'Empire' now, would it?" Claire asked—a bold provocation. She smirked wickedly, the very image of a villainess. The man she spoke to seemed at a loss for words.

This clash unfolded at the educational institute run by the empire, the Imperial Academy. Behind Claire, who stood with her arms folded, a small girl trembled on the ground—Philine.

"U-um..."

"It's okay. Let Miss Claire handle this," I whispered into Philine's ear as I took her hand and helped her stand. She seemed confused but nodded for the time being.

"Do you know who I am?!" the man demanded.

"I beg your pardon, but I've only just transferred here today. I haven't the slightest idea."

"You...you won't get away with this!" The man stammered words befitting a henchman as he glared daggers at us.

As for why all this had come to pass on our first day—let's rewind a few hours.

"These new transfer students will be joining you from today. Everyone, please give them a warm welcome." The teacher introduced us briefly before assigning our seats and beginning class. I balked a bit in surprise; I'd expected time for self-introductions.

The teacher provided no review to help us transfer students catch up, nor did they ease us in at all. First period was a social studies course, but the difficulty of the materials and the pace of instruction far surpassed the mode of instruction at the Academy in Bauer. We didn't know much about the culture of the empire either. With the exception of a few, we exchange students ended that class dead-tired.

"Class dismissed." With those brusque words, the teacher left the classroom.

Who in the world could possibly keep up with these classes?! the transfer students unanimously thought.

At that point, a crowd formed around us. The teacher was cold, but the students didn't seem much different from Bauer's.

"Hey, hey, you guys are from the Bauer Kingdom, right?"

"Is it true you had a revolution?"

"What are your names?"

"Please, allow us to introduce ourselves," Claire said.

Five Bauer transfer students were in this class: Claire, me, Lana, Eve, and Joel. I couldn't see Yu or Lene, who had been assigned to a different class.

"My name is Claire François. It is a pleasure to make your acquaintance." Claire introduced herself first. The moment she said her name, the entire classroom stirred.

"Aren't you the hero of the revolution?!"

"Is it true you outsmarted and beat a thousand royal soldiers?!"

It seemed Claire's fame had reached the empire, although the tale had clearly grown in the telling.

"I'm not that remarkable. The power of the people brought revolution."

"But you're, like, super strong, right?"

"Not even I could defeat a thousand people," Claire demurred. "That part is exaggeration."

"Hey, hey, who's stronger, you or Her Majesty Dorothea?"

As I'd expected, Claire was popular right off the bat. Yet she turned to me. "How about we finish our introductions first? Rae?"

I stood from my chair at Claire's prompt. "My name is Rae Taylor, and I'm Miss Claire's wife. Don't try to take her from me or I'll bite." I bared my teeth and growled a bit.

"Wha—Rae?!" Claire became flustered.

Sorry, Miss Claire. I have to do this to make sure everyone knows who belongs to whom!

"Huh? Is she with Claire?"

"She called her *Miss* Claire, though."

"Ooh, Rae's pretty funny!"

My introduction seemed well received. Perhaps they thought I was joking.

"N-next, then," Claire continued. "Lana?"

"Heeey!" Lana stood and winked. "Name's Lana Lahna! I'm a wicked girl trying to snatch Miss Rae from Miss Claire. Nice to meet you!"

"Huh? A love triangle?"

"Oh, man, that's gonna be a bloodbath..."

"Just like *Soap Opera.*"

Seemed like Lana's introduction had been well received, too. *Hmm? Hold on...*

"Um, did you say 'soap opera'?" I asked.

"Yeah, you know, the novel series, *Soap and Opera*? It's a masterpiece about messy relationships. I'll lend it to you sometime."

"Huh? Um, yeah. Thank you," I said. *So misleading!*

"All right, next. Eve?"

"My name's Eve Nuhn. Nice to meet you." Eve introduced herself in her trademark blunt way.

"This time it's a harsh, cold girl!"

"Hey, hey, want some candy?"

"Please step on me, Mommy."

Eve's introduction was also well received. Actually, were my ears playing tricks on me, or had there been something weird in the mix just there?

"Lastly, Joel?" Claire prompted.

"I'm Joel Santana. I'm confident in my physical strength. Nice to meet you." Joel gave a passable introduction, although I thought it could be a little warmer.

"And now we have a level-headed cool guy."

"That bluntness ain't bad."

"Please step on me, Daddy."

Joel's introduction was *also* well received. But also, come on, there was definitely one weirdo in this class.

Regardless, the students seemed welcoming enough. I'd been prepared for them to be more guarded, even for them to give us the cold shoulder, but they received us strangers amicably enough—perhaps because Nur prided itself in its diversity. As long as we put in the effort to get along, they would do the same.

"How about we introduce ourselves, too?"

"I'm Johann!"

"Wha—hey, I was going first!"

The students clamored as they introduced themselves one by one. I noticed that one person among them remained silent.

"Hey, Philine, it's your turn!"

"Ah, y-yes..."

Claire glanced at me upon hearing Philine's name. I nodded back.

"M-my name is Ph-Philine. N-nice to meet you..."

I couldn't help thinking Philine looked like a small, timid animal as she shyly introduced herself. She sat down immediately afterward and hid her face behind a book.

"Philine's actually Her Majesty Dorothea's daughter—can you believe it? They're nothing alike."

"Is that so," Claire responded.

No doubt about it, Philine was the girl we were after. I needed to think of how to engage her—

"Shut up!" A loud voice surprised us. I looked toward its source to see a rough-looking boy with his feet on his desk. "You guys are too noisy..."

"O-Otto...so you were here. Why don't you introduce your—"

"And why the heck do I gotta do that?"

"N-never mind, then..."

The classroom fell silent. It seemed Otto was something of a problem child.

"Hey, that ringlet blonde and the rest are all enemies of the empire, right? Why the heck are you getting all chummy with them?" Otto's chair creaked as he got up and lumbered toward us. A tall boy, nearly six feet already, he also sported impressive musculature. He was basically a walking boulder.

"Otto, was it? I'm Claire François. Pleased to meet you."

"Don't even try. I bet you're just some sheltered rich lady like Philine over there." Otto drew close to Claire, looking down on her from above. I itched to blast him with my magic, but Claire signaled me not to with her eyes.

"Me, a sheltered rich lady? Well, you're not entirely wrong."

"Heh, I knew it."

"But I'd rather be a sheltered rich lady than a boy so poor in the head."

Otto looked shocked for a moment before he fumed. "You tryin' to get killed?!"

"Oh, my, you really are in want of a brain. Don't you understand you'll cause a diplomatic incident if you lay a hand on me?"

"Like I care!" Otto swung his arm at Claire, but she nimbly evaded it while hooking his foot with hers, sending him to the ground.

"Y-you!"

"Oh, dear, I beg your pardon."

"You're dead meat!" Enraged, Otto swung repeatedly at Claire, but—

"Haah...haah...I'll...kill..." Each swing missed without so much as grazing her. A few seconds in and the result couldn't be clearer. Otto had lost.

"Is that it?" Claire asked, brushing off her shoulders. "I suppose you make a poor delinquent, too."

Otto seemed to be trying to deploy some sort of martial art against Claire, but he was completely out of her league. Claire had trained in the art of self-defense from a young age, and she had real combat experience from the events leading up to the revolution.

"Ugh... Fine, I'll use this!" Otto reached into his breast pocket and pulled out a long cylindrical object.

A magic wand!

"Miss Claire, look out—" I lurched forward but was beaten to the punch.

"Stop!" A figure stepped in front of Claire and shielded her. Philine.

"Huh?! What are ya doin'? Get outta the way, Philine!"

"Using magic is going too far!"

"I said get outta the way!"

"Eek!"

Otto shoved Philine aside. I saw his lips move for a moment but couldn't hear what he said.

Claire walked in front of Philine, who had fallen on her bottom, and shielded her.

"Magic? Sure, why not. Give it a shot, see what happens," Claire goaded.

"D-don't you look down on me..."

That about brings us up to the present.

"Eat this!" Otto waved his magic wand, and flame arrows burst forth from the tip toward Claire.

Claire lunged straight at them.

"Look out!" Philine's shriek echoed throughout the room. But Claire quickly cast flame arrows of her own to extinguish Otto's before running forward and kicking him in the chest.

"Guh!"

"Now then, time for your punishment." Claire smiled down on the collapsed Otto.

Ah, she's furious, I thought. *She's smiling, but she's absolutely furious.* Pushing Philine aside had been the last straw.

"W-wait! Y-you'll cause an international incident, remember?!"

"No, *I* won't. This is just a quarrel between students. Isn't that right, everyone?" Claire smiled gracefully as she cracked her knuckles. Nobody dared say anything.

Go get 'em, tiger! I thought.

"B-but you said so yourself!"

"Obviously a bluff. You really are a boy of little brain." Claire drew her own magic wand and touched its tip to Otto's forehead. She'd said she was bluffing, but no matter how you looked at it, this was the real bluff. Killing someone would *definitely* have repercussions, even if both victim and aggressor were "just" students.

"Incidentally, I'm not just *any* sheltered rich lady. I'm a sheltered rich lady with high aptitude in fire magic. Would you like a demonstration?"

"W-wait, d-don't!" Otto trembled in fear as he pleaded.

"St-stop!" Philine grabbed Claire's arm right before she could wave her wand.

"What is it?"

"I-Isn't this far enough?"

"Is it? Don't you bear him a grudge?"

"Otto is...violent sometimes, but deep down, he's a good person. He just happened to be in a foul mood today..." Philine earnestly pleaded with Claire. Tears welled in her eyes, undoubtedly from fear. Myself, I loved seeing Claire blow a gasket, but I could understand why someone else might think it frightening. Even the other Nur students had backed away.

"Very well. I'll respect your wishes and yield. Let's end our self-introductions here. I bid you all a good day." Leaving those words behind, Claire took her bag and left the classroom.

"Damn it..." Otto growled.

"O-Otto, wait, let me heal you..."

"Leave me alone!" Otto shook Philine off as she tried to cast healing magic on him and stormed out of the classroom.

It seemed the brawl had come to an end.

"H-hey, Miss Rae? Was Miss Claire always that scary?" Lana asked.

"Huh? Scary how?"

"Whaddya mean, 'how'?" Lana looked at a loss.

Hmph. Personally, I considered getting to see Claire's fury a rare treat.

"Miss Claire can be scary when angry, sure, but she's usually pretty nice. If anything, she's absolutely charming."

"Charming?"

"Yes. Observe." I pointed toward the entrance of the classroom. As if on cue, Claire reappeared, looking visibly flustered.

"I-Is something the matter, Claire?"

"Um, did Otto do something again?"

The Nur students asked gingerly—they couldn't imagine what else would have brought her back to the classroom.

To this, she responded, "...I seem to have forgotten we still have classes left."

How embarrassing. Oh, how I adored her.

Things settled down after that hectic first day, and our life at the Imperial Academy began in earnest. Classes remained fast-paced and difficult, but Claire, with her natural smarts, and I, with my knowledge of the original game, managed to keep up. The same couldn't be said for the other transfer students, though.

The Imperial Academy wasn't a boarding school like the Royal Academy. Students commuted from their own homes or, if they hailed from a different country, lived in lodging paid for by the empire. Roll call began at nine in the morning, meaning we had more time to get ready than at the Royal Academy. At least, that was the case for most students.

"May, Aleah! Hurry up and get changed. It's time for elementary school."

"They have music class today, Miss Claire. Here, take this instrument."

"I'm still hungry, Mama..."

"I'm sleepy..."

Every morning, we fought to get the kids ready for school. We had to make breakfast, brush their teeth, get them changed, and see them off, leaving barely any time to eat breakfast ourselves. This led to us cutting attendance close every morning, usually arriving between eight-thirty and nine on the dot. Our other classmates were almost always all seated whenever we arrived.

"Oh my gosh, Miss Rae's *sooo* slow. Miss Claire, too."

"Morning, Lana."

"Good morning, Lana. But you don't need to add *Miss* to our names anymore—we're your classmates now, not your teachers," Claire said.

"That's right. We're not that far apart in age either," I added.

"Aww." Lana looked displeased. "But I, like, *totally* respect you two, so I'm gonna keep at it, 'kay?"

"Suit yourself..." I said. Something about her words struck me as odd, but I decided it wasn't worth following up on.

"Morning, Eve."

"Good morning." Eve returned my greeting but immediately averted her eyes. It seemed she still wasn't a fan of mine.

"Excuse me, Eve?" chided Claire, ever the stickler for etiquette. "I won't tell you to respect us as much as Lana does, but you should at least show some manners."

"Sorry," Eve said, but she didn't look apologetic in the slightest.

"It's fine, Miss Claire," I said. "Eve and I just have something of a misunderstanding between us."

"Is that so?"

"Do you have time to talk right now, Eve? I think we got off on the wrong foot somehow." I'd never had the chance to clear things up back in the kingdom. Maybe now was a good time.

"There's no misunderstanding here," Eve curtly declared before turning her head away. Negotiations had already broken down.

This girl's so stubborn! She could hate me all she liked, but I still wanted to correct the misunderstanding. Was there a way I could force her to talk to me?

"Morning," a voice listlessly greeted us.

"Oh, Joel. Good morning."

For a tough-looking guy, he was pretty friendly. He'd stopped addressing Claire and I as formally as he had when we were his teachers, which was just how we wanted it.

"Mornings must be busy for you two, with your kids and all," Lana said.

"I suppose it is, but that also means there's never a dull moment," I replied.

"Wow, I don't think I could handle that."

Children weren't for everybody.

Our first class began at nine-thirty and went on for an hour and a half. Like I mentioned before, the contents were difficult and came quick. After taking the classes for a while, I came to realize that the curriculum progressed at a rate determined by the top students of the class, as befitted a nation that advocated meritocracy.

Otto's performance surprised me a bit.

"Let's see... Otto, could you answer this question?" The teacher asked.

"Huh? Make someone else do it."

"Do you want your evaluation to suffer?"

Otto mumbled something under his breath before standing up and walking toward the blackboard. He took a glance at the math problem before effortlessly writing out the answer.

"Done. You happy?"

"Very good. You have a good head on your shoulders, Otto. You just need to work on your attitude a bit."

"Oh, lay off."

Otto walked back to his seat with his hands in his pockets. Despite being a problem student, he was by no means dumb. His attitude remained terrible, but he listened in class and always answered the questions correctly. I'd had a bad impression of him because of the first day, but he seemed to be a truly gifted student.

I didn't remember anyone named Otto from *Revo-Lily*, so he must have been a background character. Though for a background character, he sure had a lot of personality.

Morning classes tended to end around noon. The academy had a cafeteria, but it wasn't too popular; most students brought their own lunch instead. I'll get into why later. For now, just know that Claire and I brought our own lunches. I also made lunches for May and Aleah. It wasn't too hard to make lunch for four, but having to devise meal plans daily proved to be a bit of a hassle. Oh, I missed the days of looking up recipes on my smartphone.

"Lady Philine, may we join you for lunch?"

"Oh, um..."

Philine was something of a loner and usually ate lunch by herself, which was perfect for us. Unfortunately...

"I-I, um... Excuse me!" Frightened, Philine ran away—leaving her lunch box behind.

"I know you said she was shy, but *this* shy?"

"Hmm... She's worse than I remember."

I'd thought this would work, seeing as there was a scene where you ate lunch with the girl you were trying to romance in *Revo-Lily*. Maybe there was another factor at play?

"You think it's because of what happened on the first day?" I asked.

"Come again?"

"You know, your fight with Otto."

"Oh... But I helped Philine then, so it couldn't be that." Claire frowned.

"I'm sure she knows that, but you were so dazzling—er, I mean—frightening then."

"Shouldn't you be correcting that the other way around?"

Oops. I'd let my true feelings slip for a moment there.

"But, supposing you're correct, isn't that a problem? That will make it harder to get close to her."

"Yeah. Well, nothing we can do about it now. We'll just have to take our time wooing Philine."

"Like I said, please stop using 'wooing' in that way..."

At around one o'clock, lunch break ended. After two more hour-and-a-half classes, putting us at four o'clock, we finished with classes for the day and went to pick up May and Aleah at the elementary school. I broke off from the three to do some shopping and met them back at the Bauer student dorm before beginning to cook dinner. We spent the rest of our evening the same way we did back in Bauer: playing, bathing, and then finally going to bed.

"We've grown accustomed to life in the empire," I said one night.

"Yes, but we haven't made much progress with Philine."

"Baby steps. Hey, Miss Claire?"

"Yes?"

I sensed Claire turning to face me, even with the bedroom light extinguished.

"It's been a while... Can we...?"

"Oh, jeez... What am I going to do with you... Come here, Rae."

Needless to say, our night went long.

"Excuse me... Would you mind if I joined you for lunch?"

I was eating lunch alone for a change when I heard someone talk to me. To my surprise, I raised my head to find a trembling Philine.

"Not at all—please do."

"Thank you." Philine took the next desk and pushed it up against mine before bringing out her lunch box. It was jam-packed with various ingredients, likely prepared by a palace chef.

"Your lunch looks wonderful, Lady Philine."

"Huh...? O-oh, really? Um... Thank you...?" Philine looked bewildered, like she wasn't used to conversing with others.

"Those meatballs look nice. Can I have one?"

"Uh, yes... It's really nothing special, but here..."

"Thank you very much."

I took a quail-egg-sized meatball from Philine's lunch and gave it a taste. Ah, not great. It seemed the empire's cuisine wasn't up to snuff. But that wasn't my problem.

"Delicious!"

"Really? Th-that's good."

"Then how about as thanks, I answer any one question you have?"

"Huh...?" Philine's mouth went wide, like I had just read her mind.

"I'm assuming there's something you want to ask, since you made the effort to come eat with me."

"Um, well, that's...yes." Philine was flustered. She wore a look of shame, like she had been caught stealing cookies from a jar. "I want you to teach me about Claire."

"Oh?"

Claire was currently in the neighboring classroom with Lene. She dearly wanted to rekindle their bond, but Lene had her own diplomatic duties as a representative of the Alpes to consider. Their schedules had just so happened to align today, so they were taking the chance to catch up without being disturbed.

"I'll answer what I can, but wouldn't it be better to ask her directly?"

"Um, Claire is...still too scary for me..."

Ah, figured. Seemed I was right. "What do you want to know?"

"Um, well, I was wondering what led Claire to start a revolution," Philine nervously asked. Just as I predicted—despite her fear of Claire, Philine was interested enough in the revolution to bite.

"Oh, that? That's actually a misunderstanding. The one who started the revolution wasn't Miss Claire."

"Huh? Then why is she called 'the hero of the revolution'?"

"Miss Claire played an important role in the revolution, but make no mistake—the ones who started the revolution were the people of Bauer Kingdom."

"O-oh, okay..." Philine looked conflicted. "Then let me rephrase the question. Why did Miss Claire support the revolution? Wasn't she part of the establishment, and a high-ranking noble, no less?"

"That's a difficult question to answer, but to put it simply, it's precisely because she was a noble."

"I'm afraid I don't understand." Philine tilted her head.

Mmm... Cute. "Miss Claire didn't support the revolution from the start. In fact, she initially rejected the very notion of it."

"Why did she change her mind?"

"A certain incident led her to question the system where nobles lorded it over commoners." I began telling her about the ghost ship incident that had occurred on our visit to Euclid, my hometown, going into detail about my childhood friend Louie and how he had attacked us to save his kidnapped family.

"That's terrible..."

"That was when Miss Claire truly learned what it meant to be poor. She examined her life and power as a noble, and she wondered how she could allow such things to happen."

I went on to explain how Claire had begun to think about ways to address poverty and wealth disparity, and how that, in turn, had led her to realize the deep-rooted problems with the aristocracy.

"She wanted to help the people, so she strove to find a way to bridge the gap between commoners and nobles."

"Something she could do..." Those words seemed to resonate with Philine.

"And the rest is history. Claire gained the support of the populace by exposing the corrupt nobles and then by siding with the commoners against the provisional government after the Mt. Sassal eruption."

I'd left out some details and mixed in some half-truths, but I finished my mostly true recounting of events leading to the revolution.

"Claire is so...strong."

"I wholeheartedly agree, but she couldn't do it alone."

"What do you mean?"

"Miss Claire is gifted, but even she can't do everything herself. She only managed to come this far because she had the help of many people."

If she were alone, she would have been executed that terrible day as a symbol of the corrupt nobility—leaving her name forever besmirched in the annals of history.

"To achieve something, you need allies," I said.

"Allies..."

"If you have any doubts about the current empire, Claire and I would be happy to lend our aid."

"Huh?!" Philine went stiff as a board. Maybe I'd gone too far? "M-my stomach hurts—I'll be taking my leave!"

"Um, Lady Philine?"

"Pardon me!"

And off she went. Aw, shoot... It had been going so well, too. Why did I have to rush things?

But her already knowing about Claire was a godsend. And now that her impression of Claire was more than just "that scary person," we could move on to the next step—putting them in direct contact.

"Did something happen? Philine just ran by in a hurry," Claire said, finally returning.

"We were eating lunch together. She asked about you. Things are looking up," I said before filling Claire in on what had transpired. "Philine appears to have doubts about the empire. I think we should try to raise her awareness on certain issues."

"Sounds good. Although I still feel kind of guilty, given our ulterior motives."

"Nothing else we can do." Diplomacy was never pretty. "Did you eat lunch, Miss Claire?"

"I did, with Lene. She treated me to Frater's latest item."

"Oh, really? What was it?"

"She told me to keep it a secret from you, saying she'd kick herself if you were to happen to already know it."

"Ah ha ha..."

Maybe I teased Lene too much?

"You should eat, Rae. Before the bell rings."

"Oh, right."

I ravenously dug into my lunch. The way I ate was impolite, but you know what they say—can't eat your omelets without breaking some eggs.

"But I wonder," I said through bites, "is Philine already on anyone's route right now?"

Revo-Lily had three romanceable characters.

One was Dorothea, with whom we'd had an audience the other day. That might come as a shock, considering Dorothea was Philine's mother, but that forbidden love was the selling point of the route. After seeing Dorothea in person, I couldn't help but think she would be a terrible romance partner. Yet she was somehow a popular choice with the game's players.

Being a devotee to the church of Claire, I'd initially thought I might be attracted to Dorothea too, since their personalities had some similarities. But no matter how many times I replayed *Revo-Lily*, I remained indifferent toward her. In my heart, Dorothea could never hold a candle to Claire.

Another romanceable character was Hildegard Eichrodt, a government official who got close to Philine to further her own career. Her relationship with Philine started for selfish reasons but slowly turned into true love. I thought it was a decent story. I hadn't met her in person yet, but it was likely just a matter of time.

The final romanceable character was a student of the Imperial Academy by the name of Friedelinde Eimer. She had chestnut-brown hair and reddish-brown eyes, and she was currently standing in front of me.

"*Salut*, Rae."

"Good morning, Friedelinde," Claire greeted.

"*Non, non*, please call me Frieda."

"Very well, then. Frieda it is," Claire replied.

This girl, with her peculiar way of speaking, was Friedelinde, nicknamed Frieda. She had an archetypal Empire-sounding name, but she was from another country, like us.

Today, we'd arrived early to the classroom this morning, thanks to May and Aleah getting ready quicker than usual.

"You two look *oh*-so-lovely today. Like apples to my eyes."

"Thank you very much. I have my mother to thank for that," Claire responded, unfazed.

"Um, thank you...?" I wasn't quite as cool.

Frieda's words always put me on edge. Claire magnanimously let it slide, but I just *couldn't* stand it. Like, what kind of person started commenting on another's appearance as soon as they met?

As was likely already evident, Frieda was a bit of a smooth talker. She had nothing but girls on her brain, and she spent every free moment trying to talk them up. Her eccentric behavior was borderline tolerable in the game, but actually dealing with her in person was *rough.*

"My dear *mademoiselles,* could I interest you in dinner this evening?"

"I appreciate the offer, but unfortunately, Rae and I have our children to look after."

"*Quoi?!* You two are married with children?! At such a young age?!"

"Yep. Through adoption," I replied.

Come to think of it, we hadn't told our classmates about May and Aleah yet.

"*Magnifique!* They must surely be beautiful children, like their mothers!"

"Ugh. Like I just said, they're adopted."

"*Non, non,* children take after their parents regardless of blood. How about you bring the children to dinner?"

"I humbly decline."

I wasn't letting her anywhere near my daughters. Frieda's route stood out from the others because it got pretty stalkery in the worst kind of way—you know, the full *yandere* experience.

Despite her happy-go-lucky attitude, Frieda's life was turbulent and full of strife. She was royalty from Melica, a country the empire invaded that had resisted to the bitter end, only to wind up not annexed but utterly destroyed. Frieda harbored a deep grudge against the empire, which conflicted with her love for Philine. Not everyone who came to the empire had been as fortunate as the man who'd been our guide when we first arrived.

Frieda's route had numerous game-over sequences and was infamously scary. I wasn't letting a person like that anywhere near my daughters.

"*C'est la vie.* We'll have to rain-check, then. Anyway, have you two grown used to life in the empire?" She didn't back off, but at least she showed some concern for us. Despite being a total yandere, she could be nice. At least on the surface level.

"Yes, the empire is much more comfortable than I expected," Claire answered honestly. For the briefest of moments, Frieda's face went dark before returning to her smiling facade. Claire didn't seem to notice, but I definitely did. Maybe we did need a bit of distance from her after all.

"*Oui*, the empire is very comfortable! And I hear the Bauer Kingdom is very comfortable as well!" Frieda smiled as she gave Claire a friendly pat on the shoulder.

"Claire belongs to me, Frieda. Please don't touch her so carelessly."

"Oh! Sorry, sorry. But this much is just right between friends, is it not?"

"She's right, Rae. You're worrying too much," Claire chimed in.

"Being too clingy is no good, you know?" Frieda said.

You're the last person I want to hear that from, Yandere Stalkers-dottir!

"Oh, Philine! *Salut!*"

"G-good morning..."

Philine arrived later than us, a rare occurrence. She seemed a bit down. If memory served me right, she wasn't much of a morning person and was often easily overwhelmed by Frieda.

"You look *oh*-so-lovely today. Like apples to my eyes," Frieda said.

I guess she was using that line with every girl she met today.

"Th-thank you..." Philine cowered.

My condolences. I finally had a moment of respite now that Frieda found a new target.

"Whether it be Dorothea or Frieda, all the individuals in your *Revo-Lily* prophecy seem a bit...odd," Claire commented.

"Yeah. I suppose the devs tried to make them memorable characters."

That said, I did think the game designers had gone a bit too far. In fact, so did the fanbase. A lot of people had complained they could have toned it down a bit, or that there should have been at least one morally righteous character. The fact that *Revo-Lily* was still widely regarded as a masterpiece was thanks to its brilliant writing and perfectly executed revolution route.

"Just making sure—we're aiming for the revolution route, correct?" Claire asked.

"Definitely."

Several conditions had to be met to trigger the revolution route, the most basic of which was to not be romancing any of the love interests. It was currently the fifth month, so we were some ways from the point where the routes diverged. Even so, I wanted to verify the state of Philine's affection for the romance-able characters.

"How can we check what route we're in?" Claire asked.

"We can ask *her*. Hey, Anna? Can we talk to you for a moment?" I called out to a red-haired girl sitting behind Philine.

"Morning, Rae."

"Morning. I was wondering if we could ask you some questions about Philine."

Anna frowned at me, puzzled. "Well, sure, I guess?"

"Does she have anyone she likes right now?"

"Oh, are we gossiping?" Anna leaned forward with interest.

Anna was similar to Misha in that they were both stoic characters who acted as the protagonists' buddies. She was a useful source for a great deal of information, but right now, I really needed to know Philine's feelings.

"Hmm, let me think... I don't think she has feelings for anyone in particular right now."

"I see. Then, who do you think she's closest to right now?"

"I'm thinking she's closest with Frieda. Despite Frieda's one-sided pestering, she is one of the few people I've seen Philine talk to."

Hmm. So Philine was closest to the Frieda route, then?

"How is she with Lady Dorothea?"

"You mean Her Majesty? They don't get along very well. Something happened between them, I think."

So things weren't moving along with Dorothea.

"Is that right. What about Hildegard?"

"Hm? Have you met Hildegard before, Rae?"

"No, but I heard she was hitting on Philine."

"Oh, I see. Philine's relationship with Hildegard is...normal, I suppose? She tries to hit on her just like Frieda does, but Philine seems more guarded around Hildegard."

"You don't say?" In other words, Philine had the most affection for Frieda, then Hildegard, and lastly, Dorothea.

"Oh, but there is someone else she seems to have a good impression of."

"Oh? Who might that be?"

"Claire."

"Wha...what?!" *Hold the phone!* "I thought she was terrified of Miss Claire?!"

"She is, somewhat, but she's also interested in her. It's one of those things...y'know, where the soft-spoken introvert looks up to the outspoken extrovert? Hildegard may have Claire's confidence, but she comes off as cold and calculating, unlike Claire."

This threw a wrench in things. Who would have thought the protagonist might actually fall for the villainess? ...Not that I was one to talk.

"But I'm sure she knows Claire's already with you, and the two of you aren't from the empire either. She's probably just interested in Claire as a friend."

"Right..."

So she said, but it was better to play it safe than sorry. I was absolutely prepared to fight Philine to the last breath in the unlikely event she stepped onto the Claire route. Not that I actually believed things would escalate to that point, but you never knew.

"Good grief. Things just got complicated..."

"Excuse me, Lady Philine? Do you have time to—"

"S-sorry! I've gotta go do something!"

Claire cordially called out to Philine, but the latter dashed off.

"How many times does that make? Are you sure Philine likes me?"

"She should, but she certainly doesn't act like it."

We'd tried to approach Philine countless times since discovering her interest in Claire, only for her to flee each time. I had to find a way to counteract her fear. Naturally, this didn't involve letting her *have* Claire.

"If only there were a way..." Claire pondered.

"Yeah..."

We looked at each other when suddenly—

"*Salut*, Claire, Rae! Oh dear, why the sad faces? You waste those beautiful looks of yours!"

The annoying one showed up.

"Oh, hello, Frieda. Rae and I were just wondering how to get closer to Philine."

"What's this? Is Claire trying to *rendezvous* with Philine now? Are you through with Rae?"

"Like hell. Are you trying to get hit?" I snapped.

"*P-pardon.*"

Shoot. I'd spoken my mind without thinking.

"Oh, dear me, I seem to have used some vulgar words just now," I said.

"Oh, yes. I feel like they were directed at me, but that must have been my imagination!" Thank goodness Frieda was a simpleminded girl. Or rather, thank goodness she pretended to be. "Putting the jokes aside, I think I have a way you two can get closer to Philine!"

"Really? Please do tell," Claire urged her.

"What is it?" We were grasping at straws. We'd accept help from anyone at this point.

"It's very simple! Bait her with food!"

"Excuse me, Lady Philine, is now a good time?"

"U-um, I have to go do something today as well!"

Claire tried to call out to Philine again after school, but this time—as Philine turned away to flee—I pulled something out from my bag.

"Are you leaving already, Philine? And here I was thinking you might like to try this."

Philine's feet stopped as her gaze turned back toward my hand. "Th-that's Broumet chocolate!"

"Indeed, it is."

In my hand, I held chocolate brought from the Bauer Kingdom. Broumet only did business in Bauer and the Alpes, so chocolate was largely unknown in the Nur Empire. But being the imperial princess, Philine had caught a whiff of the latest trend in the world of sweets.

"A-are you giving that to me?"

"We will, as long as you don't mind joining us for tea," Claire said.

"The cafeteria should be pretty empty this time of evening. Can we count on you to join us?" I asked.

"Um... Well, I..." Philine hemmed and hawed.

Just one more push.

"I also have this." I reached into my bag and pulled out one more object.

"Um, what is that?"

"This is a new confectionary called *rakugan*. It was announced by Broumet just last month."

"Rakugan? I can't say I've heard of it..."

I'd sent this recipe to Broumet around the time we left for the empire. Rakugan is a traditional Japanese confectionary made by pressing starch and sugar together—it's often found in Japanese gift shops. It can be molded into a variety of pretty colors and pleasing shapes, such as flowers or animals, while retaining its sweet flavor. I was confident the empire had never seen anything quite like it.

Making rakugan was surprisingly simple, as was sourcing the ingredients. I only needed powdered sugar, rice flour, and food coloring. I got the powdered sugar by using a mortar to crush sugar I'd bought at the market. The rice flour was fairly easy to buy, as rice existed in the Bauer Kingdom. The only challenge was food coloring, but I managed to make a substitute with cocoa powder and ground tea leaves for a lovely red shade.

To make the rakugan, I mixed the powdered sugar with the red food coloring while adding just a slight bit of water. Then I added the rice flour and mixed it some more before putting it all through a sieve. Time was of the essence here, as the mixture quickly hardened. I then put the sifted mixture into a wooden mold and pressed it in. Once it took form, I let it dry, and *voilà*.

You could create as many different designs as you wanted simply by changing the food coloring or mold, meaning it was quite a treat for the eyes as well.

Philine stared at the rakugan with deep interest.

"How about we talk for a while, Lady Philine?" Claire asked.

"S-sure..."

Hook, line, and sinker.

"Haaanhnnn..." Philine sounded like she was melting as she bit into the chocolate. Broumet sold many varieties of chocolates, including low-sugar ones, but the variety Philine favored made liberal use of sugar. "This rakugan is so good, too... Such refined sweetness."

I'd been worried about how well the rakugan would go over, but to my relief, she adored it.

"Was it to your liking, Lady Philine?" Claire inquired.

"Yes! I had no idea such delicious sweets existed." Her eyes shone with excitement. I had forgotten until Frieda reminded me, but Philine was actually a gourmand—especially for sweets. This got her in trouble later in the game, but that was a story for another time. One would think being the imperial princess meant she could have all the sweets she wanted, but Dorothea disliked sweet foods, leaving Philine few opportunities to try them.

I'd never imagined sweets would be the breakthrough we needed. I needed to thank Frieda later.

"I'm glad to hear it," Claire began. "I'm actually fond of chocolates myself. It's good we have something in common."

"You are? Sweets are the best, aren't they?"

"Indeed."

We'd also succeeded in getting Claire and Philine to talk to each other.

"I'm glad we could talk like this," Claire said. "You seemed to be afraid of me until just now."

"Th-that's..."

"Am I wrong?"

"I'm sorry. I *was* afraid," Philine admitted.

"It's all right. It happens quite often. I seem to invite misunderstandings."

"I don't think it's misunderstandings so much as you're flat-out scary when you snap," I chimed in.

"Rae, please be quiet."

Yes, ma'am.

"I really did want to talk to you, though," Philine said. "You remind me of my mother in some ways."

"Her Majesty Dorothea? Really?" Claire seemed perplexed.

It was true, they did share some traits. They were both confident, arrogant, and strict, but I thought Claire was far and away more mature than Dorothea. Claire had respect, kindness, and virtue, none of which Dorothea possessed in any amount.

In other words, Claire was a far more dazzling gem than Dorothea.

"I'm honored to be compared to Her Majesty. On the other hand, you don't take after her much, do you?" Claire said.

"I get that a lot." Philine laughed derisively. "I'm nothing like my mother. I'm nothing even compared to my siblings."

"Lady Philine..." Claire seemed hurt by Philine's self-deprecating words.

"How can I be more confident—like you, Claire?" Philine put on her bravest face as she asked.

Claire thought for a moment. "Well... It isn't easy, but you should focus on making small steps first. Try doing something you're good at, or something you enjoy. You might fail, but as long as you keep trying, you'll eventually improve and succeed."

"I see..."

"If you keep doing that, then eventually you'll be confident enough to walk with your head held high."

Philine appeared to slowly absorb Claire's words.

"Nobody is confident right off the bat," Claire continued. "And if they are, it's an empty confidence."

"That's true..." Philine nodded.

"Don't be afraid to make mistakes and take that next step, that next leap. You can worry about what comes next afterward."

"I think I understand now." Philine nodded deeply. "I may be shy, but I've been using that as an excuse for inaction. But if I don't try, I'll be like this forever."

"That's right."

"I think I get it now. Thank you, Claire."

"I'm glad I could help."

Philine extended her hand. Claire took it and held it tight.

"Would it be okay if we talked again sometime?" Philine asked.

"Of course. Let's be friends, Lady Philine."

"Yes!"

And with that, we'd made a connection with Philine.

Intermission—Song of the Caged Bird
Philine's POV

I returned to the Imperial Castle after parting with Claire and Rae. I entrusted my bag to a servant and began the walk back to my own room.

I was in a good mood. Claire's words had struck a chord with me and still rang fresh in my mind. I felt like there was something even someone like me could do. I felt like real change could come.

"Well, if it isn't the princess. How do you do?"

"Hello, Hilda."

Hildegard Eichrodt was a government official. She had silver hair and red eyes, and she wore a monocle, something seldom seen on a woman. Though she seemed cold and unfriendly at first, she was actually quite kind. In fact, we'd first gotten to know each other when she helped me find my lost cat.

"Home from the academy?"

"Yes."

"Welcome back. Did something good happen today?"

"Huh? Y-you can tell?" My hands flew to my cheeks. I had been smiling this entire time without realizing.

"It's not your face as much as it's the entire way you carry yourself. I'm often watching you, so I can tell when you're in a good mood."

"R-really? How embarrassing..."

How silly of me, I thought. But still, I held on to the spark Claire had given me.

"What happened? Would you mind telling me?"

"The truth is..."

I told Hilda of today's events: the novel confectionaries I received, the wonderful conversation I'd had with Claire, and even how I felt like we might be friends now. I was surprised to hear the passion in my own voice—I must really have wanted to tell someone about all this.

"And that's what happened today. Do you think there's something even someone like me can do?"

"Lady Philine, may I say one thing?" Hilda's voice was firm. I thought it a little strange.

"Um, yes?"

"I think it's best if you don't make contact with that person anymore."

"Wh-what? Why?" I was confused. Why would she say that? When Claire had finally become my friend?

"That girl is from the Bauer Kingdom. It could cause problems if you spent too much time with her."

"Problems? Claire isn't a bad person."

"That may be true, but she's still the hero of a revolution, and you're the princess. You can't be certain she didn't approach you with an ulterior motive in mind."

Her words surprised me. I was prone to forgetting I was, in fact, the imperial princess. I'd lost count of how many times people had approached me with hidden intentions, to the point that I dreaded dealing with people altogether. But even so—

"Claire is different. She actually listens to what I have to say."

"That could just be what she wants you to think. What if she's taking advantage of your weakness?"

"I..." I could say nothing to that. I knew well enough how weak-willed I could be. Claire had given me courage, and I wanted to grow closer to her, but what if Hilda was right and Claire's friendliness was nothing but a facade?

"Princess, I'll always be there for you if you need someone to talk to. There's no risk in talking to me, unlike those two." Hilda's eyes softened as her cold expression warmed into a smile. She cared about me.

"Yes... Thank you, Hilda. But I think I still want to be friends with Claire."

"Making friends is a good thing. It's sometimes even necessary in politics. But be careful not to cross a line. For your sake, and for our country's."

For our country's sake. I had no defense against those words. I had a responsibility as an imperial princess, even if I could never live up to the title. The spark Claire had given me flickered away.

"I'm terribly sorry, Princess, I didn't mean to ruin your mood. I just wouldn't be able to stand seeing your kind heart be hurt in any way."

"It's okay, Hilda. Thank you." She didn't have to warn me like this. She did it for my sake.

"Thank you for your understanding. Now then, may I walk you to your room? I'd love to hear about your day at the academy."

"That's quite all right, Hilda. I've taken enough of your time already."

"Not at all, I'd be more than happy to walk you there."

"Please, I would like some time to think alone. Excuse me."

I turned down Hilda's kind offer and briskly took myself to my room. I cleared my servants out before collapsing onto my bed, still in my uniform.

Claire...

Despite Hilda's warning, I still wanted to talk to Claire. I wanted to talk to her more, about anything and everything, even all sorts of trivial, meaningless things. I wanted to know more about her. I had a *hunch*.

Claire might be the one I need.

Despite my timid personality, I was a member of the imperial family. I cared about my country's well-being. My mother was a capable ruler, but I had doubts about the empire's future. Our current approach to diplomacy was incredibly aggressive—no, invasive, even. We'd won every war thus far, but that success wasn't guaranteed to last.

The Nur Empire had made too many enemies. Our failure to infiltrate the Bauer Kingdom's government had allowed the three-nation anti-Nur alliance to form. We were currently buying time to build up our forces, but the expenses were mounting. At this rate, we would have to recall troops from our annexed territories. And if the anti-Nur alliance were to incite other countries to fight against us, the empire would be surrounded by enemies on all sides. We would stand no chance of winning.

Invasion has its limits...

The empire *had* to choose to reconcile, sooner or later, and I believed that now was the time.

But there's no way Mother would ever listen to me.

Mother always stuck to her beliefs. Barring any unforeseen circumstances, she would never change her foreign policy.

What can I do...?

There wasn't much I *could* do, despite being an imperial princess. I wasn't resourceful like Hilda. I wasn't outgoing like Frieda.

But that didn't mean I should just sit and watch it happen.

I won't let that happen again.

A crimson memory from my youth had etched itself into my mind. I recalled the events as clear as day, despite the pain they brought to my heart, in hopes I would never forget them.

Claire...

I wanted to talk to her again. I wanted to lay bare all these worries plaguing my heart. Even now, her confident smile remained in my mind.

Oh... What's wrong with me?

My chest hurt. It felt tight whenever I remembered Claire's face. Even if Hilda were to reproach me, I still wanted Claire.

I wish tomorrow would come soon.

If I went to the academy, I could see Claire again. Yes, I would finish my business quickly so I could sleep. I would slowly ease my body out of bed and then ring the bell for a change of clothes. Then, after changing, I would study.

"I'll do what I can. Small victories, little by little."

While reflecting on Claire's words, I started to stand.

"Morning, Claire."

"Good morning, Lady Philine."

"Good morn—"

"Morning, Rae. Hey, Claire, I—"

Philine cut my greeting short with a smile before diving into a conversation with Claire. She'd been like this for a few days now, her fear of Claire replaced by infatuation—rendering me the third wheel. We wanted to encourage this closeness, but I found it hard to suppress my jealousy.

The school bell rang, signaling the start of class. Just an aside, but things like this really served as a weird reminder that the game had been developed in modern-day Japan.

"Aww. Already? See you later, Claire."

"See you." Claire smiled as Philine reluctantly departed. The moment Philine was out of sight, she relaxed, allowing herself a look of exhaustion.

"Good work, Miss Claire."

"Thank you, Rae. Philine's not a bad girl, but she's just so earnest. She can be hard to deal with."

"That's a princess for you. Sheltered upbringing and all."

Claire used to be sheltered as well, but she'd changed. She could no longer be called a villainess, ignorant of society's ills. Although, personally, I never minded seeing a bit of that old side peek through.

"I still feel guilty. It's like we're tricking her."

"We're not tricking her, Claire. We're just not telling her the entire truth."

"What's the difference?" Claire sighed. "But that doesn't mean I'm giving up. Our family's future is on the line."

"That's right. On another note, do you think Philine is cute at all?"

"Huh? Well, I suppose she's cute?"

"Guh!"

"Ah, not in that way! Objectively speaking! Objectively speaking, she's cute!"

"My wife's cheating on me..."

"Stop! People are going to misunderstand!"

The Imperial Academy didn't have anything resembling a homeroom. Instead, the teachers made announcements before class if they had anything important to convey to us. Today, they did.

"The pope will be visiting our academy next month. We'll be assigning duties to everyone in preparation."

The pope led the Spiritual Church. They usually stayed at the Bauer Cathedral, but as the Spiritual Church had followers all over the world, the pope had to travel every so often to visit different locales. According to the teacher, the pope was coming to the capital for a conference with Dorothea. I hadn't thought Dorothea particularly devout, considering how she dismissively referred to the church as a "house of worship" during our audience. I wondered what they could possibly have to discuss.

"What kind of duties will we have?" a student asked.

"You'll be clearing monsters from the pope's planned route. The military will handle the more dangerous areas, while we'll take care of the less fraught ones."

Monster extermination. Just as with Bauer's Amour Festival,

the military often lacked the personnel to tackle all the beasts alone, relying instead on support from local militias and other citizen volunteers. The Nur Empire actually had it worse than the Bauer Kingdom, being closer to demon territory. Demons sat at the peak of monster hierarchy, making monsters far stronger and more numerous in the empire's vicinity.

"Form teams of four and report your members to me after school. Now, with that out of the way, let's begin class."

Class began like normal. As always, the teacher hated wasting time on things not pertaining to our studies. The same couldn't be said for the students.

Psst! Rae, Claire! Would you like to party with moi?

Um, I-I'm here, too...

I heard two voices in my head. Had to be telepathy. The first was Frieda—using her wind-attribute magic—and the second, Philine.

Will it be the four of us, then? Claire asked.

Oui! The four of us are very strong, no? Frieda said.

Sure, but are you allowed to team up with us? We're from the Bauer Kingdom, you know?

What's the problem? Frieda asked.

Philine is a princess of the Nur Empire, Claire explained. *Is it really all right for her to work with people who were so recently the empire's enemies?*

It was a good opportunity for us to strengthen our rapport with Philine, but we had to consider her circumstances.

W-we're friends now. It should be okay! Philine said.

Yes! A-okay! Frieda said.

Color me unconvinced. I had a feeling the teacher would say no. But to my surprise, the teacher didn't object in the least when we reported our group after school. Really, Nur Empire?

While we were reporting to the teacher, I tried to negotiate exchanging monster extermination for a different task. I hadn't ruled out the possibility of an assassination attempt on the Nur Empire's part under the pretense of an incident out on the hunt. But the empire and the kingdom both had appearances to maintain for sake of diplomatic relations, so I was shot down. I swore to myself that no matter what happened, I would at least protect Claire.

"Let's go over what we're each capable of," Claire began. "I have high-aptitude fire magic and am somewhat proficient at close-quarters combat."

"I have ultra-high aptitude earth and water magic and am terrible at close-quarters combat," I said.

"What?! Rae is a dual-caster?!" Frieda exclaimed.

"A-amazing..." Philine said.

Even in a country as advanced in magic as the empire, dual-casters were a rarity.

"I only have medium aptitude in wind. But I am good at close-quarters combat!" Frieda said.

"I have medium-aptitude water magic. I'm no good at close-quarters combat."

Claire and I had already known their abilities, but we needed to keep that mum, of course.

"What type of magic are you two most skilled at? I specialize in attack magic, and Rae is an all-rounder who can do just about anything," Claire said.

Claire praised me! Yahoo!

"I am skilled in body-reinforcement magic," Frieda explained. "But I cannot use it on other people well."

"I can use healing magic," Philine said.

"In that case, Frieda and I will fight on the front line while Rae and Philine provide support from behind," Claire said.

"Sounds perfect," I said.

"No complaints from me," Frieda said.

"Me too," Philine said.

And just like that, it was settled.

"We start tomorrow, correct?" Claire asked.

"I believe that's what the teacher said," I said.

"Did you have something in mind?" Philine asked.

"I was thinking we could do some practice beforehand."

"Oh? Why practice?" Frieda asked.

All eyes turned to Claire as she continued. "We ought to coordinate our teamwork before the real thing. For safety reasons."

Like the Royal Academy, the Imperial Academy also had a field with a magic-dampening barrier that we could use to plan our tactics.

"Sounds good," I said.

"Sounds fun!"

"No problem here."

With that, we moved to the field.

It turned out our team was well balanced. I already knew Claire's strength, but Frieda and Philine could hold their own as well. Frieda's fighting style resembled Thane's in that she used magic to boost her physical abilities. But while Thane preferred to fight empty-handed, Frieda used a sword. She could even use magic to sharpen her blade, and she cut my earth dolls in half like butter.

Philine's healing magic impressed me as well. Despite only being medium aptitude, she had a wide variety of spells in her arsenal. Light wound-healing magic, sleep magic, detoxifying magic, de-paralysis magic, even concentration-boosting magic—she could do it all. Not to brag or anything, but I could dispel most debuffs with my advanced healing magic, meaning I didn't need to learn as many spells as Philine. That said, her medium-aptitude healing magic consumed less magic power than mine, so in a sense, she was the more skilled healer.

I should have her teach me later, I thought.

Incidentally, both our magics paled in comparison to the effects of the Tears of the Moon.

"This seems a good place to stop," Claire said, after we'd sorted out a few basic tactics. "We should be able to operate with these parameters. Let's give it our best tomorrow, everyone."

"I'll protect you, Claire!" I declared.

"Rae? You'll protect us too, no?" Frieda asked.

"Ah ha ha..."

I mean, sure, yeah, but a lady's gotta have priorities, you know?

We called it a day just as the sun started to set.

I woke up with muscle soreness the next day, having not exercised so hard in a long time—though let the record show that my night with Claire had absolutely no involvement in said soreness.

The afternoon of the next day, we began clearing monsters from the path the pope would travel. We planned to work at it for about an hour and a half each day, and our efforts earned us a credit in practical magic.

"Frieda! Look out!" Claire exclaimed.

"Leave it to me!"

A monster resembling a bear attacked Frieda, swinging its sharp claws at her chestnut-brown hair.

"*Non, non,* not so easy." Frieda dexterously parried the claws with her sword—throwing the monster off balance. "Now, Claire!"

"Got it!"

Claire sent a flame spear directly through the monster's now exposed side. The monster let out a cry before collapsing and fading into nothing, leaving only a magic stone behind.

"Phew. This area seems clear." Claire wiped the sweat off her brow. The weather wasn't that hot yet, but all the moving had made us work up a sweat.

"Good work, Miss Claire, Frieda. Any injuries?"

"I'm all right, Rae. Thank you," Claire reassured me.

"I'm okay, too!" Frieda said.

"The two of you are so strong," Philine remarked, astonished. Claire was one thing, being used to actual combat, but Frieda truly shone out on the field. Neither of them had yet suffered more than light abrasions.

The area assigned to us that day was populated by larger and stronger monsters, but in fewer numbers. So far, we'd taken down water slimes, grand wasps, and grizzlies, all of which proved easy to beat when fought individually.

"I wonder how the other students are doing," Claire said.

Scanning the area, we caught sight of other teams of students fighting monsters some ways away. Students of the Imperial Academy received excellent combat training, and, as far as we could tell, they handled their areas just fine.

"I hope Lana's group is okay," I said.

"I'm sure they'll be fine. I could see Lana having problems, but Eve and Joel are with her," Claire reassured me.

From what I remembered while teaching at the Royal Academy, Lana was a complete beginner at magic. On the other hand, Eve and Joel were true adepts, particularly Joel, being the son of a soldier who'd had some martial training. They *were* probably fine, but—

"I'm worried about their fourth group member."

"Oh, right... Otto."

Otto hadn't found a group until the very end, when Lana invited him to join theirs. He hadn't seemed too enthusiastic about joining, but Lana—being Lana—cajoled him into it.

The delinquent and the gyaru—now that was an amusing tag team if I had ever seen one.

"Isn't it fine? I hear Otto is actually quite strong," Claire said.

Like her, I'd heard that Otto, despite being a problem child, was as gifted a fighter as he was a student. His father apparently served as a soldier in the military. I recalled Joel's ears pricking up in interest at that little tidbit.

"They should be fine. There are other teams around anyway," Claire said.

True enough. If worse came to worst, they could run for it and get help. But I still couldn't shake this nagging bad feeling.

"Hey, girls, worrying about your countrymen is okay, but maybe focusing on the task at hand is more important?" Frieda's words brought me back to reality. Before us, a wolf-like monster with three heads growled—a cerberus.

"This one's strong. Everyone, be careful!" Philine warned.

Cerberuses were monsters with bodies as thick and solid as cows. Their sharp claws and fangs posed a problem, but even a body slam would do a number on someone. I eyed the creature before us with due caution.

"It's coming!" Claire shouted.

The monster charged the second before Claire could warn its target: Philine.

"Oh, no you don't!" Frieda cried as she leapt into its path. But the cerberus showed no sign of stopping, ready to send them both flying.

Not if I could help it.

"Marsh!" I cast earth magic on the ground before the cerberus, causing the hard earth to instantly turn to boggy mud. The monster's legs disappeared into the ground.

"Got you!" Frieda swung her sword. I was certain it was over but... "What?!"

Frieda's sword was blocked by the cerberus's snapping fangs.

"Frieda, move!" I yelled.

Frieda left her sword behind as she jumped away. The cerberus spat flame at her, missing by a hair's breadth.

"That was close." Frieda breathed a sigh of relief. Her sword was gone, caught by one of the cerberus's heads. "Hey, give it back! That sword's special!"

"Stand back, Frieda. Let me handle it."

"Oh, *pardon*. Go get her, Claire."

Claire confronted the cerberus with her wand at the ready. The cerberus eyed her, growling, waiting to see her next move.

"How about...this!" Claire instantly summoned five flame spears and shot them at the cerberus. Each one traced a different arc as they careened toward the beast.

The cerberus snarled as it took a massive leap to the side, dodging all the spears. It was nimbler than its form suggested. But that wouldn't be enough to stop Claire—or me.

"I'll stop its movements—be ready!" I instructed.

"Yes!"

I created a pitfall where the cerberus would land, and it fell straight in. No matter how nimble it was, it would take some time to clamber out. Claire looked down on the struggling monster as the François family crests appeared above her head—her signature spell, Magic Ray.

"You're done!"

A blazing beam shot from the crests, directly piercing the cerberus. The monster, now horribly charred, ceased to move. It faded away soon after, leaving behind a magic stone.

"Phew," Claire exhaled. "That took some effort."

"You were wonderful, Miss Claire!"

I showered Claire in praise as she retrieved the magic stone alongside Frieda's sword.

"Here, Frieda. Let's be careful next time."

"*Merci*, Claire. Will do." Frieda returned her sword to its scabbard.

"You were wonderful, Claire! It was like you were on the same wavelength as Rae." Philine lagged behind before catching up to us. Her expression seemed a bit muddled, perhaps from jealousy?

"Well, Rae and I have been a team for a long time now."

"Together forever!" I said.

"Um... Yes," Claire said.

"Wife for life!"

"Okay, enough with the joking, Rae," Claire spat.

I feel your love even when you berate me, Claire!

"Oh... How nice..." Philine grumbled enviously. *Was* Philine entering the Claire route?

"Lady Philine," I said.

"Hm? Um, yes?"

"She's mine."

"Ngh—y-yes..." Philine sagged her head dejectedly. I felt a bit bad, but Claire was where I drew the line.

"Shall we head back?" said Claire. "We may have handled today's combat well, but we still need to rest up and restore our magic."

"Sounds good," I said.

"No objection!" Frieda said.

"Let's go home," Philine agreed.

That was when we heard someone else speak. "Impressive. You managed to defeat the cerberus."

Startled, the four of us spun around toward the source of the voice. I hadn't noticed their presence at all.

"To boast this much power before reaching maturity... Quite impressive for humans." The figure sat, watching us from a boulder a short distance away. He wore what appeared to be a black frock coat, and he could easily be mistaken for a human if not for the bat-like wings protruding from his back. His eyes, full of intelligence, had vertically slit pupils.

"A demon!" Frieda exclaimed.

Demon—a higher order of being that ruled over monsters. This was my first meeting with one.

"Who are you?" Claire glared at the demon.

"Oh? And here I was, thinking you were a noble. Did no one teach you to give your own name before asking another's?"

The demon frowned as he ridiculed Claire, unmoving from his perch on the boulder.

"How rude of me." Claire smiled thinly, still guarded. "I am Claire François, *former* nobility of the Bauer Kingdom, as you say."

"Mmm... I see. So it *was* you. I am known simply as Aristo. Unlike you humans, we demons bear no surnames. I serve as one of the Three Great Archdemons."

Everyone froze upon hearing Aristo's words. The demon slowly stood from the boulder and stroked his chin, upon which he had something not quite resembling a beard. He watched us with an air of utter composure.

Not much was known about the enigmatic race called demons. Even I, with my memory of the original game, knew little. They were mentioned in passing in the original *Revolution* and *Revo-Lily* but never actually made an appearance in either game. Even the games' setting and supplementary material barely touched on demons, saying only that they ruled over monsters and stayed within their own territory east of the Nur Empire.

I hadn't heard the term Three Great Archdemons before, but it was clear this demon was of high standing, not just from some low-level mob. *We might be in real danger.*

"Thank you for introducing yourself, Aristo. Do you have business with us?" Claire asked.

"Mmm... No, not quite. I was in the area on some unrelated orders when I saw you humans around. I figured I might as well fulfill another task while I was here."

Aristo nonchalantly strolled toward us. He appeared unguarded, but I hesitated, not sure if I should preemptively strike.

"And what is this task, pray tell?"

"Nothing serious, Claire François. It just involves you doing one thing for me."

"And what might that be?"

"Mmm... To put it simply," Aristo sneered. "I need you to die."

"Miss Claire!" I caved in the ground at Claire's feet, causing her to plummet to safety just as a black flash of light streaked across where she had stood moments prior.

"Oh, ho. You dodged."

"Why, you fiend!" Claire's scowling visage slowly rose back into view as I returned the ground under her feet to normal.

Aristo simply stood there, unfazed. Had that really been magic just now? I'd never seen an attack like it before.

"*Madame* Claire, let's run!" Frieda cried.

"We can't fight a demon with our numbers!" Philine agreed.

I was wholly on board with this idea.

"I'd very much like to run right now, but I get the impression our friend here isn't so willing to look the other way as we do," Claire said.

"You're all free to try and run regardless," said Aristo. "I believe humans have the right to choose how they end their fleeting mortal lives."

"And I choose to stand my ground!" Claire called up ten flame spears, twice the amount she'd summoned against the cerberus earlier, and fired them at Aristo.

"Is that it?" Aristo made no attempt to dodge, taking the full impact of the barrage.

"Impossible..." Claire's eyes widened.

The demon stood there, untouched.

"Such low-level magic cannot possibly harm me. Now, cease your struggle and die." Aristo waved his hand horizontally, sending bullets of concentrated darkness at Claire.

"No!" I created a wall of earth before Claire, but—

"Meaningless."

The black bullets pierced the wall with ease, continuing toward Claire.

"Hiyah!" But right before they could hit, Frieda lunged forward and knocked them away with her sword.

"Oh, you could repel that? I must reevaluate you, then. You're stronger than I thought."

"Merci!" Frieda summoned her magic to empower her legs and instantly closed the gap between her and the demon, slashing down with her magic-veiled sword.

"Mmm... I'd prefer not to be hit by that." Aristo took a step back, dodging the blade.

Seeing this, I readied a medium-level earth attack spell. "Earth Fang!"

The ground rose to ensnare Aristo's feet, stopping his movements.

"Got you!" Frieda swung her lowered blade back in reverse. It looked like it would hit this time for sure, but—

"What?!"

"You were close. But not close enough."

Frieda's sword was blocked by nails that had rapidly grown from Aristo's hand.

"A blessed sword as well as medium-level magic... I'd best get a little serious, then." Aristo effortlessly pulled himself free of my foot bindings.

So medium-level magic only amounted to that much...

"I'll be striking from above. Block it if you can." Aristo drew back his right arm as Frieda moved to block with her sword.

I felt a sickening lurch in my gut. "No, Frieda! Dodge!"

At the last second, Frieda abandoned her attempt to block and did as I said. The blow barely missed her body but clipped her sword, snapping it clean in two. Those nails were stronger than her magic-empowered blade.

"*Oh, non*! I can't believe it..."

"Frieda, get back!"

Frieda jumped back at the sound of Claire's high-pitched voice.

"Light!" Claire unleashed Magic Ray at Aristo.

"Hmph." Aristo expelled a dark beam of his own. Light and darkness briefly clashed before canceling each other out.

"Not even Magic Ray could best him?" Claire bit her lip in frustration.

Aristo was strong. We were already exhausted from our work slaying monsters, but I had a feeling we would have been no match for him in top form either.

"Everyone!" I began. "Retreat while I stop his—"

"I won't let you." He cut me off before raising his hand to the air. Darkness began to swell around him...

And exploded forth to surround us.

I regained consciousness moments later.

The ground around us was carved into a massive crater, as if a bomb had gone off. Frieda and Philine lay gravely wounded on the ground, trying to stand and failing to.

"Miss Claire!"

"Ngh..."

Claire was on her knees before Aristo. She glared up at him in defiance, but he remained impassive.

"It's over, Claire François. Perish, for what you have wrought."

Time moved with excruciating slowness as his nails swung down.

I was such a fool. Why had I assumed we'd never encounter a demon just because they weren't in the game? Despite the very real in-world history of demons invading human territory since time immemorial? The promise I'd made to protect my family—had that just been empty words?

In desperation, I tried to cast Cocytus, but my magic was too far drained.

Just when I thought it was all over, something struck Aristo's nails away.

"I-I won't let you!"

Standing between Aristo and Claire was a small figure.

"You're..."

"L-Long time no see, Miss Claire."

The figure, clad in a nun's habit, held two short swords that glistened in the light. Beneath her fluttering wimple were silver hair and red eyes. We knew her well.

"Miss Lilly!"

Former cardinal Lilly Lilium had arrived just in the nick of time.

"I-I made it!"

"Hmph. So you've appeared again, Saint," sneered Aristo.

"Pl-please stop calling me that."

"You always seem to find the perfect timing. What's the secret?"

"Wh-who knows? Love, perhaps?" Despite her usual shy stutter, Lilly gallantly stood her ground before the demon.

"Miss Lilly..." I tried to stand but couldn't due to exhaustion. I couldn't even call on my healing magic while so tapped.

"I-It's okay, Rae. I can handle him." Lilly flashed me a smile before turning back toward Aristo and readying her two shining swords. "Why don't you turn back now, Aristo? Reinforcements are coming. I'm sure you'd rather not die here."

"You mock me. Do you think I can be defeated by some humans banding together?"

"W-with me here, I do."

"Mmm... I'll admit, you are a formidable opponent, Saint."

Aristo raised an eyebrow. He seemed wary of Lilly. "But not even you could fight me unscathed."

"True... How about we agree to a draw then...?"

"Hah. Don't be like that. Let's enjoy ourselves some." Apparently not in the least inclined to back down, he sent another salvo of black bullets at Lilly.

"Y-you know, despite what you might think, I'm actually quite busy!" Lilly wove through the bullets, occasionally blocking with her swords, as she closed the gap to Aristo. Once in range, she swung down with her right.

"Mmm... A blessed shortsword—and a real one, unlike that imitation. I'd rather not be hit by this either." Aristo leapt back, opting not to block with his nails as he did with Frieda's sword.

"Rae, use this!" Lilly reached into her pocket and threw something toward me. Four objects resembling vials rolled closer. "They're high-grade potions. Drink one and help the others."

"Thank you, Lilly." I uncapped and downed a potion, and magic power surged up within me. I scrambled up and beelined toward Claire. "Miss Claire, I've got you."

"Leave me for later, heal the others—"

"Oh, don't even. Be quiet and drink." I helped Claire swallow a potion and watched with relief as her wounds faded.

"Thank you, Rae."

"You should thank Miss Lilly instead."

"You're right." Claire staggered up and nodded toward Lilly. "I'll go back her up."

"Got it. I'll help Frieda and Philine."

I parted with Claire and headed toward Philine. I held her upright as I administered her a potion.

"I'm okay now. Thank you, Rae."

"Don't worry about it. I'm going to go help Claire and a friend of ours. Can you heal Frieda?"

"Of course." Philine nodded. I passed her the final potion and dashed off toward the fight.

"I-I'll hold him off! Support me with magic!" Lilly commanded.

"Understood!"

"Roger that!"

This was our first time fighting all three together.

Lilly advanced on Aristo with her swords. Wary of the blades, Aristo continued to dodge, still not using his nails to block.

Lilly's skill surprised me. I had seen her fight before, but that had been in the grips of an alternate personality. The real Lilly was just as strong, if not stronger.

"Insolent!" Aristo fired black bullets at her from close range.

I was certain Lilly couldn't dodge, but she did—reacting in the blink of an eye, moving with unbelievable speed. It was incredible, even considering the fact her physical abilities were boosted by magic.

"Stand still!" the demon snarled.

But dodging had left Lilly off balance. Seeing an opportunity, Aristo swung with his nails.

"Don't you dare!" Claire fired her Magic Ray, forcing Aristo to stop mid-swing and counter with a black ray of his own.

"Earth Spike!" I formed an earth spear to try to pierce Aristo, but he effortlessly avoided it by flying into the air with his enormous wings.

"Mmm... So you were all simply exhausted earlier. Your magic is leagues stronger now. It seems I'm at a disadvantage."

"Come back down here so I can burn you to ash!" Claire demanded.

"I think I'll decline. It's best I flee, especially with that Saint here."

"I won't let you!"

"W-wait, Miss Claire! Let him go. You'll want to hear what I have to say before you fight him again," Lilly said.

"Ngh..." Claire grimaced. She was undoubtedly frustrated, considering her pride. She had never been so thoroughly thrashed by an opponent. "Fine."

"Thank you, Miss Lilly," I said. "You really saved us back there."

"Allow me to express my thanks as well," Claire added. "Things would have turned dire if you hadn't come."

I'd been so sure it was all over for a moment. I couldn't thank Lilly enough.

Lilly smiled bashfully. "N-not at all! I'm deeply indebted to you two, so something like—"

"Merveilleux!"

"Eek!"

Frieda suddenly crashed into Lilly's side, nearly taking her to the ground.

"Who is this *jolie* lady? She must be an angel to save us in our time of need, no?" she prattled excitedly.

"U-um, hello?" Lilly looked bewildered. She looked to me for help, but frankly, this tickled me pink.

"What is your name, little angel?"

"L-Lilly Lilium."

"Oh, even your name is so *charmant*! My name is Friedelinde Eimer, but please, call me Frieda!"

"Um, sure... Miss Frieda."

"*Non, non!* Just Frieda! We are good friends, no?"

"B-but it's our first meeting?!"

Frieda was laying it on a little thick even for her. Was Lilly now on the Frieda route? She *had* cut a pretty gallant figure just then. I wouldn't have been in the least surprised if Frieda confessed to falling for her at first sight.

"Frieda, how about we move from this place for now?" Claire said. "I think the danger has passed for the moment, but we still need to report this to the empire...and the Bauer Kingdom, for that matter."

"Oh, *pardon*. I was too mesmerized by Lilly's beauty. Let's go back."

"Lady Philine, are you okay with that?"

"Yes, let's return." Philine nodded.

All in agreement, we hastily made our way back to the relative safety of more people.

Demons... It was hard to believe they were so strong. They were far more powerful than the monsters we had fought before. They seemed likely to surpass any opponent we'd *ever* fought.

I need to rethink my countermeasures...

I spent the journey home thinking of nothing but how I could protect Claire from this new threat.

"I-It's good to see you two again, Rae, Miss Claire." Lilly bowed deeply.

We'd returned to the Bauer student dormitory to talk after reporting the incident to the academy. I'd thought the Nur Empire would be more concerned about the appearance of demons, but it seemed to be a fairly common occurrence around here. The person receiving our report didn't react much at all to the news.

"Let's leave the pleasantries at that and get down to business. What are you doing here in the empire, Lilly?" Claire said, asking what was on everyone's mind. Currently gathered were the core constituents of the Bauer Kingdom exchange group: Claire, Yu, Misha, and me.

"R-right. I've resumed my duties at the cathedral. I traveled ahead to the empire to prepare for the pope's visit."

"Oh, I see."

Oh, yeah. We'd been slaying monsters to prepare for the pope's visit in the first place, and it wasn't like the head of a global religion could suddenly pop in unprepared. They'd send someone ahead to handle negotiations, preparations, and the like, and Lilly was apparently that person.

"So I take it you're a cardinal again?" Claire asked.

"Ah, no. I'm acting as an ordinary nun now. The pope was kind enough to forgive me, but I couldn't take advantage of her kindness more than I already have." Lilly forced a smile as she spoke. She still hadn't forgiven herself for her crimes. How very like her.

"Um, b-back on topic. My main task is to plan countermeasures for the high-ranking monsters and demons in the empire. As you likely know, the empire shares a border with demon territory, so encounters with demons are more frequent here than in the kingdom."

I'd realized intellectually that the chances of demon contact were higher here, but I'd never imagined they could be so powerful. The four of us, albeit already exhausted, had been powerless against Aristo. We would have been massacred if Lilly hadn't arrived.

A flash of memory came to me—Aristo's claws swinging down on Claire—and I shuddered.

"Are all demons that strong?" I asked.

"N-no, Aristo is special. He's part of a powerful group called the Three Great Archdemons. Meeting him was a spot of bad luck."

I felt some relief on hearing Aristo was a rare exception. I didn't know what I would do if all demons were that strong.

"Th-the Three Great Demons—no, *all* demons—generally don't leave their lands. Demons usually dispatch monsters on their behalf when they wish to fight humans."

"So why would a powerful demon turn up then?" Yu mused.

"I-It's likely because of the pope's visit. The church and the demons have been mortal enemies throughout history." Lilly bowed profusely in apology.

Was that really it? I'd witnessed the demon targeting Claire... though Aristo's words *had* made it seem like he was in the middle of another mission when he spotted us and chose to attack.

I had my doubts, but I listened as Lilly continued.

"The church cannot tolerate the existence of demons. W-we believe they can't be reasoned with and must be destroyed on sight, for their goal is to bring about the end of the world."

That sounded excessively hostile of the Spiritual Church, a religion that extolled the virtues of impartiality and benevolence. What would demons even gain from ending the world? Claire met my eyes with a dubious look of her own. It seemed she harbored the same concerns.

"By end of the world, do you by chance mean the end of human society?" Claire asked.

"No. The end of the world the demons seek is a literal one that includes their own ruin," Misha answered. As a nun, she presumably knew a few things about demons herself.

"Their own destruction as well?" Claire asked, confused.

"Y-yes. The values of demons are beyond human understanding. That's why they can't be reasoned with."

That made a certain amount of sense. There could be no negotiating with a race that wanted to destroy the world in its entirety, themselves included.

"B-because of the empire's proximity to their lands, people

here sometimes encounter demons. We're unlikely to meet any big-name demons again as long as we remain far from their borders, but let's stay cautious, everyone."

"So we just cross our fingers and pray we don't meet a demon again?" Claire grumbled.

"Well, the church has some measures to combat demons. This being one of them." Lilly unsheathed a sword. "Th-this sword is a magic tool enchanted by a water spell called Blessing. Weapons with Blessing are able to wound demons more grievously. Perhaps you're aware Frieda's sword was enchanted with a weak blessing?"

Frieda had said something about her sword being special. Aristo had still broken it in two. He really was something else.

"Th-the cathedral has ordered me to loan everyone Blessed magic tools for the sake of this mission. Since everyone here is a magic user, I'll be supplying you with wands."

A member of the church stepped forward with a bag for each of us. Lilly took a bag and opened it, revealing its contents.

"Th-the magic stones on these wands have been enchanted with Blessing. Blessing itself is water magic, but you can use any magic type with an enchanted item. Keep in mind that Blessing only has an effect on demons."

"Can you teach us how to cast Blessing ourselves?" I asked.

"Th-that I cannot do... It is one of the church's most closely guarded secrets, of an order higher than even the Tears of the Moon. Only the current pope is permitted to know it."

Lilly went on to explain that Blessed magic stones were an important source of income for the church. I could put the spell to good use if I learned it, but I understood the reasoning in this confidentiality.

"Bl-blessed magic tools are incredibly valuable, so I can only loan up to one per person. Please be careful with them."

We each received a Blessed magic wand from Lilly. Inspecting the wand, I noticed that its magic stone was colorless and transparent, rather than one of the four attribute colors. Ordinary water magic would cause the stone to turn blue. There really was something peculiar about Blessing.

"D-demons have the same weak spots as monsters, a magic stone that acts as their core. Th-the reason why is unknown, but their magic stone is often located where the human heart would be. Don't forget this."

With that, Lilly's lecture on demons came to an end.

"Thank you for teaching us, Miss Lilly."

"N-not at all, Rae."

Even so, I was grateful to learn anything that hadn't been explained in the game. She'd even armed us with Blessed weapons to boot.

"Is there *any* way I can show my appreciation?" I asked.

"Th-there's no need for that, I was just doing my job... But, um—"

"What is it? Request away!"

"Well, um, I was thinking, you see, if you're free right now, maybe we could have tea toge—"

"Gladly! We have so much to catch up on anyways," I said. That was such a small request. I was willing to talk for as long as she wanted.

That was when my...you know, my *wife* loomed over with a frightful face. "Hello, Lilly. I hope you wouldn't mind me joining your tea party, would you?"

"O-of course not. I definitely had no intention of trying to get closer to Rae while you weren't around and—guh."

Miss Lilly... Your true thoughts are leaking out.

"Honestly..." Claire sighed. "I can't let my guard down with you."

"Lilly, you harebrained fool," Lilly muttered. "You messed things up again..."

"Miss Lilly?"

"Um, Lilly?"

"Ah. I'm sorry! I'm sorry!"

It had been a while since we'd heard Lilly's involuntary cursing.

"Miss Manaria helped remove my second personality, but lately, the words just find their way out again..."

"It's fine," Claire assured her.

"If anything, you wouldn't feel like Miss Lilly without that," I said.

"I-Is that how you guys see me?" Lilly asked through tears.

We invited the teary-eyed Lilly to our room and talked away until dark. We ate dinner together with May and Aleah, after which Lilly got ready to go home.

"I-I'll be going then. L-Let's have our lover's rendezvous some other time, Rae."

"Just hurry up and leave," Claire spat.

They squabbled briefly, and then we bid her goodbye.

"Are your injuries feeling better now, Claire?" Philine asked the next morning in our classroom. She'd been lavishing Claire with concern ever since our fight with the demon, even though she had been heavily injured as well.

"Thank you for worrying, Lady Philine, but as I said yesterday, I'm completely fine." Claire was doing her best to be nice, but the endless worry understandably tired her out.

"So you say, but are you truly sure? While your body may have healed, I worry you might still be scarred by the memory of the event."

"I am not so soft. If anything, I feel the opposite. I want nothing more than to defeat Aristo, should we ever cross paths again."

"Goodness..."

They went on to have essentially the same exchange every morning since.

I knew it was a good thing that we'd become friends with Philine, but I couldn't help feeling like the girl was weird. She was too friendly. And also too close. Like, way too close. She kept making just a bit too much physical contact with Claire, raising all too many red flags in my eyes. Her feelings for Claire were definitely not those of friendship.

I'd seen this person before—every time I looked in the mirror, as a matter of fact.

"Excuse me, Lady Philine? For the umpteenth time, Claire is mine. Think you could stop clinging to her like that?"

"Ah. R-right. I'm sorry, Rae, things just kind of happened..." Philine put her hands on her blushing cheeks and squirmed.

What do you mean, 'things just kind of happened'? I thought. I swore to not let my guard down with this girl.

"You're imagining things, Rae. Lady Philine and I are friends. This level of intimacy is completely normal." Claire wore a thin smile as she took the mediating role.

"Th-thank you, Claire!" If Philine were a dog, her tail would have been wagging furiously right now.

Um, Miss Claire? What are you, some thickheaded light novel protagonist? She's clearly fawning all over you.

"Lady Philine, you're a member of the imperial family, right? Don't you have a fiancé or something?" I asked.

"No, not yet."

"Really? How unexpected. I figured an imperial princess would have a political marriage arranged for her." At least, that was what Claire had said. I wasn't too familiar with high society.

"Mother prefers to conquer through force rather than politics..." Philine muttered sadly. Certainly, Dorothea seemed the type to take what she wanted rather than negotiate for it. Not that I thought she was all brawn and *no* brain.

"So, yes, I currently have *no* partner right now." Philine glanced at Claire.

"O-oh... Is that so," Claire said.

"Why did you try to announce your availability to Claire just now?" I demanded.

Philine was definitely, *definitely* interested in Claire. What happened to her being a shy character? I mean, sure, this was still nothing compared to *my* advances, but still.

"Me? Announce? I'm just being friendly with Claire, that's all..."

"I think you're being a little *too* friendly though..."

"Am I? Oh, dear..." Philine put her hands on her blushing cheeks and squirmed for the second time.

Stop that. It's not cute. Okay, it's kind of cute, but you're not fooling me! I straightened, fed up. Time for a curveball. I was sick and tired of this. "Lady Philine, is it your intention to start an illicit relationship with Miss Claire?"

"Wha—Rae?!"

"I-I don't love her or anything..."

Whoa, who said anything about love? Don't just go putting words in my mouth! This is why ditzy princess characters are insufferable...

"What would the imperial family think if they found out about you flirting with a taken woman?" I asked.

"The Nur Empire practices polygamy," Philine said matter-of-factly.

"Uh..."

Oh, right. The Empire had different marital practices than Bauer. Here, monogamy wasn't enforced, and same-sex marriage was recognized—the latter largely due to *Revo-Lily* being a yuri game.

"Besides, you two aren't legally married yet, right?" Philine asked.

"Y-yes, but, um..."

"Besides, as a member of the imperial family, I'm a much better match for Claire, a former noble."

Huh? Why do I feel backed into a corner all of a sudden?

"That's not it, Lady Philine." Claire stepped in to chide her. "It's true, Rae and I are neither legally married nor from similar social backgrounds."

"So I'm right," Philine said.

"But I've come to realize something, you see. Marriage isn't just a political tool or a way to repay the parents that raised you. Marriage is for your own happiness."

"Your...own...happiness...?" Philine murmured.

"I'm not saying entering a political marriage or marrying to make your parents happy is wrong, but it's also important to marry someone special to you."

"I...see."

"In that regard, Rae is perfect for me. Even if we are not legally married, she is my irreplaceable partner. Please understand that." Claire, now completely finished, smiled sweetly. In contrast, I wore the smuggest look ever.

"I see... I understand."

Even Philine had to reconsider after hearing all that. She was a reasonable girl who'd just gotten a bit carried away by making a close friend. Now, we could all go back to—

"I understand completely. I would like to formally announce my interest in being Claire's partner."

Come again?

"Wh-what are you saying, Lady Philine? Didn't you hear what I said?" Claire asked.

"Of course. I believe I can *also* be an irreplaceable partner you won't regret being with."

Her curveball left both Claire and I speechless.

"I understand now that Rae is a special person to you, Claire. So I'm going to try my best to be the same thing to you."

"W-wait, that wasn't what I was getting at!" Claire exclaimed.

"It's okay. Remember what you taught me? Little by little."

"That's completely out of context!" Claire was flustered.

Had Philine always had this reckless side? I suddenly saw a bit of her mother in her.

"In any case, I promise to become a fine lady you can both be proud of," Philine proudly declared.

Claire and I looked at each other, thinking, *What just happened?*

It seemed I had a love rival now. And, of all people, it had to be the one person whose cooperation we needed most.

Good grief, I thought, exhausted to the core, when Yu suddenly appeared. It wasn't often she visited different classes.

"Claire, Rae."

"Hello, Lady Yu. Is something the matter?" Claire asked.

"A letter arrived from the kingdom. Bad news." Yu looked grave. "Ex-chancellor Salas Lilium has escaped from prison."

11
The Assassination of the Pope

"**S**ALAS ESCAPED?"

That sly schemer... I knew nothing good would come of pardoning him. There was trouble brewing, I was sure of it.

"But how?" Claire asked. "I thought he was confined in a special high-security prison?"

"Someone from the kingdom is here to explain what happened. Come to the exchange student lounge after classes."

"Understood."

Having delivered her message, Yu returned to her own class.

"Miss Claire..."

"I know. I have a bad feeling about this..."

"Oho, Claire, Rae. Have you two been well?"

"Father?!"

"Master Dole?"

When we went to the lounge after classes, we found my father-in-law, Dole François, waiting for us. Apparently, this was the messenger Bauer had sent to bring us the news.

"Where are May and Aleah? I can't wait to see how much they've grown."

"They're in our room," Claire answered. "It hasn't even been two months since you've seen them, you know."

"And? Children grow so much in a short span of time. Why, I remember when Claire was little—" He was about to launch into a story about Claire's childhood when Yu politely interrupted.

"Excuse me, Dole. Might you convey the news from the kingdom? We're still not aware of what's going on."

"Oh, dear, you'll have to excuse me. My daughter and granddaughters are just far too adorable—"

"Father, please cut to the chase."

"You lack patience, Claire. You're just like Melia in that regard," Dole said with a tinge of melancholy—Melia being Claire's deceased mother. He cleared his throat before continuing. "Salas Lilium disappeared from his high-security prison cell beneath the palace around the middle of last month. It's assumed he somehow broke out."

In other words, he'd escaped shortly after we left the kingdom. The prison was the same one I'd been temporarily held in after the incident with Yu's gender reveal. It should have been far more closely guarded than an ordinary prison.

"We don't know how he escaped, but we can assume he had help from someone influential within the palace. Our number one suspect is, well..." Hesitant to finish, Dole looked at Yu.

"My mother, I suppose?" Yu said, to which Dole nodded. Yu sighed, looking unsurprised.

"Unfortunately, yes. Lady Riche and Salas seem to have, uh... history with each other." Dole was skirting the truth.

"It's all right. You can say it, Dole. Mother was in love with Salas. Even after he was imprisoned, she met with him regularly."

Salas was popular with women, for reasons that escaped me. Thane's mother, the late Queen Lulu, had carried on an illicit affair with him—just like Riche, it seemed. The late King l'Ausseil had been a wise king, but apparently he lacked whatever it was women looked for in a man. Personally, I'd liked the late king a hundred times more than Salas. All Salas had going for him was his looks.

"She's just a suspect. We have no proof. But she has taken some rather suspicious actions of late. We're keeping an eye on her."

"Father, what do you mean by 'suspicious actions'?" Claire asked.

"Well, you know how Riche relinquished the title of queen dowager?"

"Of course. I recall she returned to the church as a cardinal?"

To remind readers who might have forgotten—Riche was formerly a cardinal of the Spiritual Church. She'd married King l'Ausseil as part of a political union meant to strengthen the king's control over the church. Riche had been queen dowager for a time after late King l'Ausseil's passing but soon gave up the title and returned to the ministry. Within the church, her position was technically equivalent to Yu's, but being the former queen dowager gave her authority second to only the pope.

"Lady Riche has dipped back into politics ever since she resumed her position as cardinal. She'd been gathering supporters within the church while undermining the influence of the current pope," Yu explained.

"I think I see where this is going." Claire looked at Yu with concern. Dole nodded with a worried expression.

"Sorry, can someone explain?" I hadn't a clue what was going on.

"Lady Riche probably hasn't given up on Yu. Now that making Yu the king has failed, she's trying to make her the next pope instead."

Well, that made sense. The cat was out of the bag now: whatever the royal family might claim, the people knew Yu was a woman. Combined with how well received Thane's rule had been, Yu had little to no chance of ever succeeding the throne. But both Yu and Riche held positions of power within the church, and Riche additionally had her former supporters to draw on. The Spiritual Church favored women, considering them more naturally spiritual than men, and the previous top choice to succeed the pope, Lilly, had removed herself from consideration. Riche must have thought the time was ripe.

"But the current pope is still young, right? It'd be a while before Yu could take over," I said.

"About that..." Dole frowned. "It's just a rumor, but...I hear there is concern that some individuals intend to assassinate the pope."

"What?!" I exclaimed. That was no laughing matter.

"You heard the pope is due to visit the Nur Empire next month, right? I suspect an attempt will be made then." Dole's expression was bitter as he shook his head in abhorrence.

"Couldn't we have Lady Riche arrested, then?" I asked bluntly.

"We can't," Claire answered. "She's a cardinal of the church and the former queen dowager. It's hard to lay a hand on a lady of her influence."

"She's shrewd, too. I'm sure she has people do all her dirty work for her, hence why we've yet to find a single piece of hard evidence against her," Dole went on.

I supposed they would have arrested her a long time ago if they could. Riche pulled strings from the shadows the same way Dole had when he was a noble. He no doubt understood better than most how hard it would be to catch her red-handed.

"That being said, we're actually not a hundred percent sure that Lady Riche is the puppet master," Dole continued.

"Isn't the circumstantial evidence damning enough?" I asked.

"The problem is that Lady Riche volunteered to be in charge of security for the pope's visit. If she were the mastermind, she wouldn't need to take such a risk."

I saw his point... If something were to happen to the pope on her journey, Riche would be the first person to take the blame.

"Maybe it's a diversion?" I asked. "Or maybe she took the job precisely to discover the gaps in the pope's security?"

"It's possible, but I'm not so sure. She says she wants to put the actual security detail under someone else's command. Well, more specifically..." For some reason, Dole looked directly at me. I had a sinking feeling in my stomach. "She wants you to be in charge, Rae."

Say whaaat? I couldn't help but mentally retort.

Trouble was *definitely* brewing.

"Thank you for coming, everyone." Former queen dowager and current cardinal Riche Bauer greeted us with a warm smile.

We were at Ruhm's main cathedral. It was smaller than Bauer's but still quite large. With me were the same people who'd met with Dorothea: Yu, Misha, and Claire.

Riche had come to the empire to prepare for the pope's visit, arriving around the same time as Lilly. She summoned us the day after our talk with Dole.

"It's been a while, Mother. I hope you've been well," Yu greeted her mother as the three of us knelt on the ground, heads bowed.

"Thank you, Yu, I have. Everyone, please, be at ease."

I raised my head and looked at Riche. She'd shielded her face from view with a fan the last time I saw her, but I got a good look now. Her eyes, blue like Yu's, seemed to smile softly. Her golden hair, which had hung long when I last saw it, lay hidden beneath her wimple. The habit she wore was different from Lilly's and Misha's, as it was elegantly embroidered in the same style as Yu's, signifying her position as cardinal. She'd given off an unfriendly impression when we last met, but now she seemed gentle—perhaps indicative of her current mood.

"Now then..." Riche began. "I summoned you all here today to ask something of you."

The four of us already knew what was coming.

"As you've likely heard, the pope is coming to the empire next month. I wish to enlist your help as escorts."

Dole's words were spot-on.

"Especially you, Claire François. I want you to be in charge of guarding the pope."

"*Me?*" Claire asked, taken aback.

Huh? That was strange... According to Dole, it should have been me. Had Riche changed her mind?

"While I'm ashamed to admit it," Claire began, "the truth is I don't know the first thing about security escorts. Certainly there must be somebody more suitable than I?"

"Oh, dear... But the Pope herself requested it. Is it really not possible?" Riche made a troubled face, cranking up the pressure.

"Well... If Rae and Misha can assist me, then I'll accept."

"Oh, thank goodness! Of course, that would be fine. In fact, I had something to request of Rae as well."

"What is it?" I asked, puzzled.

Riche called for an attendant, who arrived carrying something. "What I'm about to show you must stay a secret. Not a word of this must leave this room."

With profound reverence, the attendant held up what looked to be a framed portrait.

"Is that...me?" I blinked in confusion. Pictured within the portrait was none other than myself. But why was a picture of me being handled with such religious zeal?

"Not you, Rae," said Riche.

Then who?

"This portrait is of the pope, Her Holiness Clarice Répète III."

The four of us let out a gasp of surprise. This went beyond simple resemblance—her face was practically a carbon copy of mine.

It could have been a coincidence. Lilly had once mentioned seeing someone with a face like mine on her travels, so maybe my face was just common in this world? Come to think of it, when I'd first met Lilly, she'd thought I looked familiar. Perhaps she had been reminded of the pope.

"As you can see, the pope and Rae look identical to one another. For that reason, I want Rae to act as her body double," Riche explained.

A dangerous request. Dole claimed the rumors of the pope's impending assassination had some truth to them, so it was safe to assume being her body double meant risking my life. And while Riche's request was reasonable if she had the pope's well-being in mind, if we did as she asked, we might well be playing into her hands.

"There is something I would like to ask, if I may."

"Of course, Claire."

"Are you not at all concerned that the pope and Rae are so similar in appearance?"

"Ahh, that. It's a closely guarded secret, but it is understood that those who look like Rae—er, rather, the pope—are born every so often. We believe them to be blessed by the Spirit God. Many popes throughout history have borne this face. The church goes to great lengths to watch over those who bear these features."

So my face held some significance in this world... But why? Was it because it was the face of the *Revolution* protagonist?

"Perhaps you were once under the care of the church, Rae," Riche said.

"Uhh, is that right..." I muttered.

Come to think of it, Elie—a look-alike of mine whom Lilly had run into—had been adopted by the church. If I hadn't been adopted by my parents, I might have met a similar fate.

Well, putting matters of my face aside for now, there was one other thing I wanted to ask. "I have a question, if I may."

"Go ahead."

"Is it true? Is there a group with designs on the pope's life?"

"That's..." Riche hesitated. I wasn't sure what to make of this. "It was Dole, wasn't it? His lips are far too loose. Well, no matter. I would have told you regardless. Yes, it's true, there are rumors that some people intend to take the pope's life."

Riche shook her head, as if the very thought were abhorrent. "Some malicious gossip has it that I'm the ringleader of said plot, but that is simply untrue. The pope is the leader of the Spiritual Church. To hurt her would be to invoke the wrath of followers the world over."

In other words, she was saying she wasn't that foolish.

"The role of a body double is a dangerous one. But you are the only one who can do it, Rae. I wouldn't ask this if you merely resembled her; I'm asking because I'm confident you can protect yourself if worse comes to worst."

High praise indeed.

"So please accept this request. For the pope." Riche bowed deeply, shocking Yu and Misha. I would later learn they had never seen her bow to anyone before.

"All right. I'll do it," I answered after deep consideration. We had no way of knowing who was planning the assassination, but my best chance of stopping it came in working within the church.

Sticking my neck out like this would have been unthinkable of the old me. It seemed I'd changed because of Claire.

"I'm...surprised," Riche said. "I was sure you would resent me too much to accept. I tried to have you killed after the incident with Yu's gender. I'm sure you noticed."

She was talking about how my food had been poisoned while I was imprisoned. For my part, I was surprised to hear her admit it.

"Considering the circumstances, it was only natural you'd hate me. I prioritized Lady Yu's feelings but disregarded yours," I said, which seemed safe. I wasn't sure if her words were an act, but I wanted to avoid making enemies if I could.

"It seems I have misunderstood you, Rae Taylor... Please forgive me for the foolish mistakes I've made." Riche bowed deeply once again. "Claire, Rae, I'll be leaving the pope's safety to you both. If anything happens, I'll take responsibility. Please do your best. Yu, Misha, please support them in any way you can."

We dropped to a knee and lowered our heads once more before being dismissed.

"You're being stubborn, Misha!"

"No, you're just too emotional, Yu!"

Claire, May, Aleah, and I were eating dinner when we heard loud arguing from the room over.

"Are Lady Yu and Sister Misha fighting?"

"Their voices are scary..."

May and Aleah voiced their concerns with worried faces. Actually, if Misha lacked the composure to use her wind magic to muffle the sounds coming from their room, the argument was pretty heated.

"Go check on them, Rae," Claire said.

"What about the cleanup?" I asked.

"I can do it—just hurry up and go."

"Right, going."

I said, "Don't worry," as I gave May and Aleah a quick pat on the head and made for the room over. I rang the doorbell, and their arguing abruptly stopped, after which I heard footsteps approach the door.

"Oh...Rae."

"Good evening, Misha. Is something wrong? It sounded like you two were having a disagreement."

"I'm sorry you had to hear that. It's nothing serious." Misha smiled as she spoke, but her naturally red eyes were red in a different sense.

"Forgive me for prying, but would you tell me what's wrong?"

"That's..."

"Why not, Misha? Let's share our thoughts with Rae," Yu said from inside the room, having heard our exchange.

"Come on in..." said Misha.

"Thank you."

This was the first time I'd been in their room since we arrived. They'd furnished it since then, making it much cozier than before. Being members of the church, they both had a number of relics and prayer objects here and there, but their overall lifestyle seemed modest.

"I'll put on some tea," Misha said.

"Oh, no, I'm all right."

"It's fine. I need to go cool my head a bit."

Misha went to the kitchenette to prepare some tea. The awkward atmosphere that lingered from their fight began to ease as the scent of tea wafted into the room.

"I'm sorry, Rae," said Yu. "I didn't realize we were loud enough for you to hear us."

"It's fine. I'm more worried about you two. Neither of you are the type to raise your voices like that."

"We were just...exchanging opinions about Mother."

"Yu kept insisting we shouldn't trust her," Misha said, returning to the living room with a tray of teacups and a displeased look.

"And I *still* think we shouldn't. There's a high chance Mother was involved in Salas's escape. It's only natural not to trust her."

"She's your own mother!" Misha insisted. "We don't know if she's conspiring, but as her daughter, you have to at least have some faith in her!"

"Faith in her? When all she ever did was force her desires on me?"

"Even so—"

They broke into bickering again.

"All right, stop, both of you. Let's take a moment to calm down," I interrupted.

"You're right... Sorry," Yu apologized.

"Sorry..."

The couple wore uncomfortable expressions, perhaps embarrassed. They had a habit of getting lost in their own little world regardless of who else was present—whether it be flirting or arguing.

"In short, Lady Yu distrusts Lady Riche, while Misha wants to trust her?"

They nodded.

"You agree with me though, right, Rae?" said Yu. "Mother only ever thinks about herself. This time is no different."

"Leaving her personality aside, I think Lady Riche is trying to act in your best interests," Misha said.

"Like when my best interests somehow involved forcing me to live as a man?"

"That's..."

"All right, all right, that's enough." I stopped them yet again as they rapidly approached a third shouting match.

Seriously, what a handful these two could be.

"We don't yet have enough information to know for sure whether to trust Lady Riche." I kept my voice level to try to enforce calm. "Salas's disappearance is fishy, but it's still a mystery. Jumping to conclusions now will only hurt us down the road."

Misha and Yu listened quietly. They were both sensible people who understood my logic. But feelings could so often run counter to reason.

"I think I understand how you feel, Yu," I continued. "You lost your freedom because of your mother. You can't bring yourself to trust her."

"That's right."

"But...!"

"On the other hand, I don't understand your sudden change of heart, Misha. You were never fond of Lady Riche." Misha had even helped us break the curse on Yu in defiance of Riche's express desires.

"I'm still not fond of her. Even in the convent, we don't get along. She tries to separate Yu and me at every opportunity—even compelling Yu to use her own influence to defy hers... But this can't be right. No mother and child should have to feud like this. Lady Yu matters more to me than anything else—that's why I can't bear to see you estranged from your mother like this." Misha's true feelings spilled from her lips. "I'm not saying every family gets along. If this were someone else's family, I'd likely agree with Yu. But this isn't someone else. It's Yu. And I want Yu to be happy."

"In other words, you believe Yu needs to reconcile with Lady Riche to be happy?"

"At the very least, the two of us will never be happy together as long as Lady Riche stands opposed to us."

"So, it's less about wanting to trust Lady Riche and more about ensuring Yu's happiness?"

"Yes."

Now I got it. I turned to look at Yu. "Lady Yu."

"Yes?"

"I understand where Misha's worry comes from now. Lady Riche is a very influential person who tries constantly to separate the two of you. You can see how this is a problem, I'm sure?"

Yu remained silent.

"So now I ask you: Why do you still distrust Lady Riche? I understand you resent her for how she caged you before, but you've been freed. You've said yourself that she relented once you abandoned your right to the throne."

I still distrusted Riche myself, but Yu's point-blank rejection of Misha's words—to the point of having an open shouting match—was odd.

"It's because...I can't forgive her for how she treated my dear Misha."

"At the convent?"

"Yes. Misha is my everything. And I won't forgive anyone who hurts her, even if they are my mother."

Now I got Yu's feelings, too. I looked between them.

"So let me get this straight... You two are arguing because you love each other."

They went silent. They stared at their feet as their cheeks reddened. As for me? I was done with this whole mess.

Get a room, you normies!

"It's clear you two had each other's best interest in mind, so how about you try sorting this out again—honestly this time? Not being upfront with each other is what led to this misunderstanding in the first place."

"You're right..."

"Sorry..."

It seemed my work here was done. "I'm going back to my room. Try not to get too impassioned again, okay? Oh, but getting *passionate* in a different sense might do you two some good, you never know!"

"Rae!"

Misha shot me a glare while Yu simply laughed defeatedly.

Leaving them to their own devices, I returned to my room.

"Everything all right? Nothing too serious, I hope," Claire said worriedly.

"Nothing at all. Just a lover's spat."

Honestly, what a couple!

We began preparations the following day. There was much to do: delegating tasks, scheduling shifts, and reviewing the floor plan of the town hall in which the conference would take place. Of course, we were exempt from attending the academy while we worked. I worried about our grades taking a hit, but it seemed they would overlook our academic performance on account of the circumstances. We still had to take tests, of course, so we needed to keep up with studying whatever we missed in class.

"The name's Hildegard Eichrodt, but please call me Hilda."

During this time, we finally grew acquainted with the last romanceable character from *Revo-Lily*. She introduced herself as the head of security on the empire's side.

Obviously, the church wasn't preparing for the pope's visit alone. With the empress in attendance, the empire needed security measures, too. Much of the empire's strength lay in its military, due in part to its extraordinary investment in magical research. This stood in stark contrast to the Bauer Kingdom, which had initially neglected magic. In fact, the empire's Department of Magic Technology was so influential that they were second in power only to Dorothea herself. And Hilda had deep ties to that department.

Hilda came off as a sharp and capable person. She wore a monocle, seldom seen on a woman, and her silver hair and red eyes reminded me of Lilly. But in contrast to Lilly's timidity, Hilda emanated ferocity. Philine claimed Hilda was scary at first glance but genuinely a nice person—but I knew Hilda's real personality. She was nothing but raw ambition and would stoop to anything to achieve her goals, even feigning kindness toward Philine.

To Hilda, Philine was nothing but an opportunity to increase her own power.

"This is the empire's security plan," said Hilda. "Please review it."

That said, she did excellent work.

This meeting was held in a shared conference room reserved for those working the security detail. The room was quite large;

it had to be, to accommodate all the people involved. Desks and chairs had been arranged in rows, and the lists of required materials covered the walls.

"Thank you, Hilda. This is the church's security plan. Let's compare notes and assist each other."

Claire led the church's security team with Lilly acting as support. As Claire was inexperienced in these matters, Lilly had been assigned to assist. Their combined efforts had allowed planning to progress smoothly.

"Will Her Holiness grace us with her countenance this time?" Hilda asked.

"Unfortunately, she will not. Her Holiness does not often reveal herself to others."

See: Claire's and my surprise at the pope's true face. She was typically hidden by a bamboo blind whenever she talked to or met people. Even when she moved, she rode in a palanquin.

"Oh, dear. It will be difficult to convince Her Majesty of this... I wouldn't be surprised if she slices open the blind to forcibly reveal the pope's face. Her Majesty Dorothea is short-tempered, after all. Even the conference staff are terrified of her." Hilda shrugged, but her expression seemed far less bothered than her words implied.

"You don't seem *too* concerned," Claire said.

"Well, truthfully, I doubt even Her Majesty would do something so impolite to the pope in the current climate. Inviting the ill will of the Spiritual Church's followers would only cause trouble for the empire."

"You have a lot of faith in Her Majesty," Claire said.

"Of course. Her Majesty loves nothing more than rationalism. Barring unforeseen circumstances, she won't transgress, not against the pope." Hilda smiled reassuringly.

Yeah, okay, but why are you trying to reassure us when you brought the possibility up yourself? I thought.

"By the way, have you met Philine?" Hilda asked.

"I have," said Claire. "She's very sweet. You wouldn't think she was the daughter of someone as stern as Her Majesty Dorothea."

"Ha ha, everyone says that. But the two are actually quite alike."

"Oh? How so?"

"She's strong-willed, like her mother. She stumbles from time to time and loses heart over small things, but when it matters the most, she stands her ground." Hilda sung Philine's praises, and to be honest, I agreed with her. "I hope everyone from Bauer will get along with Philine. Especially the two of you, who led the revolution."

Hilda's lips loosened into a smile, her cold demeanor suddenly warm. Countless players fell for that smile in the game.

But I wouldn't be deceived. I had a feeling that behind the scenes, Hilda was telling Philine the exact opposite—warning her not to get close to us, so she could stay number one in Philine's mind.

"Of course. We hope to be good friends with her." Claire had studied Hilda's personality in preparation for our stay in the empire. She knew Hilda was likely feigning friendliness, yet she managed to respond with a superb smile of her own.

"Incidentally..." Hilda lowered her voice. "I'm sure you've heard the rumors about a group aiming for the pope's life? I can safely say the culprit isn't associated with our government in any way. As I noted, making an enemy of the church would be terrible for us. And while this entire affair somewhat embarrasses Dorothea, she understands we have no choice at present."

The objective of the pope's visit was to dissuade the Nur Empire from continuing military aggressions. War brought suffering, and with the three-nation anti-Nur alliance taking shape, a mighty war loomed on the horizon. Consequently, the pope wasn't just visiting the empire. She had just finished holding a similar conference with Thane in the Bauer Kingdom, and she planned to visit Sousse and the Alpes after the empire. According to Lilly, she grieved how violent the world had become.

Dorothea had intended to refuse the meeting, as she believed religion had no place in politics, but the empire wasn't in a position to do that. They were already staring down the barrel of a potential war with three other nations. Earning the enmity of the Spiritual Church on top of that would be reckless.

"We hope the church will take adequate steps to protect her Highness's safety, too. If anything were to happen to our empress, however unlikely, it would be a great blow to our people," Hilda said.

"Understood."

"As for your former chancellor, was he ever caught?"

"That... No, unfortunately we are still looking for him."

So the empire knew of Salas's escape.

"It would be a relief to catch him before the pope's visit," Hilda said. "Just so we have one less thing to worry about."

"I agree wholeheartedly."

"I've heard through the grapevine that he has strong ties to someone high up in the church. Unexpectedly, it seems the one plotting to harm the pope is—"

"That's enough, Hilda," Claire interrupted before Hilda could lay out a direct accusation. "We're no fools. We have already devised countermeasures for this matter you're so concerned about, so let's end the baseless speculation there."

"I apologize. That was rude of me." Hilda bowed slightly.

Now that I thought about it, Salas had originally been working with the empire. They probably didn't want us asking them too many questions either.

"All is forgiven," Claire said. "As co-head of security, I understand your concerns."

"Thank you. Now, shall we review the plans?"

This first meeting between security teams went on to finish without a hitch. Having been in charge, Claire was understandably exhausted by the time we returned to the dormitory.

"So many unexpected things keep occuring... What happened to our plan to manipulate the empire?"

"Nothing we can do about it. The circumstances have differed too drastically from my book of prophecies," I said as I ran a comb through May and Aleah's hair. May's hairstyle resembled mine, while Aleah's took after Claire's. May had always preferred her hair short where Aleah liked hers long, so the styles fit nicely.

"But still, something must be done. We might as well start with what's ahead of us," Claire said.

"I'll be there for you."

Finished with the girls, I combed Claire's hair. She had quite a few split ends. *Must be from stress.*

"Thank you, Rae."

"Anything for you."

Repeatedly dropping kisses on her head, I swore to myself again that I would ease her burden, if even just the tiniest bit.

Preparations continued steadily, and before we knew it, the day of the pope's arrival was upon us. The sky was clear, the air brisk, and the earth warmed by the sun's gentle rays. Claire and the personnel she led awaited the pope at the western city gate. Lilly had responsibilities elsewhere, but Yu, Misha, and Riche stood with us.

"She's late..." Claire mumbled. Transportation in this world wasn't punctual down to the minute like in modern-day Japan, but the pope was an hour late—long enough to make us worry something had happened en route.

"Are you concerned?"

"Of course. What if the pope was assas—ahem! There's that rumor to consider." Claire stopped herself before saying "assassinated." While information pertaining to the issue had been shared with the security team, we had to watch what we said while in public earshot.

"Who knows, maybe she slept in."

"Why, Her Holiness would never. She's not you, Rae."

It appeared Claire was still on edge.

"You're horrible! Just who do you think wakes up early every morning to make everyone breakfast and lunch?" I covered my face and pretended to cry.

"H-huh? Wait, I'm sorry. I didn't mean it like that, Rae. I really do appreciate what you do, okay? It was just a slip of the tongue. I'll take it back, so please don't cry—"

"No! I'm hurt! I won't stop crying until you kiss me!" I continued to pretend-sob.

"Wh-what are you saying?! W-we're outside, I can't kiss you when there's people watching..."

"No. I. Won't. Stop! Not until you kiss me!" I tried adding a tantrum to my act, but—

"Rae...you're not actually crying...are you?" Claire stared at me with glazed eyes.

"Tee-hee."

"Don't 'tee-hee' me. We don't have time for your games—this is serious business."

"I did it precisely because it's serious business, Miss Claire."

"Quit joking around," Claire huffed.

"You're being too doom-and-gloom. Look, I read in a book a while back that in times like these, you should assume the worst-case scenario and therefore take the best-case action to address it. Shall we try it?"

"Sounds easier said than done... All right. What's the worst-case scenario?"

"Let's say...it's the pope already being killed."

"Then what's the best course of action from there?"

"How about sending someone to go check?" I offered, when we were suddenly interrupted.

"Emergency!" someone called. "The pope and her entourage have been attacked by a pack of monsters! Requesting aid!"

Everyone snapped to attention.

"How many, how strong?!" Claire swiftly asked.

"About ten mid-strength monsters!"

"Dispatch security units one through three. The rest are to stay and defend the gate." Under Claire's orders, the reinforcements quickly assembled. "Will you go for me, Rae?"

"If that is your order."

"Go. I'm counting on you."

"Yes, ma'am!"

I joined the reinforcements, which consisted of about fifty soldier priests from the empire's church and a hundred imperial soldiers. I was the only Bauer student. Sped up by those who could wield wind magic, we took off from the city at a blinding pace.

"They're in sight!" a voice exclaimed from the front.

Ahead, the pope and her entourage were encircled by monsters, barely managing to defend themselves with a perimeter defense.

"Attack!" the leader of the reinforcements ordered.

Most of our units were composed of mages, but I spotted some swordsmen in the front. The mages in the back rained down magic, instantly taking out a third of the monsters, which were too distracted by the prey in front of them.

"Don't let up!"

The military escorts guarding the pope promptly repositioned to catch the monsters in a pincer attack. The number of fiends rapidly dwindled.

As the last of the monsters were slain, the pope's escorts voiced their relief. "W-we're saved..."

"Not yet!" I shot an ice arrow at a shadowy figure creeping behind them.

"Feh... So there's a sharp one among the bunch."

The shadowy figure avoided my attack by beating the large wings on its back and bursting upward into the sky.

"A demon?!"

"I don't care what you humans call me, but I have a name: Platos. Remember it."

"Platos?! Isn't that one of the Three Great Archdemons?!" a soldier exclaimed.

Platos—unlike Aristo, his fellow Great Archdemon—wore nothing but animal skins. His speech and attitude were rough, strikingly unlike the calculating Aristo.

Wasn't meeting big-name demons supposed to be super unlikely? Yet here I am, facing a second!

"Taste my strength and die!" Platos slammed a club into the

ground, sending ripples through the earth that knocked the soldiers down. "Eat this!"

He raised his hand into the air, and stone spikes exploded from the ground. It was the medium-level earth spell known as Earth Spike, but the number of spikes he summoned was irregular—more than a hundred, all bursting forth at once.

"Muddy Soil!" I used my earth magic to change the spikes to soft mud moments before they could pierce our flesh. Stopping more than a hundred Earth Spikes took a toll on me, even with my ultra-high aptitude magic, but I had no choice. It was that or be slaughtered.

"Not bad. Bet you're Rae Taylor, huh? One of the humans that idiot Aristo let slip away."

I felt a disturbing lack of magic left in me...right as I caught Platos's eye.

Shoot.

"I bet Aristo spent too much time playing around with you, huh? Well, I ain't like that. I'm gonna end you nice and quick!" Platos charged toward me as he swung his club.

He's fast!

"Stop!" Soldiers stood in the way of Platos, readying their lances, swinging their swords, and firing their magic.

"Move!" The demon didn't even flinch. Their attacks bounced off him as he tore through, knocking the soldiers out of the way. "Hnnh—die!"

He grinned, confident in his victory, as he swung his club at me.

"Judecca! Earth Spike!"

I froze Platos in place mid-swing, then attacked him with the same spell he'd used earlier, forming my trademark combination technique: Cocytus. But before Earth Spike could connect, Platos wrested free of the ice through sheer strength and flew into the air.

"Whew. You nearly screwed *me* of all people... Man, and right after I was done bragging. You humans are freaks." Platos glared down at me from above. "But hey, know what? I bet you're at your limit. You humans got crazy small magic reserves. Just those few spells probably got you near empty."

As much as I hated to admit it, he was right. After countering his hundred-something Earth Spikes and then casting two of my strongest spells, my magic was nearly depleted. That wasn't to say I was completely tapped, but I only had about one, maybe two casts of a spell that could damage him.

I was about to consider retreat when a dignified voice rippled through the battlefield.

"Fill."

Light began to envelop the area, the illumination somehow palpable and soft. Power swelled in me where it touched. Fallen soldiers rose one after another. I, too, felt my magic power restored in its entirety.

From near the pope's palanquin, a clergyman called out. "Her Holiness the pope has granted us her blessing! Today, we shall not know defeat! Stand and slay the demon!"

In unison, the escorts, the soldier priests, and the soldiers responded with a war cry.

Was that...a wide-range healing ability? Does such magic exist? I wondered.

"Hmph. Couldn't finish you off. Whatever, let's just call it for today. Later." Seeing us recovered, Platos indifferently prepared to retreat.

"Chickening out?" I called after him.

"Hah! Wait until you can hold your own against me before talking smack," Platos spat with derision. I would much rather have taken him down right then, but he didn't take the bait. The demon left, flying to the east.

"Was that Her Holiness's power?"

"It's a miracle!"

Here and there, the soldiers began to exclaim words of praise for the pope. They'd been near death moments prior. I hated to think of what would have happened if the pope hadn't saved us with her magic.

"Rae Taylor, this way, if you would." The clergyman who had rallied the soldiers beckoned to me. I approached, though I didn't yet know what for. "Thank you for buying us much needed time. Her Holiness's magic is powerful but takes time to prepare."

Have I seen this person before? I was pretty sure he was a bishop.

"Oh, no, if anything, I should be doing the thanking. The pope's magic saved us all," I said.

"You flatter me," a voice answered from within the palanquin.

"Y-Your Holiness?!"

"It's fine, Bishop Rhona. It's only a matter of time before she and I must see each other."

The blind on the palanquin lifted, and as it did, I came face-to-face with a girl who looked exactly like me, though the aura she exuded was unmistakably different.

"It's a pleasure to meet you, Rae Taylor. I am the pope." The girl's voice was alarmingly monotone, and her expression didn't so much as twitch.

She was Clarice Répète III.

"Thank you very much for coming to our aid earlier."

We welcomed the pope at the empire's main church. Claire and I faced the pope's palanquin as we knelt on the ground, though she had her blind lowered, so we couldn't actually see her face. Adjacent to the palanquin were Riche, Yu, Misha, and then Lilly, as well as other members of the church. Everyone looked tense, thanks to the recent attack.

In contrast, the pope thanked us in a calm—no, a mechanical voice, one that lacked inflection and was devoid of emotion—yet, somehow, was not uncanny in the slightest. Her face was identical to mine, as was her voice, if I listened carefully enough, but we had entirely different airs.

"Thank you for gracing us with your presence. My name is Claire François, and I am in charge of the security for your visit.

I am relieved to see Her Holiness was not harmed earlier," Claire said as she formally introduced herself.

"I've heard nothing but good things about you. Everyone praised your handling of the recent situation as well."

"Thank you very much."

Claire conducted herself with utmost decorum. She never ceased to amaze me in formal situations, ever the perfect lady. It was hard to think she was the same person who grew flustered every time May and Aleah cried at home—not that I did any better in that case.

"Your partner is very strong," said the pope. "I likely wouldn't be here if it weren't for Rae Taylor."

"Thank you very much for your kind words." I bowed deeply together with Claire.

"I'm sure you've already heard from Cardinal Riche, but it seems there are those who desire my death. While it pains me to know some believe I have not fulfilled my duties as pope, I cannot afford to pass from this world yet. Will you lend me your aid?"

"Of course, Your Holiness. We'll do everything in our power to protect you."

"Thank you very much. Now then, I must now speak on a different matter. I ask all clergy other than Cardinal Riche, Cardinal Yu, Lilly, and Misha to take their leave."

The members of the clergy whispered to one another in confusion.

"I'm sorry, did Her Holiness not make herself clear?" Riche's sharp, sagacious voice ripped through the murmurs. She'd spoken softly when she summoned us the other day, but I thought this tone sounded much more authentic. But that was probably my bias talking.

At her urging, the clergy members vacated the area.

After making sure all but those specified had left, Riche said, "Now then, let's swap Her Holiness and Rae. Misha, the blind, if you will."

"Certainly." Misha lifted the bamboo blind, revealing the Pope's small frame sitting on a modest white chair. She wore a white vestment embroidered with golden threads.

"Your Holiness, I beg your pardon, but may I ask you to leave your seat so we can begin exchanging clothes?"

"Understood." The pope's expression never flickered as she stood and slowly walked toward us.

At the risk of sounding narcissistic, I simply must make clear that the pope was bewitchingly beautiful. While we had the same face, she exuded an aura of mysticism I simply couldn't match. There's a fine line between the chilling and the divine, and her indifferent, emotionless visage wavered over it, but it landed, in the end, at divinity. Perhaps being the pope meant she had to maintain constant control of her expression?

Such were my thoughts when I heard a thump.

No one spoke.

She tripped. The pope had tripped. And squarely on her face, at that. Unable to process what had just occurred, Claire and I stared, our mouths agape. The idea of offering a hand didn't so much as surface in our minds.

Then, as if nothing had happened, the pope stood and resumed slowly pacing toward us with her coolly composed expression.

Then another thump.

She fell a few steps thereafter. On her face. Again.

"Your Holiness?!" Claire regained her senses and rushed to the pope's side to help her up. The pope, still expressionless, took her hand and stood.

"Forgive me, I'm afraid I'm not athletically inclined."

But you're just walking? I thought. *Can walking really be considered something athletic?*

Her vestments did seem heavy, and they dragged on the floor as she walked. No sweat appeared on her brow, but she seemed to struggle to move. I'd thought it strange that she walked so slowly, but perhaps that was just as fast as she could go?

Or maybe she's just really physically weak? I pondered.

She eventually reached me and took a single deep breath, like she had accomplished a great feat—despite merely walking forty feet or so.

"Now then, Misha, Lilly, please help her change," Riche said.

"Certainly."

"Y-yes."

Lilly rushed over to the pope and began stripping her heavy vestments off, piece by piece. I stripped my own clothes and donned the vestments passed to me by Misha. *Oh, they* are *pretty heavy.* Perhaps because of their ornamental nature, the vestments restricted my ability to flex my limbs and were difficult to move in.

While I still thought the pope frail, these clothes *were* partially to blame.

"Please wear these if you would like, Your Holiness." It would be outrageous to make her wear my used clothes, so Claire handed over a washed set we'd brought from home.

"How are these worn?" The pope looked at my clothes in puzzlement, like they were a foreign object.

"I-I can help you change."

"No, Lilly," Lady Riche cut in. "If Her Holiness is to live as Rae for the time being, she needs to learn these things. Please teach her."

"Please do, then, Lilly," the pope asked.

"Y-yes."

The pope seemed to lack basic common knowledge, as if she'd lived under a rock her whole life. I guess she'd just been born with a silver spoon in her mouth, leaving her no need to learn such things? Thankfully, she seemed to get the hang of normal clothing quickly. She moved her arms and legs about curiously, looking very cute—was that also narcissistic of me to say?

"It's light and easy to move in. A bit cold, however."

"Please wear this if you're cold, Your Holiness."

"Claire, if I'm to live as Rae, I need you to treat me like her."

"Oh... B-but, of course. You should wear this then, Rae."

"Yes, Miss Claire." The pope put her arms through the jacket Claire handed her. I always added "Miss" when I said Claire's name, and it seemed she would do the same to maintain cover.

"Rae—I mean—Your Holiness, take care to watch your speech and behavior as well," Misha warned me.

This might be a whole lot more tiresome than I anticipated.

It had been a few days since my swap with the pope.

The conference with Dorothea was still days out, but the pope always had various small tasks she needed to see to. I generally left them to others and focused on not blowing my cover, which was easier than I thought, as the pope rarely saw people herself. Even so, on the rare occasions I did have to deal with someone directly, I occasionally slipped up and spoke unnaturally or mistook the order of formalities.

"Ugh... I'm exhausted."

Finished with meeting clergy from the empire's church, I returned to the room that had been supplied to me and sloppily sprawled onto the bed with a deep exhale. Keeping up the facade was difficult because, to no one's surprise, my personality was the polar opposite of the pope's; it took everything I had to prevent myself from fooling around. Of course, the worst part of everything was not having Claire by my side.

When this is all over, I'll toy with Claire to my heart's content! I promised myself, when I heard a knock at the door.

I hurriedly got up and sat neatly on the bed.

"Come in."

"Pardon me, Your Holiness." Riche entered the room. She

peered at me, eyebrow raised for a brief moment, before fixing her expression. "Your duties are concluded for the day. Good work. I brought a change of clothes."

She brought out some plain, unadorned vestments that acted as casual wear and unfolded them for me to see.

"Furthermore... Please take care not to lie down with your formal vestments on, or they'll grow wrinkled."

Ah. She'd seen right through me. Yeah, I supposed the real pope wouldn't be flopping around on a bed like this.

"I'm sorry, Lady Riche."

"Try again."

"Riche."

"Yes, Your Holiness."

Riche smiled in contentment after I hurriedly corrected myself. She began helping me change clothes.

"That said, I understand you must be exhausted. Acting as the pope must not be easy, having to be composed all the time." She spoke with consideration, her voice low enough that only I could hear.

"Oh, yes. Especially since I usually act like a wild animal."

"I'm sure that's not true. I hear your grades in etiquette were quite high back when you were a student."

As the outer tunic was lifted off, I responded, "I can't hold a candle to real nobles. We live in different worlds, after all."

"Well...that's all in the past. Now, there's no distinction between noble and commoner," Riche muttered, sounding unsure whether the change was for better or worse.

"I recall you were originally a member of the church?"

"Yes. But if you trace my lineage back, I descend from prominent Bauer aristocrats." Naturally. No common-born clergywoman, not even a cardinal, could so easily become queen.

"Was it difficult adjusting to life as royalty?"

"Oh... In its own way. I learned etiquette at the church, but the formalities expected of the royal family were much more complex. I had to practice so much." She sounded nostalgic. "But I had help. I know you don't like him too much, but back then, Salas was good to me."

So he'd actively supported Riche even before she became queen?

"Everyone only speaks ill of him since his imprisonment. Of course, not even I can forgive his ties to the empire, let alone what he tried to do to the kingdom. And yet, I don't think it right to deny what he did for the kingdom either."

Her words had some truth. Salas had been an excellent chancellor who brought stability to Bauer. Even the late King l'Ausseil's push for meritocracy would have ended before it began if it weren't for Salas's help in making it a reality.

"He used to be a dreamer with a beautiful ideal in his heart. But that all changed because of her... Because of Lady Lulu." The queen before Riche. The one who'd had an affair with Salas that resulted in the birth of Thane. "Lady Lulu was constantly falling in love with new people. A typical noble lady, if you will. She seduced Salas all too easily, naive as he was."

My impression of the events was quite different, but I knew

when to keep my mouth shut. Instead, I asked a different question. "Did you love Salas?"

She didn't respond for a time. Only the sound of rustling clothes filled the room.

"Personal feelings matter little in a political word. I was l'Ausseil's wife, and so I could never be wed to Salas. That was all."

Her words sounded like they were meant for herself rather than me.

"At any rate, I became queen, then gave birth to Yu... She gave my life meaning. I'm sure you...and Yu don't think too highly of me, but I truly do love her."

Her expression softened when she spoke Yu's name. I would remember the look on her face for a long time to come.

"What I did to her was unforgivable. I don't know if I even have the right to call myself her mother anymore. But everything I've done, I did with her best interests in mind. And no matter what anyone might say, that is the truth." She stared intently at me as she spoke. I felt sincerity in her words.

"What do you think of Misha?" I asked.

Riche wore a thin smile upon hearing my question.

"I think Misha is a wonderful girl. Her family used to be nobles of good repute, and she cooperated with us in hiding Yu's true gender. You might not believe me, but I was certain she would be Yu's future spouse. That is, until her house fell to ruin." She spoke nostalgically, as if envisioning a young Yu and Misha together.

"What about now?"

"Now...I'm not so sure. Yu's a woman now, but she still wants to take Misha as a lifelong partner. I just can't understand why one would choose to love someone of the same gender. I'm sorry if I offended you."

"It's all right. I don't mind."

Straight people might never completely understand how queer people felt—and vice versa. Neither party was at fault.

"And yet, I do envy you and Yu. You both chose to live lives that were true to yourselves, choosing your paths despite knowing the hardships ahead. I think you're all wonderful. I really do."

Her words took me by surprise. I thought she simply loathed our kind of love, but to hear her admit she didn't understand it, and even envied it...

"Perhaps the times are changing. When I was your age, whom I loved or married wasn't my decision to make. They say the elderly tend to look back fondly on the past; I think it's because we envy our younger selves, who had yet to make the mistakes we've made now. It's easier to wish to change your past than to acknowledge what you've done."

Her words didn't match her still youthful appearance. Her voice seemed to age when she spoke of the years long gone.

"Rae, one day you'll become an adult and understand what it means to be trapped in the past. There will be children who show you the world to come, and then you'll understand how enviable—yet oh-so-brightly—they shine."

The words she spoke this day would stay with me forever. Even after what would come to pass, I would still look back and think on the truth of Riche's words.

Intermission—Adultery (Accidental) Claire's POV

A few days had passed since the pope and Rae swapped roles, and things seemed to be going well for Rae, considering she hadn't exposed herself. The same could not be said for us.

It was evening, almost time for the guards to change shifts.

"Don't you think Miss Rae's been kinda quiet these last few days?" Lana—who was helping with guard duty—asked, full of suspicion. By her side, Eve looked over toward us, doubtful as well.

"Not at all. I'm just as I always am," The pope responded. Her words resembled the sort Rae might say, but her tone remained flat and emotionless.

"Th-that's right. Oh, I know, she's probably just tired from guard duty." I tried my best to work up an excuse.

"Hmm, really? Something's not right... Was Miss Rae always, like, this expressionless?"

There it was—my biggest cause for concern. Unlike Rae, who was incredibly emotive, the pope's face never so much as twitched. We couldn't avoid arousing suspicion.

"Th-the truth is that Rae and I have been fighting for a while now. That's why she seems a little stiff."

"Ohhh, I see, I see. Hey, Miss Rae, if you're bored with Miss Claire, then why not start a secret relationship with me?" Lana said, joking around with Rae—who was actually the pope—like she always did.

Seeing Lana's suspicion pass, I breathed a sigh of relief—but I was getting ahead of myself.

"What do you mean by 'secret relationship'?" the pope asked in her impassive voice. My blood pressure shot through the roof.

"Whoa, whoa, whoa! Are you giving me the okay? Oh, my gosh, this is my lucky day!"

"Filth..."

Lana seemed to be in a state of euphoria while Eve made no effort to hide her disgust. My concerns just kept growing.

"Whatever are you saying? Rae would never cheat on me," I said.

"Whaaat, but you said yourself that you were fighting. I'm not lettin' an opportunity like that slip by, you know?"

The pope's deadpan eyes stared at me. It didn't seem like she was going to lift a finger to fix this mess. It was up to me to drag us out of it.

"W-we may be fighting, but that doesn't change the fact we both love each other deeply," I said. "We're just having a small...tiff."

"Yeah, but isn't, like, a 'small tiff' already a reason to end things? What's the point in forcing a relationship that's not working out?"

"Lana... Just what kind of relationships have you been in so far...?"

I wasn't even inquiring about her relationship history—just expressing my exasperation with her dismal view of love.

"In the first place," I continued, "why are you so interested in Rae? You've been approaching her since the first day of class." Rae told me she had no recollection of ever meeting Lana prior, so why was she so infatuated with her?

"Huh? I mean, like, c'mon—Miss Rae's *sooo* cute and smart! And I just *love* how clingy she can be."

"Oh. Well, I'll give you that."

Cute—check.

Smart—couldn't disagree.

Clingy—absolutely correct.

"Besides, I feel like Rae would never cheat romantically, but she would be totally up for a purely physical affair."

"N-nonsense!" I rebuked Lana, not least because I didn't want the pope to hear any more on this topic.

"Is there a difference between a romantic affair and a physical one?" the pope innocently asked, tilting her head.

I'm begging you, Your Holiness, please don't pay her any heed!

"*Absolutely!*" sang Lana. "A physical affair's not cheating if there's no love!"

"You know that's not true! Keep spouting nonsense and I'll burn you!" I raged.

"Oh, no, help me!" Lana said in a deadpan voice as she hid behind the pope. "Save me, Miss Rae!"

"Miss Claire, it is wrong to burn someone for mere jests. That would not be moral conduct," the pope chided me.

"It was a joke... You really take such matters seriously, don't you?"

I felt like I was surrounded by enemies, no ally in sight. *Rae, I feel your absence keenly. Come back soon.*

"Aha! You like me too, Rae! I knew it! So how about you and I get dinner tonight?"

"No, thank you. May and Aleah are waiting for me at home."

"Aww, figures. Kids add an extra challenge to the pick-up game. But that just makes it even better!"

"Goodness, do you ever stop spouting nonsense? Oh, look, it's time for shift change already. Good day, Lana, Eve," I said.

"See you later, Lana, Eve."

"Laters!"

"Goodbye..."

We parted company with the two and hurried home.

"Mother Claire, Your Holiness, welcome home!"

"Welcome home!"

May and Aleah greeted us as we returned to our dormitory. *Ahhh,* I thought, *nothing is better after a day's work than seeing those smiles.* I hugged them both and rained kisses onto their cheeks.

They already knew about the switch between Rae and the pope. They'd actually realized something was different before I even had a chance to explain on the first day, simply taking one glance at the pope's face and asking—

"Who's this person?"

"Where's Mother Rae?"

I was surprised—they tended to be comparatively lukewarm around Rae, but I suppose they were paying attention to her all the same. Rae would be ecstatic to hear it. I couldn't wait to tell her.

"I've prepared dinner!"

"Aleah's amazing! She's just like Mama Rae."

"Thank you, Aleah."

"Thank you very much."

The pope and I both thanked Aleah. While I was ashamed to admit it, neither I nor the pope could cook. I had considered hiring someone with the funds provided by the church when Aleah suggested she do the cooking herself.

I worried whether she could handle it at first, but all doubt went out the window on the first day, when she lined the table with irresistible dish after dish. She'd only been taking lessons from Rae for a month, but she proved an exceptionally fast learner. Of course, May helped her sister a little, but it was mostly Aleah.

We changed, ate, bathed, and played with the children. Before we knew it, it was time to sleep.

"May, Aleah, time for bed."

"Okay!"

"Yes, Mother."

They said their good nights and returned to their room.

"They're good kids," the pope said. Her face was as devoid of emotion as usual, but something about her felt gentler than usual.

"Yes. I'm proud of them." I truly was, from the bottom of my heart. At first, I'd been worried about whether I was equipped to raise them—but those worries had long since passed. I had misunderstood what parenthood was in the first place.

Parenthood wasn't just raising a child. Parenthood was watching over a child as they raised themselves. We weren't meant to force our children to become something, but rather to help them grow into what they wanted to be. At least, that was my take on it. Naturally, I still believed in a certain level of discipline to ensure their safety.

"Now then, shall we go to sleep ourselves?"

"Yes."

We headed to the bedroom and got into bed. The room, originally meant for Rae and me, only had one bed. This unfortunately meant the pope and I had to sleep together. At first, I'd had misgivings about sleeping beside a woman who looked identical to Rae, but the pope was a quick sleeper—unlike my mischievous wife—so I adjusted soon enough.

"Good night, Your Holiness."

"Good night, Claire."

That was when I felt something soft touch my lips. I sat up in shock.

"Y-Y-Y-Y-Your Holiness?!"

"A...physical affair...isn't cheating...right?" She spoke drowsily before she drifted into sleep completely.

I was in turmoil.

Oh, Rae! Please, forgive me!

With this new strangeness hanging over my head, I prayed for Rae to visit me in my dreams as I closed my eyes for the night.

Three days remained until the conference. I was getting used to my role as body double, albeit with the occasional verbal slip-up here and there.

But I don't think I could ever get used to this food...

Despite being the leading figure of the church, the pope's meals were incredibly modest: hard bread, bland pottage with beans, a boiled egg, and some fruit. It was basically the same diet Claire and I had lived off of for some time after the revolution. The church didn't forbid the eating of meat, so I could only assume this was part of their religious self-discipline.

"I shall now begin the poison testing," said the attendant by my side.

My appetite, already low because of the bland food, sank even lower at the mention of poison. I understood it was a necessity, though, given the pope's status and the rumors.

I couldn't just use my detoxifying water magic either, as the empire had a poison called cantarella that was resistant to it. I'd been able to detoxify the old variant used on Thane, but if the variant Louie used—or a newer variant, for that matter—was mixed in my food, I'd be dead. It was easy to think magic was all-powerful, but it had its limits.

The attendant who was testing my food for poison was a nun by the name of Sandrine. She took regular care of me as well. She seemed to be a fervent believer in the pope and had been doing this work since a young age. She looked like most other nuns, about the same height as me, her eyes soft and kind. I'd say she was in her twenties. She was also a bit thin, perhaps from this diet the clergy lived on. Come to think of it, every clergy member I had seen so far was on the thinner side.

"It's safe." After trying a part of all my food, Sandrine returned to my side on standby.

"Thank you, Sandrine."

"Not at all. This is merely part of my duties," she said with a warm smile.

I felt a pang of guilt as I spooned the pottage into my mouth. Sandrine was unaware of the swap and still thought she was risking her life for the pope. If she were to be poisoned and die, it would be for some stranger she had never heard of. I didn't quite like the thought of that.

"Your first order of business will be meeting with Lady Riche to discuss the coming conference."

"Understood."

I didn't meet very much with people, in part due to being a double. The majority of my work was handled by Riche. In fact, she did a lot of things, such as handling the conference preparations, collecting information the pope would need for the conference, and keeping me up to date on Claire and the real pope—as well as May and Aleah. It was thanks to her that I could focus on my role without those worries.

I continued listening to Sandrine recite the day's agenda while finishing my meal. *Maybe I should ask for different options*, I thought, as I moved to get changed. My heart sank when I thought about having to wear those heavy vestments for another day.

"I think you've gained a little weight, Your Holiness," Sandrine said. Her words startled me. I shared the pope's face, but our figures weren't quite the same. "It must be because of the empire. I'm sure they're giving you the best quality ingredients out of consideration for you."

Thankfully, she explained away the difference herself. Whew.

"I'll do the buttons on your back," she said as she moved behind me. It was annoying how you couldn't don these vestments alone. The buttons were too far back to reach. Maybe I could get Broumet to start selling zippers...

"I graciously thank thee for bestowing the honor of touching Her Holiness's body," I heard Sandrine whisper from behind me. Every time she touched me, she offered her gratitude to God and kissed her rosary. No doubt, she was doing it today as well. But she was taking an unusually long time.

"Is something wrong?" I asked.

Suddenly, I felt the presence of strong magic behind me. I tried to turn, but I found my neck compressed, unable to breathe. Something thin and cord-like had wrapped around my throat.

"San...dri...ne...why?!"

I abandoned searching for an answer and devoted myself to finding a way out of my predicament. Survival first—interrogation later.

I summoned a bead of magic as fast as I could behind my back and fired, sending Sandrine flying straight to the wall.

I gasped for air while eyeing Sandrine warily. Her gentle

expression was nowhere to be seen, her eyes now glazed over and her hands gripping a rosary. That rosary—it had to be what had choked me. Any normal cord should have snapped; I suspected it had been specifically made to double as a garrote. In fact, some strange light emanated from it—was it a magic tool?

Interrupting my thoughts, Sandrine charged, cord in hand. But she was slow. She expected to be facing the physically frail pope.

"Gotcha." I grabbed her right wrist and twisted it, applying pressure on the joint. I'd figured it was about time I learned some practical combat skills, so I'd had Claire teach me the basics of martial arts.

Sandrine resisted for a while, but she gasped with pain and released the cord.

"Sleep." I pressed my fingertip to her forehead and cast another of my trademark water spells, the same one I'd used on Claire during the Commoner Movement. It was strong enough to make even the magic-resistant Claire faint—so of course, there was no way a simple nun like Sandrine could resist.

"Phew..." I was out of the woods. I picked up the rosary and thought about calling for someone when—

"Your Holiness!"

Someone came bursting through the door.

"Lady Riche..."

"Are you all right? I heard a noise and came as soon as I could!" Riche spoke between gasps. She had run here full speed. "Y-you're bleeding!"

"Huh? Oh... I must have been cut when I pushed her back." I couldn't see, but apparently there was a scar around my neck.

"Did Sandrine do this?"

"Yes, but I have a feeling she wasn't herself."

"Is she still...alive?"

"Don't worry, she's just unconscious." I couldn't have her dying on me before I could collect information.

"Such a terrible scar... I'm so sorry. I thought I had removed anything that could be used as a weapon, but I hadn't considered a rosary," Riche said worriedly as she started to cast healing magic on me.

That's odd, I thought as I stashed the rosary underneath my vestment. *But I can't jump to conclusions yet.*

Following Riche, clergy members came pouring into the room.

"What happened?!"

"Your Holiness, are you safe?!"

"Sandrine did this?"

Things were getting noisy in here. A soldier priest pinned Sandrine down as she began to rouse.

"Ngh... Where...am I?"

"Sandrine, you are under arrest for your attempt on Her Holiness's life."

"What?! I would never!" she insisted.

"You still feign innocence? I see no reason to wait for a trial. Execute her here." Riche's harsh words took me by surprise.

"Wait," I said, disturbed. "We still need to question her."

"That'll take too..." Lady Riche cut herself off. "Her crime is clear. I see no reason to waste time."

"Lady Riche, *I'm* fine," I whispered in a voice only she could hear, but she didn't stop.

"Execute her, on the spot!"

Riche left me with no choice.

"Are you disobeying the orders of your pope?" I asked coolly.

This was my last resort. Those words wouldn't have meant anything if the two of us had been alone, but Riche had the onlookers to consider.

"Forgive me... We will obey Her Holiness's decision." Starting with Riche, everyone began to kneel before me.

Ugh. This feels terrible.

After that, Sandrine was questioned by the church. She claimed she was in the middle of changing me when she blacked out. She also seemed to blame herself greatly, as—no matter the true circumstances—she had attacked the pope, and she even now wished for her own execution.

I ordered the questioning to be carried out with at least one member from the church and one member from the Bauer Kingdom always present. I suspected Sandrine wasn't the sole perpetrator, which left her at risk of being silenced by conspirators to hide information.

I visited Sandrine a while later.

"Why did you go so far as to save me after what I did to you?" she asked me through tears.

I couldn't think of a good response, so I simply answered, "Do I really need a reason if it's you, Sandrine?"

Overcome with emotion, she started sobbing even more.

Your Holiness, I might have accidentally put you on the Sandrine route. Sorry!

I made it clear to the others that Sandrine should not be punished until the full circumstances behind the case were made clear.

"Have this analyzed for me." I also covertly handed Sandrine's rosary to a Bauer Kingdom clergy member on the side—without Riche's knowledge.

Intermission—The Anatomy of a Smile Pope Clarice Répète III's POV

"Your Holiness, what's wrong?"

"Is something stuck on our faces?"

The young twins—named May and Aleah—looked at me skeptically. No, perhaps skeptically wasn't quite it. They simply regarded me with unbridled curiosity.

I was living in Rae and Claire's room for the time being. Claire was currently out, leaving me alone with May and Aleah. I had no knowledge of housekeeping tasks, so I looked after May and Aleah instead—although it might be more appropriate to say they looked after me.

"Nothing is wrong. I was simply thinking about how cute you

two are," I answered truthfully. As pope, I did not often have the chance to freely express myself, and this was a good opportunity to learn. I'd been taught to watch my words, expressions, and even my thoughts to best serve the church, but I'd never thought of it as a burden. This was how I'd been raised. My purpose was to be the symbol of the church. It was what I had been *created* for.

"Are you praising us? Hey, hey, are you praising us?"

"Yes." I nodded, causing May to smile happily.

However, Aleah seemed a little put off. "You're supposed to smile if something's cute."

"Smile?"

"Yeah. Even if you say we're cute, we don't know if you mean it with a face like that. If anything, it's scary."

"How does one smile, Aleah?"

"Huh?" Aleah looked at me in surprise, caught off guard by my honest question.

"Do you not know how to smile?"

"I do not."

"Haven't you smiled before?"

"Not that I can recall."

"Oh, no! May, we need to do something!"

The twins began conferring. Smiling seemed to be terribly important.

"I know!" May began. "We just gotta do this!" She began tickling my sides.

"Huh? Aren't you ticklish?"

"It is very ticklish."

"But you still won't smile."

"It seems not."

"Then you join too, Aleah! Two is better than one!"

"Okay!" Aleah joined in the tickling. But it didn't seem to change anything. "She still won't smile?"

"I thought that'd do it..."

I didn't smile. I was ticklish indeed, but it didn't result in a smile. The two girls continued to try various things, but to no avail.

"I'm sorry, girls," I said.

"It's okay. I guess some people just don't smile very easily."

"But the two of us smile all the time, don't we, May?"

"Yeah..."

"But, Your Holiness, you really think we're cute, right?" May asked.

"Yes."

"Then I'm sure you'll smile one day! Because Mama Rae always says 'cute is justice'!"

"Cute is justice?" The connection between justice and smiling eluded me. Just how deep down the rabbit hole did smiling go?

Claire returned home soon after, and our conversation came to an inconclusive end. But the fact that I couldn't smile lingered in the back of my mind.

The next day, I visited a convent in the empire with Claire. I wasn't supposed to go out often, since I was being targeted, but staying cooped up at home wasn't something Rae would do. That being the case, I asked Claire to bring me to the convent.

I'd picked this place because I heard there were many children here.

"Look, it's Miss Claire and Miss Rae!"

"May and Aleah, too!"

"Hello, everyone. Have you been well?" Claire said.

"Yes!" they all cried.

Apparently, Claire and Rae often visited a convent in the Bauer Kingdom, helping through donations and charity work. They'd continued this work in the empire and were already familiar faces at this establishment.

"Now, now, children. Let's not cause trouble for Claire. Welcome, Miss Claire, Miss Rae."

"I hope it's okay we've come by again, Kaja."

"Of course. The children were waiting for your visit."

"Really? That's good to hear. I brought some sweets for everybody."

"Yay!"

Claire handed over the basket she'd brought, and the children shouted in glee.

The nun known as Kaja looked troubled and said, "Oh, dear. That's not how you show your gratitude, children. What do you say?"

"Thank you very much, Miss Claire, Miss Rae!"

"You're very welcome. May, Aleah, go ahead and play with everyone."

"Okay!"

"Yes, Mother."

The children carried the basket to the yard. There, they sat down next to a flower bed and began divvying up the sweets.

"Miss Rae, is something the matter?"

I looked blankly back at Kaja. Had I done something considered unusual?

"You don't seem very energetic. Normally you would go and play together with the children. You seem...different today."

It seemed those who knew Rae well could feel something off about me. It wasn't too surprising; no matter how alike we looked, it didn't change the fact we were separate people, even if this body had originally been *hers*.

"Do I often play with the children?" I asked.

"Huh? Um, yes, I believe so?" Kaja answered.

"It's because you're a child at heart," Claire chimed in. "Playing with children is right up your alley."

"Do I smile when I play with children?"

"Why, of course you do! You smile so happily," Kaja said.

"I see..."

I stepped away from Kaja and Claire and walked toward the circle of children. As I came close, the children looked up at me.

"Hello, Miss Rae!"

"Miss Rae, are you eating, too?"

"There's enough for everyone!"

"Come sit with us." Aleah took my hand and pulled me into the circle. "We're playing house with the sweets."

"I'm the big sister!" May said.

"And I'm the mommy!"

"I'm the father."

"I don't wanna play house. I wanna play tag!"

"We can play tag after," Aleah said. "We just got snacks to eat, so we might as well play house, too."

I listened, fascinated by the conversation. Despite their young age, their communication was complex. They had a range of vocabulary, intonation, and expression; I couldn't even begin to imagine the degree of permutations and combinations they could use to communicate. It made me feel light-headed, but not in a painful way. It felt pleasant.

I'd asked to come here to see more children and experience more of the same cuteness I'd observed in May and Aleah. But I now understood children were unimaginably complex and full of intriguing surprises when placed into groups.

I'd learned something new—children were far more than just cute.

"Are you gonna eat?" A shy little girl held out a sponge cake to me. I'd noticed her sneaking glances at me for a while now. How was I supposed to react?

"Wow, Julia. You're usually so scared of Miss Rae."

"Miss Rae isn't scary today."

Julia plopped herself down by my side and smiled up at me. Every person I'd met since swapping with Rae had described me as strange or odd. Julia's kind words, the first positive evaluation I had received, warmed my chest. But that warmth couldn't last long, for that was not how I had been made.

And yet, before I knew it, my hand was on her head, gently

patting her. Children's hair was soft and thin. She giggled and shut her eyes as if ticklish.

"Are the sweets to your liking, Mother Rae?" Aleah asked impatiently, perhaps because I had yet to eat my sweet. She'd made all the sweets we brought today. She claimed they were nothing compared to Rae's, but they looked wonderful to me.

"It's delicious..."

The sweetness of the sugar and the richness of the butter filled my mouth as I bit into the sponge cake, followed by a citrusy smell wafting up to my nose. It was a brand-new experience for me, as I hadn't had many chances to eat something sweet.

"Was it to your liking?"

"Aleah's sweets are good, right?"

"Aleah made this?"

"Awesome!"

"It's just like Rae's."

The children seemed to agree it was delicious as well. I felt joy knowing I had shared the sensation with them.

The children and I played various games together. They teased me for my low stamina, saying things like "Rae's so weak today!" I felt joy well up inside me countless times, and every time, I had to snuff it out.

"Goodbye, everyone. We'll come by again sometime."

"Thank you. Until next time."

"Bye-bye!"

Kaja and the children waved goodbye as we left the convent.

"How was it, Your Holiness? I'm sure you don't often get to do things like this," Claire said.

"Indeed."

As pope, I mainly met with nobility and high-ranking officials. Of course, I did visit convents and the less fortunate, but those were mainly politically motivated performances. Playing with children like this was a first for me.

"I learned a lot today." I meant it. Today, I had learned things I might have gone my whole life without knowing. My chest was tight with emotions I had never felt before.

"Oh, my. Look, Your Holiness," Claire said with a chuckle. I looked to where her finger pointed and saw the children waving goodbye.

Julia was there, waving her small arm with vigor. I waved back to her. Seeing this, she began to wave as hard as she could.

"Your Holiness, do you know what face you're making right now?"

"I do not, but I imagine it is the same as always."

"He he... You're smiling."

"Oh...!" I touched my face. The corners of my eyes had lowered, and the sides of my mouth had risen together with my cheeks.

So this was what it was to smile.

"Let's come again sometime," Claire said.

"Yes, definitely." I might not be able to come again as Rae, but I swore to myself I would come, regardless. "Thank you for today, Claire."

"Not at all. I'm happy we came as well." Claire smiled sweetly. *I'm sure she smiles more when she is with Rae.*

I looked at her warm smile and made a wish, knowing full well such a wish could never be granted.

I wish them the strength to brave the truth of this world.

The day of the conference was finally upon us. I had assumed the pope would attend as herself, but it seemed the one sitting behind the blind would be me, while Misha used her wind magic to project the pope's voice.

"Empress Dorothea would fly into a rage if she knew about this, but we have no other choice," Riche explained in a pained voice. The church was reluctant to deceive, but, well...

I sat behind a blind that had been set up in the conference hall. We awaited Dorothea and her people, who were scheduled to arrive later than us. Security guards stood around the blind, among them Claire, Lilly, Misha, and the real pope, posing as me. The pope would be standing just behind the blind as well, so even if she moved her lips, Dorothea wouldn't be able to see her.

"Her Majesty Empress Dorothea has arrived."

Dorothea entered through the door, clad in her usual pitch-black armor. I could only presume it to be her formal attire. Her mantle waved as she strode to her seat, stopping before it to name herself.

"Dorothea Nur. Let this conference be productive." She gave

a brief introduction before sitting. The advisor by her side turned pale, but the empress remained composed. Egocentric as always, doing what she believed to be logical.

"Clarice Répète III. Thank you for meeting with me today."

In contrast, the pope took her time to speak. She'd abandoned most formalities, likely out of consideration for Dorothea.

The pope continued, "Before the conference begins in earnest, there is one thing I would like to ask."

"Speak."

"Did you make Sandrine attack me?"

The conference hall stirred at this frank accusation. I was surprised, too. No matter how straightforward Dorothea liked to be, this had to cross the line.

"Hmph... So the rumors were true. Well, I did not order it. Though I doubt you'd place much weight in my words."

"I believe you. I do not think you the type to lie."

The conference opened with this intense exchange. The atmosphere in the hall grew tense, everybody sitting on the edge of their seat.

Dorothea suddenly erupted into laughter. "The current pope is amusing indeed! I've taken a liking to you!"

"Thank you very much."

Both sides, the empire and the church, heaved a sigh of relief as the tension dissipated.

"I have no interest in taking your life," said Dorothea. "There's nothing to gain in the church's enmity. I guarantee your safety as long you remain in my empire."

"Thank you for your reassuring words. Shall we begin?"

As planned, I extended my hand below the half-raised blind. Dorothea met my hand and gripped it. Hard. *Really* hard—ow!

"Hmm... I see." For reasons beyond me, Dorothea wore a knowing sneer.

The discussion continued smoothly after that. The pope admonished the empire for their aggression while Dorothea objected, demanding the pope stay out of their domestic affairs. I sat alert, but nothing of note occurred. Only near the very end did something unexpected happen.

"On another note, is it customary for you to use a proxy when meeting with dignitaries? Don't you think it a little insulting, even with your life being targeted?" Dorothea sneered. The conference hall lurched into its most intense state of apprehension yet.

Was the jig up?

"What do you mean?" the pope asked.

"So you choose to feign ignorance? Fine. I'll overlook it. But I can't do the same for that woman." Dorothea looked to the side of the blind and smiled—directly at Riche. "You must be wondering why your magic tool won't activate."

"Wh-whatever are you talking about?" Riche responded.

"That ring you've been trying to activate is a magic tool, is it not? I'm sorry to inform you that it's not going to work."

"Wh-what?"

"Your hint proved useful after all, Rae Taylor."

Dorothea looked back at the blind and grinned. Riche did the same, but with a face bitterly warped.

"Rae, you couldn't have..."

"I'm sorry, Lady Riche. I had the teleportation magic tool you tried to bring swapped out."

"Y-you!" Riche's face twisted with indignation. It seemed she was behind the plot after all. "H-how did you know?"

"Your behavior after Sandrine's attempted assassination was odd. You called the rosary the weapon, but you never saw the rosary itself."

"B-but the marks around your neck made it obvious!"

"You'd think of a cord or a rope, then. A rosary is quite a leap of logic."

Riche bit her lip in frustration, trapped by her own mistake. "I see... So you had already figured it out. Then the order you gave at the time was to seek retribution against me?"

"Not at all. I really hoped I suspected you wrongly and that I could trust you."

"You're naive. If I were you, I would have had me killed at the moment of doubt."

"I couldn't. Not Yu's mother."

"You..." Riche's eyes widened.

"Enough of this charade," Dorothea said. "Hilda, arrest her."

"Right away." Hilda ordered her soldiers forward. Riche seemed to resign herself to her fate, showing no signs of resistance.

But things never could go that easily.

"Oh, no, no, no. We can't have that, can we, Lady Riche?" A familiar voice dripping with malice echoed through the hall.

I knew that voice. "Salas!"

"Where are you?!" Claire demanded.

"Why, hello, Rae Taylor, Claire François. And goodbye." Magic filled the hall as Salas's condescending voice echoed around us.

"Hilda, sitrep," Dorothea commanded.

"Right! I-It's…" The color drained from Hilda's face. "Teleportation magic! Something is teleporting here!"

"Hmm…" Dorothea turned on Riche. "You. What do you know of this?"

Riche didn't respond, but one look at her face made it obvious she knew what was going on.

"What are you doing, Mother?!" Yu yelled at the top of her lungs.

"It was all for your sake, Yu." Riche gave us a broken, joyless smile.

The next moment—it appeared.

"A demon. Interesting…" Dorothea sounded genuinely amused.

The demon that appeared before us was unlike its comrade in human clothing, Aristo, as well as the one who'd looked like a human barbarian, Platos. This one had an enormous black body that gleamed with a metallic shine, the upper half humanoid, the lower half insectoid.

"Name yourself, demon," Dorothea began. "I shall grant you the right to speak as a parting gift before I send you to the next world."

"I am Socrat, of the Three Great Archdemons." The upper humanoid half of the demon pointed toward me. No, not toward me—but behind me, toward the real pope. "We come only for her life. Comply and yours shall be spared."

Socrat crept closer toward the pope.

"All hands, battle formation! Rae, you too—the body double plan has failed!"

The guards obeyed Claire's swift commands. I leaped past the blind and joined everyone else.

Standing at the front, the soldier priests flailed their morning stars at Socrat.

"Hindrances." Without so much as slowing his stride, Socrat used the first of his three pairs of legs to sweep the soldier priests aside, sending them flying against the wall.

"Get back! We'll stop him with magic!"

Seeing melee combat prove nigh impossible, Claire ordered a change in tactics. The soldiers unleashed an onslaught of magic bullets. The hall was big, but it was still indoors; Socrat couldn't dodge with his large frame. Sure enough, the magic bullets hit their mark.

"Did I not make myself clear?" The demon stepped out from a billow of smoke, his pace unchanged—not recoiling one bit from the attack.

"Well, how about this?!" Claire readied her Magic Ray. Unlike during her confrontation with Aristo, she was in peak condition. "Light!"

"Darkness."

Claire let off four rays of light, but they were intercepted and swallowed by four rays of darkness—which continued to fly at her.

"Miss Claire, look out!" I jumped to push Claire down just before a streak of darkness whizzed over her head. The darkness collided with the wall behind us, destroying—no, *erasing* it from existence.

"He's too powerful..." Claire muttered. Everyone could see that Socrat's magic far outstripped Claire's Magic Ray.

"That magic... You must be Claire François. You'll be next after the girl, so wait your turn." Socrat spared a sidelong glance for us as he continued his deadly advance toward the pope.

"Your Highness!" I yelled.

"St-stop right there!"

Standing before the pope was Yu. The other soldiers had completely lost their will to fight.

"Icicle Blade!" Yu's sword took on a chilly glow. As I once explained, Yu's nickname was the Prince of Ice—although, I supposed Princess of Ice would probably be more appropriate now. Her wimple fluttered in the air as she closed the distance and sliced at Socrat's front leg. "Nngh?!"

The blade couldn't penetrate his carapace, inflicting only a superficial wound. Socrat kept moving, about to trample Yu.

"Socrat?! What of our agreement?!" Riche shrieked.

The leg about to crush Yu halted.

"Ah, indeed. I shall honor the agreement and overlook this one. Now, be gone." With a swing of his leg, Socrat sent Yu flying through the air. Lilly bolted forward and caught her.

"Uhh..."

"Stay with me, Lady Yu!" Lilly began to heal her, but Yu's wounds weren't minor. We'd exhausted nearly everything we had, yet not one attack had done meaningful damage to Socrat, who stood mere steps from the pope. We watched in horror, thinking all hope lost.

But it wasn't over yet.

"Did you really think I'd let you do as you please, demon?" Unsheathing her two swords, the woman sneered like a wild beast eyeing its prey.

Empress Dorothea—bearer of the title Sword God—now stood in Socrat's path.

"Another hindrance?" Socrat casually swung his front leg at Dorothea. He'd cut down everyone he'd hit thus far, the impact rivaling that of a battering ram.

"Hm?"

Something flew through the air. Yet Dorothea still stood. An object hit the ground with a shuddering thud—Socrat's front leg.

"What?!"

"I don't know who you meant to address with your drivel, but you're in my presence now. *Kneel.*"

Something flew again. The end joints of Socrat's remaining four legs were cut away.

"Y-you—?!"

"I am Empress Dorothea."

Accompanied by a sharp slicing sound, one of Socrat's human arms flew off. To my eyes, it didn't seem like Dorothea had moved at all. She appeared stock-still, standing at rest with her two swords lowered in front of her, yet the proof of her actions lay in Socrat's halved limbs.

"Hmph, this will not do." Socrat leapt back to the safety of the wall behind him, allowing his legs to begin regenerating.

"Too slow." But Dorothea was faster. She already awaited him at his landing point. This time, I saw her take the time to ready her swords, positioning herself to intercept him. "Sever."

A high-pitched shrill rang out as Socrat was bisected cleanly down the middle. An instant later, Dorothea landed on the ground, and the two halves of Socrat's body crashed down behind her.

I hadn't seen her swing at all. Impossible as it seemed, Dorothea had just overwhelmed a high-ranking demon with her skill in swordplay alone.

"This is...the Sword God," Claire muttered deliriously by my side. The title wasn't for show. Dorothea's strength quite literally surpassed the realm of man.

"How unexpected. You're quite powerful." Socrat, whom I'd thought dead, spoke nonchalantly. The two halves of his bisected body melted and pooled together before clumping into a mass, his carapace re-forming.

"Hmph. I suppose a Three Great Archdemon wouldn't die from something like that," Dorothea muttered, unamused.

Socrat had reconstituted, smaller than before but without any wounds.

"So you're the Sword God. I heard you were strong, but to this degree? I should have listened to my subordinates."

"Don't worry about that. In a moment, you'll have no further regrets."

"Because you will have killed me?"

"Exactly." Dorothea walked calmly toward Socrat.

"I'll admit, your skill with the sword is divine. But how will you handle this?!" Socrat opened his mouth wide, and a thick beam of darkness spewed out.

"Your Highness!" Hilda screamed.

"What?!" Socrat watched in confusion as Dorothea closed the distance by lunging entirely into the dark beam. Her two swords blurred, and in the next moment, Socrat's head fell to the ground.

"Too bad. Magic has no effect on me." Dorothea crushed Socrat's head underfoot.

The empress possessed a unique ability called Magic Nullification. This ability had allowed her to single-handedly annihilate an entire battalion of Sousse soldiers. In an era shifting toward magic-focused combat, such an ability was unequaled.

But the ability was a double-edged sword. While magic attacks were meaningless against her, support magic and healing were ineffective, too. She was abnormally strong but could only ever fight alone. I found it kind of sad—strength that only made one lonelier.

"Goodness, such stupendous power." A neck grew from the stump of Socrat's decapitated head.

Look who's talking, I couldn't help thinking.

"Fill." The pope used her area-of-effect healing ability. The collapsed soldiers began to rise, their wounds healed.

"Freeze." I cast my own area-of-effect freezing spell, Judecca. I'd normally never cast it while an ally stood near the enemy, but I didn't have to worry about Dorothea—she would be untouched.

"You even have tactical talent. I want you even more now," Dorothea said.

"Just hurry up and hit him!" I shouted.

I opted not to use Earth Spike, instead relying on Dorothea to deliver the finishing blow. Understanding my intention, she sliced the frozen Socrat into fine pieces.

But even that wasn't enough.

"The moment after you learned magic doesn't affect her, you mercilessly attacked while she was in range... You're bold, Rae Taylor." Socrat regenerated for a third time, smaller again. How many times did we need to do this? "Oh, dear... I imagine I could handle the empress alone, but dealing with Claire François and Rae Taylor alongside the Saint and the pope is a bit much for me."

He hesitated for a moment—or at least, he pretended to. "Ahh, but of course! Let's see how well you can deal with this."

I sensed a surge of magic power as his body unnaturally swelled. He looked like a balloon on the brink of bursting.

"You're going to self-destruct?!"

His laugh creaked and echoed through the hall. "Well, *I* won't die. But everything within two hundred feet of my body will be wiped from this earth."

He's serious! "Miss Claire, get behind me!"

"But the others!"

"Quickly!"

I raised multiple layers of tungsten carbide barriers and pushed Claire down behind them.

What followed was a roar louder than the eruption of Mt. Sassal.

When I next opened my eyes, I was greeted with a gruesome sight. The meeting hall was nowhere to be seen, wiped off the face of the earth as Socrat had claimed. Socrat himself was gone, presumably having fled.

Not a single one of us had come out unscathed. If there was a silver lining, it was that the pope, Misha, and Claire had each respectively been protected by Dorothea, Lilly, and me—so at least the main constituents of the conference were not severely injured.

However...

"Mother! Why?!"

Yu was injured as well—but not lethally so, as Riche had protected her daughter with her own body. Yu frantically began trying to heal her mother, who lay on the floor in a pool of blood, but it was clear that she was beyond saving. The lower half of her body was shredded. She had moments left before the shock and blood loss took her.

"Ah... Yu... You're all right..."

"Mother... You... Why..." Yu stammered, the words stuck in her throat, as her mother looked up at her absently. She had too many things to ask, too many things to say.

"Yu... I'm sorry. In the end, I couldn't do a single thing for you."

"That's... That's not true..." Yu gripped her dying mother's hand, desperately trying to let her mother know of her presence.

"I thought...if I couldn't give you the throne...I could at least make you pope... But I failed... I'm sorry."

"I...I never wanted such a thing! I just... I just..."

"What is it, Yu...? You're getting harder to hear..."

"Mother!"

Riche's life faded ever further. Even Yu understood her time was running out.

"Your Holiness, please heal her!" Yu cried.

But the pope only shook her head. "Doing so now will only extend her suffering."

"No... This can't be..." Yu's eyes clouded with despair.

"Yu... Live freely after I die... Find...your own...happi..." Riche passed away before she could finish. Yu watched in a daze, slowly realizing she was gone.

Misha dragged her injured body along the floor and embraced Yu from behind. Yu leaned against her and began to cry.

And so the attempt on the pope's life ended in failure.

Starting with Yu, every person close to Riche was investigated. Gradually, the whole picture became clear.

The mastermind was Riche after all. She tried to make Yu the pope by killing the current one. By becoming head of security, she learned the inner workings of the security arrangements and

smuggled in a magic tool to summon a demon. This plan had failed, but Salas had finished it for her. Based on the testimony of those who'd helped Riche, Dorothea and I had also been targeted for assassination—Dorothea because she posed a threat to the Bauer Kingdom, and me, because I had lost Yu her right to the throne.

Salas's whereabouts still eluded us. We found testimony of Riche helping him escape prison, but the trail went cold after that. We only knew for sure that he had been at the conference hall, presumably disguised with a magic tool, and had disappeared in the aftermath. He had also caused Sandrine to attack me. An expert from the kingdom looked into it for me, confirming the rosary's role in the attack. Salas had switched the rosary Sandrine always kissed before touching the pope's body, replacing it with one embedded with a hypnotic suggestion to kill the pope. Was nothing sacred to that man?

With this, the church acquitted Sandrine, freeing her of all suspicion. I wondered if she would go back to poison tasting for her beloved pope. Maybe she'd be surprised to find the pope suddenly thinner again, now that we had switched back, although I heard Aleah's cooking had allowed the pope to gain some weight. Perhaps our swap would go unnoticed.

Yu endured a thorough investigation, but her innocence was more than evident. Every single one of Riche's conspirators unanimously testified that Riche planned everything without Yu's knowledge.

This was nothing more than conjecture, but I suspected some part of Riche had expected things to end like this. Just as Dole had said—if she'd really wanted to, she could have acted without leaving a trace of evidence behind. I believed she'd left a trail on purpose so suspicion would never fall on Yu.

Not that we'd ever know the truth now.

On the surface, Yu continued on, the same as ever. She fell into a depression for some time, but she soon recovered her usual tender smile. Yet every now and then ever after, I spied Misha gazing at her with sorrowful eyes.

About a week after the incident, Claire and I were spending the evening relaxing in our room when we heard shouting from the next room over.

"Rae..." Claire nudged me.

"Going."

I took myself on a visit to the room next door. I rang the bell, and shortly thereafter, Misha appeared. Her naturally red eyes were even redder than the last time I'd interrupted their shouting match.

"Sorry," she murmured.

"And good evening to you, too. Can I come in?"

"Um..."

I pretended not to see Misha's tears and waltzed on through the door.

"Hey, Rae. Sorry, were we too noisy again?" Yu looked as she ever did, wearing a composed smile.

"What's going on?"

"Misha says I haven't smiled since the incident, which obviously can't be true."

Weird thing to claim, I thought. *You're even smiling right now.*

"You're forcing yourself," Misha accused. "You can fool the others, but you can't fool me."

"You're overthinking it, Misha. I'm fine already."

"You're lying!"

It wasn't like Misha to get this worked up. I realized the difference might be something only she, having been by Yu's side for so long, could discern.

"How could she?" Misha cried. "Your mother! How could she be so foolish as to make her child feel this way?"

Her stance had shifted since their last argument. She had to feel betrayed for having urged Yu to put her trust in Riche. From Misha's perspective, both the incident with Yu's gender and the assassination attempt appeared to be sheer selfishness on Riche's part—actions she'd taken without a shred of consideration for Yu.

"Even so, Mother cared for me. I'm sure of it." Yu's voice was tinged with a mixture of resignation and love.

"Lady Yu..." Misha could do nothing more than look sadly at her.

"Mother was wrong. What she tried to do was unforgivable. Her actions only ever hurt me."

"Then why—"

Yu cut her off. "Because now...I think I understand. That was her way of trying to show her love." Yu interrupted Misha's next attempt to speak as well. "What she did was wrong, but it wasn't *just* selfishness. She did it all for me, even if she never understood what I truly wanted. As twisted as it was—it was love."

Yu smiled as she spoke. Misha stared at her, stunned.

"I didn't understand her. I thought she only wanted to hurt me. But I was wrong. There's no doubt in my mind now that the one who gave her life to save me was someone I could call my mother." Yu clenched her right hand, perhaps remembering her mother's final moments.

Seeing this, Misha overlapped her own hand onto Yu's. I had a feeling she no longer thought Yu's smile fake. There would be no further misunderstanding between them.

"Mother and I never truly understood each other. I regret that now. That's why I never want that to happen to us." Yu took Misha's hand and stared deep into her red eyes. "Thank you, Misha, for always being there for me. I want to be with you for the rest of my life, till death do us part."

"Lady Yu!" Tears spilling from her eyes, Misha dove into Yu's arms. I had never seen her cry like this before.

"I'm sorry I made you worry. I'm sure I'll make you worry from here on out, too. Will you stay with me regardless?"

"Yes! Always." Misha continued to nod wordlessly as Yu gently stroked her hair.

They would be fine now. That being the case—

"Um... Should I...go?" I gingerly suggested. I'd come over because I was worried about them, but I'd ended up not doing a single thing. The lovebirds were deep in their own world again.

"Ah. Sorry, Rae! The mood was just kind of right—and before I knew it, this happened," Yu said.

"Don't give me that! Do you have any idea how awkward it is to see your friends profess their love to one another?"

"What? Like you did during the revolution?" Yu teased.

"Wha—well, that's..." *Ugh. Why did I ever think I could best Yu at her own game?* I sighed. "Anyway, I take it you two are fine now?"

"Yeah, we're fine. Right, Misha?" Yu grinned.

"No, we're not fine. If you really meant what you said, then prove it to me, right here and now," Misha challenged.

I couldn't believe my ears, and neither could Yu, whose eyes had gone wide.

"Prove it?"

"Yes, prove it."

"Hmmm... Well, there you have it, Rae. Gonna stay and watch?"

"Good night!" I turned on my heels and fled the room.

A brief instant before I turned, I saw their shadows overlap.

"How were they?" Claire asked. She was waiting for me in our room, looking concerned.

"I feel stupid for even worrying..." I chuckled. "Hey... Tonight, can we, you know?"

"Hm? Oh—jeez... Don't try to seduce me, it's time to sleep."

"I can't sleep. I need to work off my frustration over what I had to deal with over there."

Plus, I was still in Claire withdrawal from my time acting as the pope's body double. Normally, I'd be able to reel myself in, if only just barely, but I just couldn't do it after watching those two flirt.

"W-wait, if we're going to do this, then do it properly—"

"Nope."

I sealed her lips with mine and allowed my desire to take over my body.

"Love is blind"—perhaps that was the phrase that best described Riche. I didn't agree with many of the choices she made, yet as someone who also lived for the sake of love, I couldn't help thinking she'd shone oh-so-brightly when she made her final choice.

If it were me, would I be able to give my life for May and Aleah like she had for Yu? What if it were Claire's life on the other end of the scales?

I chose to run from such torturous thoughts, instead allowing myself to be lost in Claire's body.

Even if such a time must come, for now—please allow me to feel your warmth a little longer.

Things Gained, Things Lost

The Bauer Kingdom was in a period of transition.

The revolution had sent ripples through the land, affecting not only the nobles but also the commoners. The future ahead looked uncertain. We'd succeeded in thwarting the Nur Empire's schemes and achieved a bloodless revolution, but that didn't mean life was suddenly changed for the better. On the contrary, the eruption of Mt. Sassal and the chaos surrounding the revolution had devastated most people's quality of life.

In other words, we were going through tough times.

I released a long sigh. *I know things are tough for us all, but still...*

Claire wasn't with me at the moment. She was off working to establish the new government. I wished I could help—and I did, in my own way—but I was a layman when it came to politics. I knew well enough that I had no role to play in something as significant as establishing a brand-new government. The most I could do was be Claire's errand girl or do what I was preparing to do right now—tend to her when she came home tired.

I was in the Academy dormitory kitchen making cream stew. Goods were in short supply, so I had to limit my ingredients. Vegetables, in particular, were hard to obtain due to the volcanic ash from Mt. Sassal having ruined multiple harvests. Most of the ingredients left in the kitchen were bottom of the barrel. The Academy had definitely seen better days. Regardless, I found a scrawny carrot and an onion to cook with. Meat—a valuable source of protein—was also hard to come by. Even so, I'd managed to obtain some chicken and was thinking about the best way to prepare it.

"Rae," a familiar, high-pitched voice called out to me. I turned.

"Welcome back, Miss Claire. You're early today."

"Our session got a bit heated today. Everyone agreed to call it a day and cool our heads."

"Is that right? Sounds rough."

"It really is." Claire sat on a chair and rubbed her eyes. I stopped cooking for a bit, washed my hands, and brought over a towel I'd warmed with hot water.

"Here, put this over your eyes. You'll feel better."

"Thank you. Ahh... This feels great..." Claire stayed like that for some time. It must have been a tiring day. "Today, we were discussing whether women should be allowed to vote. I, of course, said we should, but many others insisted otherwise."

"Figures."

Women's suffrage was so natural a right in modern-day Japan, it was hard to imagine not having it. But things weren't so simple in this world.

"They skirted around the issue on account of my gender, but it's clear the men all shared the same doubt: 'Do women even understand politics?'"

Such a statement sounded utterly nonsensical to me and my inherited sensibilities, but I had to remember that Japan and the kingdom were very different. Firstly, the literacy rate and level of education among women was low. I kid you not—things were so bad that if you asked a woman for their opinion on politics, chances were they'd answer, "What's a politic?" Of course, women from the now-deposed nobility and well-educated commoners might be well versed on the subject, but they only made up a fraction of the nation's women.

The second problem was that there were too *many* women. A lot of men had been conscripted for the war with the Nur Empire, leaving a greater ratio of women than men. In light of this critical lack of education in a majority of the populace, the government might not even function if women were given the rights to vote.

"Despite the issues, I believe we need to at least give it a shot. There might be some bumps in the road at first, but I'm sure it'll gradually work itself out," Claire insisted.

If we waited for the country's education system to evolve to serve women as well as it did men, we'd be waiting a long time. Besides, participating in local politics didn't just require a formal education—it also required an awareness of the issues that plagued our day-to-day lives, of which all women had plenty.

But Claire's logic hadn't convinced the big shots of the new government.

"Their misogyny runs deep," Claire said sadly.

"Indeed." I hugged her from behind. She relaxed, leaning onto me.

We stayed like that, basking in each other's warmth for some time.

"Mmm. It smells good. What's for dinner?" she asked.

"I made cream stew."

"Sounds delicious. Wasn't it tough finding ingredients with things as they are?" Claire was no longer an ignorant noble. She knew full well how scarce food had become, and she understood how difficult it must have been for me to prepare dinner.

"Anything for you. Now, let's return to our room and eat."

"Thank you, Rae, I really do appreciate all you do for me."

Those words alone made everything worth it.

I returned to our room and set some stew and a baguette on the table in front of Claire. Normally, we'd have some salad to go with our meal, but I'd splurged on the stew today, so this was it. I set out my own portion and then took a seat.

We put our hands together and said, "Bon appétit."

"My! The chicken is so juicy! How'd you find such good chicken?"

"The chicken's nothing special. Just ordinary breast meat. The real secret is in the preparation."

"And what's that?"

"I rubbed it lightly with salt and cooking wine, then left it to sit. After that, I coated it in flour." Breast meat tended to dry out when you cooked it, which made the prep extra important.

"That's it?"

"That's it. I hope I curbed the dryness a little."

"A little? I thought I was eating thigh."

"Such kind words." I was glad she enjoyed it. With a little thinking, even the most meager ingredients could become something delicious. Of course, I'd take better ingredients over this any day.

"Whew... That was delicious. Thank you, Rae."

I made some coffee for Claire, who flipped through a newspaper as she drank. I turned my back to her and began washing the dishes. Alas. I enjoyed cooking, but I didn't care much for the washing.

"Rae."

"Yes?"

"When are we doing...'that'?"

"Hm? What's 'that'?" I responded confused, not looking back.

"You know... Our wedding."

"Wha—" I almost dropped a plate. "Our wedding? You're not teasing me right now, are you?"

Times weren't exactly great—not to mention that this would be a same-sex marriage. There were so many reasons why it wasn't realistic to have a wedding, at least not right now.

"Oh? Do you not want to marry me?"

"I do!" I responded instantaneously. Of course I wanted to marry her. The problem was whether we *could*. "I thought the constitution they're drafting didn't recognize same-sex marriage."

Done with the dishes, I sat down across from her.

Claire folded up her newspaper. "You're right. Legally, we can't get married."

"So why bring it up now?"

"Because I don't think a wedding itself poses any legal issue."

"Go on..."

"Regardless of what the law might recognize, I believe a wedding is an occasion where two people who love each other can reaffirm their bond, witnessed by their family and friends."

What Claire was describing was similar to what we called a civil wedding in modern-day Japan. Wedding ceremonies could be held in a variety of ways: there were traditional Japanese weddings where you made your vows before Shinto gods, Buddhist weddings where you made your vows before Buddha—and many other kinds, including civil weddings.

Civil weddings weren't religious ceremonies but occasions where you and your partner said your vows to each other in the presence of your family and friends. They were popular among the younger generation in Japan, but hearing Claire suggest one took me by surprise. It was so starkly opposed to the old-fashioned beliefs of this world that she usually subscribed to.

"I agree, but where would we get the money?" I asked.

Weddings involved banquets. That cost money, and it wasn't like the invitees could just take a day off work, with the current state of the country. I wouldn't be surprised if many found themselves unable to attend.

"Let's keep it small. Most of the people we know have some

position in the new government. I'm sure they can afford to attend the ceremony."

"Now that you mention it, yeah..."

"Of course, I'll pay for your parents to attend. There's no point in a wedding without them."

"No, let me pay for them."

Most of Claire's aristocratic assets had been seized after the revolution. The only reason she could maintain her current lifestyle at all was because the citizens had raised some funds for her in recognition of her contribution to the country. In truth, I currently had more savings than her. I'd suggested we share our assets when we moved in together, but she refused. Right now, we were splitting living costs but managing our own personal expenses ourselves.

"Let's meet halfway and split it. I just want to make sure your parents can attend, no matter what," Claire said.

"Right..."

She kept talking, making plans for our wedding. Happy as I was to hear her do so, I still thought it might be better to wait until circumstances improved. But I also didn't want to rain on her parade. I'd just let her keep going and see what happened...

"Who else do we need to invite? There's the royal siblings, Lene, Lambert, Misha, Father... Sister and Cardinal Lilly might be a bit difficult."

"The royal siblings, Lady Manaria, and Cardinal Lilly probably can't come."

"I understand Sister is too far away and Cardinal Lilly is still under investigation, but why the princes?"

"Did you forget you're an ordinary citizen now? Royalty can't just show up to our wedding."

"Ahhh... That's right."

Despite her best efforts, Claire still sometimes forgot she wasn't nobility anymore—perhaps because she spent so much of her time meeting with members of the new government, debating them on equal footing. Despite being a citizen, her social circle remained composed of powerful people.

"I should have known that... Oh, well. That means the only ones we can invite are your parents, Father, Lene, Lambert, and Misha."

"What about your noble friends?" I asked.

"Some of us still write, but I doubt they can come. It's taking all they have to adjust to life after losing their titles."

I could only imagine the shock of losing the wealth and privilege one had enjoyed since birth. I wouldn't be surprised if many former nobles had been rendered homeless. Many had the funds to survive life as a common citizen—it was just a question of whether they *could*.

"Maybe it's better to wait for the situation to improve," I said. "That way we can invite your friends, too."

"You've been pretty against the idea for a while now. Were your words about wanting to marry me a lie?"

"Of course not! I really do want to marry you!"

"Then why are you against it?!"

For reasons beyond me, Claire seemed in a rush to marry. I grasped her hand and asked, "Miss Claire, why are you hurrying this?"

She was silent.

"We've already confirmed our feelings for one another. Something like a wedding can wait. So why?"

"I'm...worried."

"Huh? Am I doing something to make you worried? Tell me what it is, I'll fix it!"

"That's not it! There's nothing wrong with you... What's wrong is...me."

"What do you mean?"

Claire was the epitome of perfection and cuteness. What could *possibly* be wrong with her? "I'm no longer a noble..."

"Okay, yeah?" At a complete loss, I accidentally gave a ruder response than I intended.

"That's it. I'm no longer a noble. No status, no prestige, no assets—all I have is an education no longer fit for my station and meaningless pride. How much longer could you love such a person...?"

"Oh, Miss Claire..."

How could I have not noticed?

Some part of me wanted to believe Claire had grown accustomed to her new life. But she was a former noble—and a high-ranking one at that. *Of course* she would have insecurities about becoming an ordinary citizen. All this time I'd spent telling myself I was supporting her—did I ever stop to really look at what she was feeling?

"Miss Claire, everything's going to be okay."

"Rae..."

I stood and hugged Claire from behind, trying to ease her

worries, even if just a bit. "Even if you're not a noble anymore, my feelings for you are unchanging. I didn't fall in love with you because you're a noble." I spoke from the heart.

"I know... That's just how you are. But what about your family? What about Lene or Misha?"

"Miss Claire..."

To her, being a noble was a way of life—one she'd once quite literally chosen to die for. She welcomed her new life with me, but it didn't change the fact that one of the pillars she'd founded her identity on had disappeared.

"Miss Claire, you should run for election."

"Huh? Rae, what are you talking about? We're discussing our wedding right n—"

"I know. But I have a feeling if we hold a wedding as you are now, you'll regret it."

"Why?"

"What you need right now is a new way of life. Something to give you purpose, something that'll guide you. Until you find that, these worries will stay with you."

Claire grew silent. Something told me she'd already been aware she was searching for a new pillar to lean on in her life. I wouldn't lie—I kind of wanted to be that pillar. Somewhere in me was a dark desire to lavish my affections on a version of Claire that was completely emotionally dependent on me. But that wouldn't be right for her. If, by some odd chance, I were to die, then she would truly be left with nothing to support her. I couldn't allow that to happen.

"I think...I understand what you're trying to say," Claire murmured after a long silence. Her face lit up as her determination gradually returned.

"So how about it?" I asked.

"No. I'm not running for election."

"Huh?"

Claire smiled at my confusion. "I think joining the new government as a politician would be respectable work, one that could give my life new meaning."

"So why not do it?"

"Because it wouldn't be right. If I, a symbol of the old system, were to take office, then the revolution would have no meaning."

I had no good counter. Examining the history of the world would show you many examples of former government officials staying in power after revolutions or coups. But that wasn't what Claire wanted. That being the case, I would simply have to respect her decision.

"But I'll look for something. A new way of life." I could tell Claire's worries had been dispelled.

"Yes. And I'll be there to help you." I kissed Claire on the head. She giggled, ticklish.

I hoped she'd find a way to live the life she wanted to lead. And when that day finally came, we would get married. I would wait, no matter how long it took, because the only one for me was my ever-so-marvelous Claire.

Wedding

CLAIRE HAD ONCE TOLD ME a wedding wasn't so much about the ceremony as much as it was about our own feelings. What truly mattered were the vows to live your lives together, vows that you made before friends and family. I think I understood what she meant now.

"Nervous?" Claire stood by my side, looking amused—relishing my rare moment of anxiety. Her face was covered by a veil.

"I think so..."

"So even you have moments like this. I was under the impression you weren't afraid of anything."

"That's not true. There are lots of things I'm afraid of."

"He he... I suppose even you're only human in the end."

"To give an example, I'm afraid of you when you're drunk."

"I don't recall being so terrible!"

"You were so cute, it was scary."

"A-again with your jokes... Enough, it's time. Don't worry, it'll be fine." Claire held out her white-gloved hand and squeezed mine. I squeezed back.

Today was the day of our wedding.

Some time ago, Claire abruptly said, "Hey, Rae. Don't you think now's a good time?"

We were sitting outside on the terrace as the sky grew dark. May and Aleah ran around the yard with Ralaire. I'd been thinking of calling them in soon when Claire suddenly popped the question.

"I'm sorry, good time for what?" It was a good time for many things. We'd grown accustomed to our new life and were currently taking a short break from teaching.

"Do you not remember?" Claire frowned. "Our wedding. Don't you think it's about time, now that I've found my own way of life?"

"Oh, right."

We'd become teachers at the Royal Academy since that discussion, and mothers to May and Aleah. It was safe to say Claire had indeed figured out what she wanted her life to be.

"My school friends have also settled into their new lives, so they should be able to come. We even have proper salaries now; I imagine inviting your parents won't pose a problem." Claire tried her hardest to sell the idea to me. She looked absolutely adorable.

She had to be an angel sent from heaven.

"Yeah," I said. "Now might be a good time."

"So...?"

"Yes." I stood and walked toward Claire. I got down on one knee and took her hand. "Will you marry me, Miss Claire?"

Claire looked shocked for a brief moment before erupting into a wide smile. "Yes!"

"Are Mama Claire and Mama Rae getting married?"

"Will there be a wedding?"

Two sharp-eared twins came riding over on Ralaire.

"Yes, we're having a wedding. Will you two attend?" I asked.

"Yeah!"

"Of course!"

The two girls began to chant, "Wedding!" over and over. I suddenly felt embarrassed.

"Now that we're settled, we need to start preparing. How does holding the wedding in two months sound? Enough time?" I asked.

"Sounds about right to me. We're not doing anything too fancy."

From then, the two of us spent day and night planning our wedding. We decided to hold it not in a church but in a restaurant affiliated with Frater. We were swearing our bond to our friends and family, not God—not that we *could* use a church, given that the Spiritual Church didn't approve of same-sex marriage. Regardless, Lene's influence nabbed us a pretty lovely venue.

We sent invitations to Dole, Lene, Lambert, Claire's school friends, my parents, and Misha. We decided not to invite the royal siblings or Manaria, given the difference in our social status now that Claire was an ordinary citizen, but we still wrote them letters letting them know we were getting married. Unfortunately, we also couldn't invite Lilly, as she was off wandering who-knew-where.

"It seems we'll have to rent our wedding attire," I said.

"Looks like it. I wish I knew how to sew for times like these."

"I'm not sure an entire wedding dress is something anyone would consider sewing on their own..."

Claire would later go on to learn sewing in earnest, but that's a story for another time.

Two months passed in a flash and before we knew it, the day of our wedding was upon us. Our guests arrived at the restaurant, their lively chatter audible all the way from the dressing room Claire and I waited in. We'd had the restaurant prepare a buffet, so the guests enjoyed food and drink as they chatted.

"It's almost time, Miss Claire, Rae."

"Got it."

"Thank you for all your trouble, Lene."

Lene—the young proprietress of Frater, a trading company that was practically a household name in the Alpes and the Bauer Kingdom—was our mistress of ceremonies for the night, garbed in a modest dress that complemented ours. She and her brother Lambert had amassed a small fortune through their trading company, but even though she now technically had higher social standing than either of us, she remained loyal to Claire. She'd helped us with a number of things, not just finding us a venue. Even now, she was personally running the show rather than delegating it to a subordinate.

"Not at all. I have to say though...you two look beautiful." Lene was overcome with emotion as she dabbed her eyes with her handkerchief.

Claire wore a pure-white mermaid-line wedding dress, while I wore a white pantsuit.

"Claire being beautiful goes without saying, but I'm not so confident I look acceptable," I said.

"Nonsense," Lene said. "If you kept that mouth shut, anybody would find you wonderful."

"Is that a compliment?"

"Of course." Lene smiled.

"The stage is set. All that's left is for you two to make your entrance," Lene's brother, Lambert, prompted us, garbed in a morning coat and holding open the door.

It was time for our wedding to begin.

"Shall we, Miss Claire?"

"I suppose we shall, Rae."

We held hands as we made our way through the door.

We were greeted with applause as we made our way to the front.

"Everyone, thank you for gathering here today."

Claire started with an opening speech, and I gazed at her profile. Her contented smile made me emotional as the memories of all the trials we'd faced leading to this moment came to my mind.

"Today, Rae Taylor and I will marry. While our union may not be recognized by law, I believe what we share to be something greater."

The guests applauded Claire's confident declaration.

"As many here likely know, my first impression of Rae was—to put it plainly—the worst. And yet here I am, marrying her. It just goes to show that life is full of surprises."

The guests burst into laughter as Claire recounted the past.

"But as I am now, I don't think I can imagine a life without Rae. To the one who stayed by my side and supported me through it all, I want you to know that I'm truly glad I met you." She looked deep into my eyes. None of what she'd just said had been in our rehearsals.

That's not fair, Miss Claire. What am I supposed to do with these feelings all of a sudden?

"Mama Rae, are you crying?"

"Did Mother Claire make you cry?"

May and Aleah approached with a handkerchief.

"I'm all right, you two. Just got a little too happy."

"Mama Rae's being weird!"

"How odd!"

The mood in the venue returned to normal, thanks to the twins.

Now's not the time to get overly emotional, I thought as I wiped my tears.

Claire continued her speech with a smile. "I wish for everyone who gathered here to stand witness to the bond Rae and I share. We vow to live proudly, sincerely, joyously, and happily together for the rest of our lives."

Applause again. As we waited for the applause to die down, Claire took my hand.

"Once again, thank you all for coming. Please, enjoy yourselves to your hearts' content."

The venue roared with applause as we bowed our heads to the guests.

"Congratulations, Miss Claire!"

"I'm so happy for you!"

"Thank you, Loretta, Pepi. I'm glad you two could make it."

The first ones to congratulate us were two girls I didn't recognize. I assumed they were former nobles based on how naturally they wore their party dresses and the way they carried themselves.

"But still... To think you would marry *her*..."

"We've done some terrible things to her..."

Hm? Have I met these two before? "Miss Claire, who might these two be?"

"E-excuse me?! Do you not remember us?"

"Even after all the torment we put you through?"

They looked so alarmed by my question. I felt bad, but I truly couldn't recall them at all.

"These are Loretta and Pepi, our classmates from school. Don't you remember? You used to tease them a lot."

"Ohhh!" Thing One and Thing Two from Claire's entourage. Yeah, no surprise I didn't recall them. "I remember now. Pardon my rudeness."

"No, perhaps it's best if you don't remember..."

"What we did was terrible. Could you find it in you to forgive us?"

"Well, to tell the truth, there's nothing to forgive," I said. "I don't remember a thing."

"Ah, but of course! You were always a peculiar one, after all..."

"Unbelievable... I apologize for my rudeness, but just what do you see in her, Miss Claire?"

They seemed genuinely worried for their friend.

"I love her for her virtues, even if I am alone in understanding them," Claire said.

"Oh, my!"

"To think I'd ever hear you speak so fondly of another!"

"Rae's actually quite endearing once you understand her. A little *too* endearing, sometimes... I always have to worry about her attracting the eyes of others; it's happened more than I care to admit."

No, that's all your misunderstanding, Miss Claire!

"You better—er... Please, take good care of Miss Claire, okay?"

"You absolutely must make her happy!"

They left those words behind as they departed.

"You have good friends."

"He he. I do, don't I?"

I had once seen Claire's entourage as a single entity, but I now understood that Claire had enjoyed real, living, breathing friends back at the Academy. No wonder she'd been so upset when I first started pursuing her.

"You know, it's thanks to you that they weren't executed," Claire said.

"But also partially my fault the aristocracy was deposed."

"Come on now, none of that." Claire smiled wryly.

The next ones to congratulate us were Lene, on break from running things, and Lambert.

"Congratulations on getting married!"

"Congratulations, Miss Claire."

"Thank you."

Lene hugged Claire as she cried tears of joy. "I just know Rae will make you happy."

"Oh?" Claire said. "What makes you so sure?"

"Call it a maid's intuition."

"I see."

Lene seemed to put a lot of stock in me for some reason.

"You've grown so much. I remember when you were little and threw tantrums whenever the tiniest thing didn't go your way."

"Oh, stop it, Lene. You sound like my parent."

"Why not? Just for today. You used to be such a handful when you were younger. Why, I remember—"

Claire looked like her soul was leaving her body as Lene dredged up the past. My wife was just the cutest.

"Please, leave it at that, Lene. I'm about to lose all face here."

"What's wrong with that? You're not a noble anymore."

"I'm still in front of my beloved!"

"You catch that, Rae?"

"Already etched in my memory."

"Augh! You two!"

Lene and I teased Claire to our hearts' content. Such a scene had seemed impossible at one point. Back when Lene and

Lambert were first exiled, we'd said goodbye for what we thought would be the rest of our lives.

"Hey, Lene."

"Yes, Rae?"

"Are you happy with the way things are?"

Lene blinked in surprise at my question.

"Of course. I have Lambert, and two people very important to me are getting married!" She smiled broadly.

"We are gonna be just as happy as you two, if not more!" Lambert said, putting his arm around Lene.

"Oh, my, is that a challenge?" Claire asked.

"I suppose it is. May the better couple win." Lene shook Claire's hand before returning to her post.

Before she left, she handed us some letters—and quite a few at that. Among them were messages from royalty: Rod, Thane, Yu, and Manaria. The contents of the letters all congratulated us on our marriage—save for Manaria's. Her letter contained this one sentence alone.

"Come to me if you split up. I'll welcome you both with open arms."

Get real, I thought.

There were some other letters, but only one of them really stood out. It was a worn-out letter with a single name on the envelope—Lilly. Written in immaculate handwriting, the letter explained that in the course of her aimless wanderings, she'd stopped by Manaria's place and learned of our marriage. She gave us her congratulations, followed by a postscript.

"P. S. Is the mistress spot still open?"

"There never was one!" Claire said, about to tear up the letter. Thankfully, I managed to calm her down. "Goodness... If only you weren't such a womanizer, Rae."

"Huh? It's my fault?"

"Whose else could it be?"

What did I do?! I thought. Still, seeing Claire get jealous was adorable in its own regard.

The next to congratulate us was Misha.

"Congratulations, you two."

"Thank you very much, Misha."

"Thanks."

Misha had shown up in her nun's habit rather than a dress, but she wore it so naturally that she didn't stand out at all. That was a former noble for you.

"Yu wrote a letter, but she also wanted me to convey something in person. She says your marriage has the blessing of the Great Spirit."

"But I thought the Spiritual Church didn't approve of same-sex marriage?" Claire said.

"You're right, the *church* doesn't. But the original scripture itself never condemns it. According to Yu, all are equal in the eyes of God."

"How very like her." Claire smiled.

"I agree," I added.

"She's done nothing but look for trouble ever since she left the royal family." Misha sighed deeply.

"Are you worried about Yu as her partner?"

"Partner? Me? You realize the gulf in status between us, right?"

"You could say the same of Miss Claire and I."

"That's...true, but..." It appeared Misha still had doubts about her relationship with Yu.

"Why don't you just take the plunge and go for it?" I asked.

"It's easy for you to say."

"It is. I've done it, after all."

"Oh, right." Misha smiled bitterly. "That's enough about me for today. Congratulations, you two. I mean it. Come by the convent sometime."

"Yes, of course."

"Catch you later, Misha."

Misha left, not staying to attend the party.

"Congratulations, Claire, Rae." A composed voice congratulated us. It was Dole, accompanied by May and Aleah. He'd mellowed out greatly since his time in politics. Not a trace of his former arrogant noble facade remained.

"Congratulations, Mamas!"

"Congratulations, Mothers."

"Thank you very much, Father, girls."

"Thank you very much," I agreed.

We exchanged hugs with Dole and the girls.

"Rae... I really can't thank you enough."

"I haven't done much at all, Master Dole."

"Nonsense. If things had gone as I originally planned, a great deal more blood would have been spilled during the revolution. Neither Claire nor I would be here to see the new era."

"But it wasn't through my efforts alone. We achieved this because of you, Claire, and many others."

"You're far too modest."

"You just give me more credit than I'm due."

Neither of us gave an inch until—

"Grampa, are you and Mama talking about something hard?"

"We're hungry."

May and Aleah tugged on Dole's clothes.

"Ha ha ha, sorry, sorry! All right, what'll it be? Grandpa will grab you two whatever you want."

"Crème brûlée!"

Dole broke into a grin, becoming the very image of a doting grandfather. The mastermind who'd once supported the revolution from the shadows was long gone.

"Oh, one last thing. Claire?"

"Yes, Father?"

"Do you love Rae?"

"I do."

"Well, judging by what I've seen from long before the revolution, she loves you at least a hundred times more. Do your best to reciprocate those feelings."

"I'll keep that in mind..."

"Very good." With that out of the way, Dole left for good this time, bringing May and Aleah with him.

"Seems like not even you're a match for Master Dole." I grinned.

"Indeed."

We giggled before seeking out the last group we needed to meet with.

"Congratulations, Rae, Claire. You both look wonderful."

"Congratulations."

A youthful woman and a reticent man congratulated us as we approached.

"Thank you very much, Mother-in-Law, Father-in-Law."

"Thank you."

My parents. They had prepared their best clothes and traveled all the way from Euclid just for our wedding. But that wasn't all.

"I'm glad we made your wedding clothes in time."

"I'm sure they're nothing compared to what a former noble is used to."

"Not at all. What you made for us is wonderful," Claire reassured my parents.

In case you've forgotten, my family were tailors. Claire and I had planned to rent our wedding attire, but my parents had offered to make them for us instead. We paid for the materials and labor, of course, but it was still nothing short of an incredible feat that they'd sewn them from scratch in the span of two months. It was starting to dawn on me that my parents might just be masters of their craft.

"Thank you, Mom, Dad," I said.

"Of course. Anything for you, dear."

"Mm-hmm."

Tears began to leak out of their eyes.

"You were always a bit odd as a child, but you've grown up so splendidly. I guess our job as parents is really over..."

"Of course she turned out wonderful. She's a lost child of the spirits, after all." My dad wrapped an arm around my mom, the latter's tears showing no sign of ending.

"That's not it," I began. "I'm your child and your child alone. And I've always been proud of that."

They weren't my biological parents. They weren't even the parents that had raised me, Rei Ohashi. But I knew, from the memories of the Rae Taylor I also held, that the love they had for me was real. It was thanks to them that I could be who I was today.

"Rae..."

"I see... Thank you, Rae, our beloved daughter." My dad hugged me tight. "Miss Claire, please take care of Rae."

"Of course. I know we're going to be very happy together."

"Thank you." My mom hugged Claire.

Today, we'd become a family in the truest sense.

"Everyone, I'm sad to say it is time for the banquet to come to an end. But before it does, our brides would like to show you all something." Just as the first empty trays began to appear and the guests' spirits were buoyed by alcohol, Lene made an announcement.

Huh? Was there something else left? I thought. I looked at Claire in confusion, only to find her equally perplexed.

"Our two brides would like everyone to bear witness to their vow of eternal love!" Lene smiled impishly. Excited cheers came from the guests.

Ah... I see what Lene was doing.

Claire looked like a pigeon nailed by a BB gun. I figured I should help her out.

"Miss Claire, they're waiting for the kiss to seal our vows."

"Ohhh, yes, that... Wait, *what*?!" Claire looked visibly flustered. She was the very definition of cute. "K-kissing isn't something you do in front of other people!"

"It is at a wedding."

"Th-that's true, b-but...!"

"Ready? I'm starting."

"W-wait! Let me sort out my feelings fir—"

"Not happening." I put my hands on Claire's shoulders and looked solemnly into her eyes. Claire shifted in her seat before regaining her composure.

"Miss Claire."

"Yes..."

"I love you."

"As do I, Rae."

"I vow to love you for as long as I shall live."

"And I vow to support you for as long as I shall live."

The venue erupted into cheers as our lips met.

"There's no turning back from here, Miss Claire."

"That's fine. I have no intention of turning back."

"Are you absolutely sure?"

"That's what I should be asking you."

There was neither artifice nor elegance to our words. But that was fine. We were perfect as we were.

"Let's be happy together, Miss Claire."

"No. We'll *definitely* be happy together, Rae."

We sealed yet another vow with one more kiss.

Sweet, Sweet Alcohol

"**W**HEW..."

"Are they asleep?"

"Yep, out like a light."

It was just past nine o'clock, and I returned to the living room after putting the children to bed to find Claire waiting for me. Having finished bathing, she was already in her pajamas, sitting alone at the living room table and enjoying what seemed to be a drink. On the table sat a bottle that held about a liter of a tawny liquid.

"What's that, Miss Claire? I thought we were out of juice." I had plans to go to the market for some more tomorrow.

"This? It's alcohol," Claire said plainly.

"Huh?" I froze.

Alcohol? As in, alcohol-*alcohol?*

"Miss Claire! You can't be drinking that!"

"Hm? Why not?"

"Because you're under twenty!"

"Okay? And?" Claire looked at me quizzically, after which I remembered—the drinking age in the kingdom was fifteen. In other words, we could drink with no legal repercussions whatsoever. In fact, we had good reason to, as some kinds of alcohol were cheaper than water—though I suspected what Claire was drinking was of the premium variety.

"It was a gift from Lambert. It's quite quaffable."

"How nice of him. Try not to drink too much though; it's not good for your health."

"I know. Always in moderation."

I suspected Claire had been drinking at aristocrat parties and other social events since before she was of legal age. She probably knew her limits better than I did.

"How about I make some snacks to go along with the drink?" I offered.

"No need for that. Just come join me."

I saw no reason to refuse, so I fetched a glass and sat down with her. She poured me some of the drink, which looked like mead.

"Cheers, Rae."

"Cheers." After clinking glasses, I gingerly brought the alcohol to my lips.

While mead contained honey, it wasn't necessarily sweet, as the fermentation process broke down the sugars. It was closest to beer in terms of taste, although beer wasn't really ever sweet, so perhaps that was a poor comparison. This mead seemed to have spices mixed with it—perhaps cinnamon? Claire was right; it was *quite* quaffable. An uncomplicated yet delicious drink.

"How is it?"

"Delicious. Not harsh at all."

"Isn't it? Lene remembered the brewery I was fond of and had Lambert deliver it."

"Oh, really."

That was Lene for you. Even if she was no longer Claire's maid, she still respected Claire as her master.

With gratitude toward Lene in our hearts, we drank glass after glass.

"Hey, Rae... This is happiness, isn't it?" Claire spoke softly, as if in a dream.

"Huh?" I looked at her in confusion, only to see her whole face lit up in a smile.

"There's you, and May, and Aleah... Every day feels like I'm living in a dream."

"It's not a dream. This is the future you've earned."

"The future *we've* earned. Clear distinction, Rae." Even after a few drinks, she remained as sharp as always. She didn't think for a moment that this happiness was hers alone.

"How's teaching going?" I asked.

"It's rewarding work, though the students can be awfully unruly at times." Contrary to her words, she sounded utterly delighted.

Claire and I had begun teaching at the Royal Academy. The students were no longer predominantly children of nobles but talented children chosen from the populace at large—a sign the Academy was changing. The curriculum had also begun to focus less on culture and etiquette and more on specialized fields of magic.

"I can't have my way in all things, like I could when I was a noble. But I suppose that's what makes life so enjoyable now."

"Is that so? I'm glad to hear that." I'd secretly been a bit worried that Claire's pride would negatively influence her teaching, but it seemed that wasn't the case. I was happy to see she found meaning in her new work.

"How about you, Rae? Are you enjoying life as is?"

"As long as you're with me, life's perfect. It's also nice that May and Aleah have warmed up to us." I was content to just have Claire in my life, especially after I had come so close to losing her. May and Aleah opening their hearts to us was wonderful, too. It was as Claire said—this really was happiness.

"Good. Although, there's one thing I'm dissatisfied with."

"Oh? What?"

Claire set her glass down before looking at me sheepishly. "I feel like you're not as assertive recently."

I choked on my drink. Her words reached my ears but ran just shy of reaching my brain. What had she said just now? "I'm sorry, could you repeat that?"

"Ugh! I said I'm sad because you haven't been all over me lately!"

I understood her words clearly this time, but now I couldn't believe they had come out of her mouth. Had the haughty Claire just said what I thought she did?

"Miss Claire... Are you drunk?"

"I am not drunk!" she said, but her face was utterly red and her speech was turning slurred.

Come to think of it, no drunk person ever admits they're drunk.

"How many glasses have you had?"

"What? There's still half a bottle. Something this light wouldn't get me *drunk*."

I checked the bottle to find it nearly empty. I'd only had two glasses, meaning around eighty percent of the missing liquor had gone down Claire's gullet. She was so far gone that she couldn't even tell how much she'd drunk.

"Miss Claire, let's call it a day here."

"Nooo! I wanna talk with you more." Claire pouted.

She avoided my hand as I tried to reach for her glass and took a large gulp.

"Miss Claire..."

"You were so aggressive back when we were students, clinging to my side, saying 'Miss Claire! Miss Claire!' Oh, how cute you were."

Now she was being outrageous. If I didn't stop her here and now, she would die of embarrassment later.

"Hey, Rae. Do you love me?"

"I do."

"Really, really?"

"Really, really."

"He he... I see." Claire smiled, as if in a trance.

Oh, man. While I did love her usual determined smile, I was weak against this kind that she so rarely showed. It took everything I had to restrain myself.

"Come on, Miss Claire. It's time to go to bed."

"Nooo! I wanna flirt with Rae more!"

I was struck dumb. What was this being made of pure cuteness before me?

Claire was always adorable, but something about her right now was *unreasonably* cute. I supposed the alcohol was making me feel a certain kind of way, too. My judgment was weakened. If this went on, I might make a mistake. Claire and I were close, but it didn't feel right to let alcohol dictate my urges.

"Raaae?"

"Y-yes?"

Her sickly sweet, coquettish voice called my name. It suddenly became far more difficult to resist the temptation to give in. I thought my heart would stop beating at her irresistible cuteness.

"Will you kiss me?"

"We should stop here. I don't think I can resist your temptations any further."

"Why do you need to resist? Rae is mine and I am yours." Claire tilted her head teasingly. I felt the last of my good judgment start to crumble away.

"Claire, I really do love you."

"He he. Thank you, Rae. I love you, too."

"That's why... You can't keep saying such adorable things, or else I might really do something."

"Eh he he, really? That makes me happy." Claire's smile was that of a goddess's.

I didn't care what happened anymore. I tried my hardest. Everything was Claire's fault for being too cute.

I stood and knelt by Claire's side, taking her hand.

"Miss Claire, may I carry you?"

"He he, so you've finally come around? Of course, with pleasure." She kissed me. I used magic to supplement my strength and lifted Claire's dainty little body up.

"To the bedroom?" I asked.

"Yes."

All that was left was to spend the night in each other's embrace.

Or so I thought.

"Ah."

"Oops."

I stood there in shocked silence.

"What's the matter, Rae? Weren't you taking me to the—?!" Claire noticed as well.

Peering out from the children's bedroom were two sets of eyes.

"They found us, Aleah!"

"We've been caught, May!"

They cried out without an ounce of guilt.

"Why are you two awake?" Claire asked.

"We could hear Mama Rae and Mama Claire having fun from our room—"

"—so we were watching to make sure nothing bad happened."

Claire and I gasped, mouths agape. Try to imagine, if you would, how we felt at that moment.

"What are you going to do now?" May asked innocently.

"Are you going to play in the bedroom?" Aleah followed up.

My head, ablaze with lust just moments prior, had completely cooled off. I imagined Claire had sobered up in a hurry, too.

"We're not going to do anything. Just say 'goodnight,' then go to sleep," I reassured the two.

"Really?"

"That's dull."

"That's why you two better go to sleep, too. Stay up too late and you won't be able to play as much tomorrow."

"I don't want that!"

"We're good girls, so we'll go to bed."

With that, the two girls obediently crawled back into bed. There was one thing left to do before I could truly breathe easy.

"Hey, Miss Claire." I looked down at Claire in my arms to see a look of great shame on her face. "I take it you've sobered up?"

"Yes." Her voice was faint.

I get it. I want to crawl into a hole, too. "Let's add a new rule."

"Agreed."

In this house, we had some ground rules. That night, a new one was added: Drink responsibly.

Birthdays

THE END OF THE RAINY SEASON finally came to the Bauer
Kingdom, and with it summer. The Academy was on break,
so we spent the day relaxing as a family.

Claire and I were helping May and Aleah with their studies.
They had been taught basic reading and writing at the orphanage,
but they hadn't had much time to familiarize themselves with it.
Even so, they proved to be fast learners and could now write as
well as anyone in their age group.

"Mama Claire, what's this say?" May asked from atop Ralaire.
She'd taken a liking to sitting on the water slime as of late.

"That says 'birthday.'"

"What's birthday?" May asked curiously.

"I know what it is," Aleah cut in with a proud look. "It's a day
to celebrate someone being born."

"That's right, Aleah. Do you two remember when your birthday is?"

"I forget. Do you remember, Aleah?"

"Of course. It's the thirteenth day of the twelfth month."

Dates in this world were based on the solar calendar, just like in my world, but they ran a bit simpler. This world had twelve months, each with thirty days.

"That's right. We'll celebrate your birthday then."

"Yay!"

"Sounds fun!"

Claire watched the two fondly as they rejoiced before looking my way. "Come to think of it, I don't know Rae's birthday."

"Of course you wouldn't. Not even I know my birthday."

"What do you mean?"

"Did you forget? I'm a lost child of the spirits."

"Ah..."

As a young child, Rae Taylor had been found wandering Euclid and taken in by the couple who adopted her. Hence, my true birth date was a mystery.

"So you didn't celebrate birthdays?" Claire asked.

"Commoners don't have the financial leeway to celebrate birthdays. At most, we celebrate New Year's and the Harvest Festival."

Bauer commoners were poor and tended to have many children. Celebrating birthdays regularly could put a real dent in a household's finances. Extravagant birthday parties were a luxury that only nobles enjoyed.

"I see... Then what was your birthday in your previous life?"

"My previous life?"

"Yes. I believe you were from a well-off family, were you not?"

Some time ago, just before the revolution, I'd told Claire

how I'd once lived in another world. She seemed to remember the details quite clearly.

"Let's see... The calendar in the other world was a bit different, but in this world, I think my birthday would equate to around the nineteenth day of the seventh month?"

"That's right around the corner! You should've said something sooner!" Claire said angrily.

"Is it Mama Rae's birthday soon?"

"Are we going to celebrate?"

We'd caught the children's attention. They seemed to be quite taken by the topic of birthdays.

"It's fine, we don't need to worry about my birthday. Let's just use the money on your birthdays."

"Absolutely not!" Claire protested. "You're a precious member of our family. We have to celebrate your birthday!"

"Yeah!"

"Indeed!"

I gave in, unable to resist all three of them. Birthdays weren't exactly something I'd looked forward to in my previous life, especially when I'd reached an age that didn't make me want to acknowledge I was getting on in years. Even now, I couldn't say I was too thrilled about celebrating my birthday.

"We only have three days until Rae's birthday! May, Aleah, let us get to preparing!"

"Okay!"

"Yes, Mother!"

"Um... What should I do then?"

"You don't need to do anything special, Rae. Just do your usual chores, like you normally do." It seemed Claire and the girls would be handling the preparation themselves. "Things are going to get busy around here!"

The next three days went by quickly. Claire and the twins cut and folded colored paper to decorate the rooms, making our house suddenly feel a lot more festive. Claire seemed to be planning a surprise for me, but, as I wasn't part of the preparations, I wasn't allowed to know what it was. I felt a little left out, yet I found myself actually starting to grow a little excited.

"Happy birthday, Rae!"

"Happy birthday, Mama Rae!"

"Happy birthday, Mother Rae!"

We decided to celebrate at dinnertime.

"Thank you, Miss Claire, May, Aleah." I hugged them each individually with all my heart.

"Now then, let's sit down and eat," said Claire. "Today's dinner is quite the feast... Although Rae is still the one who made it. Sorry."

"Ha ha, it's fine. Thanks for covering the cost of the ingredients."

"It wouldn't be much of a birthday party if I didn't." Claire had insisted she would cook right up until the very end, but unfortunately, cooking happened to be one of the very few—if not only—things she was still hopeless at. She settled for covering the cost of the ingredients, allowing me to go all out for the first time in a long while, as we'd kept meals on the frugal side ever since the revolution.

Today's dinner consisted of roast beef, potato salad, onion soup au gratin, baguette, and crème brûlée.

"Time to dig in."

"Would you please wait a moment, Rae? May, Aleah, can you fetch it?"

"Okay!"

"Yes, Mother!"

The two girls disappeared to their room, immediately returning with something in hand.

"Here you go, Mama Rae!"

"It's your birthday present!"

They politely handed me a wrapped package.

"Can I open it?"

"Uh-huh."

"Of course."

I wonder where they got the wrapping paper? The clumsy wrapping made clear that the twins had done it themselves. I carefully unwrapped the present, taking care not to tear the paper in case it could be reused.

"Oh, a portrait?" Drawn in crayon on paper was a picture of me. I took up the whole space and had a big smile plastered on. Was this how they saw me?

"We worked really hard to draw this."

"How is it? Does it look like you?"

"It looks just like me! Thank you, May, Aleah." Nearly moved to tears, I hugged them again. The twins hugged me back, smiling.

I had the best daughters in the whole wide world.

"I also have something for you." Claire handed me something as she blushed profusely. That face alone was a gift in itself.

"A handkerchief?"

"It's nothing special, but I hope you like it." Claire was being beyond modest. The handkerchief was embroidered with myriad small flowers. It was far fancier than the sort an ordinary citizen would usually possess, more befitting of a noble, its beauty so fine you might hesitate to even use it. She had doubtless embroidered it herself.

At the edge, I found delicate writing: *For my beloved Rae, from Claire.* And to think she'd done this in only three days! This was nothing short of a treasure.

"Thank you, Miss Claire."

"He he, I'm glad you like it."

I honestly hadn't even expected to receive a present, so I was caught off guard by all of this. If May and Aleah hadn't been there, I might have cried.

"Let's eat, shall we? I'm sure Rae's cooking will be delicious."

"Mmm, it's yummy!"

"Ah! May's already eating!"

"He he!"

The four of us enjoyed a boisterous birthday dinner together.

"The birthday went by so quickly."

"Indeed," I replied.

May and Aleah were already fast asleep. After helping them get to bed, Claire and I quietly drank tea together.

"Did you enjoy it?"

"I did. This was the most enjoyable birthday I've ever had, previous life included." I'd gotten along with my family in my previous life, and birthdays had been pleasant. But celebrating with the family you'd made for yourself was a joy all its own.

"He he. Glad to hear it."

"Thank you for today, Miss Claire." I meant it. Thanks to Claire, I'd learned how wonderful it could be to spend your birthday with the ones you love.

"If it weren't for you, I'm sure my life would be dull indeed. Thank you for being born, Rae."

"Miss Claire..."

Her words had a special meaning—she was saying she loved our current life more than her old life as a noble, where she had enjoyed everything she could have ever wanted. That made me unbelievably happy to hear.

"I actually...have one more present left for you..."

"What is it?"

"You have to guess," Claire said bashfully. I had an idea of what she meant.

"Today's been so much fun, I don't know if I can control myself tonight," I said. "I might just devour you whole if you're not careful."

"I'll allow you to try, just for today. But I get the feeling the one who'll be devoured won't be me."

"Is that a challenge?"

"It might be."

I grabbed Claire's hand and headed to the bedroom.

As for her last present? Let's just say it was wonderful.

Holy Night Festival

TODAY WAS THE TWENTY-FOURTH DAY of the twelfth month. In the modern world, today would have lined up with the day called Christmas Eve.

But this was the world of *Revolution*. There was no Christmas here—or so you might think. Instead, you see, we had this holiday called the Holy Night Festival.

"The prevailing belief is that the Great Spirit descended to the earth on this day. That's why the Holy Night Festival is an important event to the Spiritual Church."

"Uh-huh." I already knew that, but I let Claire talk anyway. She looked so cute when she haughtily explained things to me.

As you might have guessed, the Holy Night Festival was a game event modeled after Christmas. Yet another aspect of Japanese culture inserted into the world-building—although I suppose Christmas was originally European in origin.

"So what do you do on this day?" I asked.

"Well, nobles often held marvelous parties and invited guests, but I believe the common—ahem, the citizens didn't celebrate so lavishly."

As a noble, Claire did seem the type to like parties.

"To my knowledge," Claire continued, "citizens would decorate their rooms and set up fir trees, then invite family, friends, and lovers over to exchange gifts."

"Oooh, that sounds wonderful."

It sounded exactly like Christmas in Japan. I'd thought it might be a bit different, since I'd heard Christmas in Western countries was more of a quiet affair spent with family. Christmas in Japan was a party, kind of like New Year's Eve in the west, while New Year's Day in Japan was generally the quiet family event.

"Will we be celebrating like citizens?" I asked.

"Of course we will. Do you have any idea how much it'd cost to hold a party and invite people?"

"That's true." We'd have to reserve a place, pay for food, and prepare entertainment for the guests. We weren't poor by any means, but that wasn't feasible on the salary of two teachers. If we had that kind of money, I'd rather use it on Claire, May, and Aleah first.

"But I do want to have a small celebration with our family."

"As do I, Miss Claire."

Spending the Holy Night with family without having to worry about guests sounded pretty great. A good way to end the year with the ones you love.

"We can afford to indulge ourselves with a feast, I think. Can you do the cooking, Rae?"

"Of course. Leave it to me!" I struck my chest with pride. This was a good opportunity to show off my stuff.

"All that's left are the presents, then. For us and the kids."

"Let's go shopping first thing tomorrow." We could leave the two children behind and go on a shopping date. No impure motives—we just needed to keep the presents a surprise from the girls.

"Sounds like fun..."

"Sure does," I said. Although I did relish the thought of a little alone time with Claire for other reasons as well.

"All right, here it comes!"

"Whoa!"

"It's huge!"

On the night of the Holy Night Festival, Claire, May, and Aleah sat around the dining table as, wearing oven mitts, I carried an herb-roasted whole chicken over and set the heavy platter down on the table with a thud. Many dishes were already set out in addition to the chicken: roast beef, green soybeans and burdock potage, root vegetable salad, and a decorated cake.

I'd learned the herb-roasted whole chicken recipe from my mother in this world, but I'd added salt, pepper, and extra herbs to make my own deluxe version. The roast beef was lovely, especially as it was our first time having beef in a while. The potage was made with green soybeans and burdock that was boiled, mashed, mixed with milk, and then seasoned with salt and pepper. I made the salad by cooking up lotus root, carrots, potatoes, and onions, then covering them in dressing for a simple but flavorful dish. The decorated cake—the highlight of the spread—was a bit misshapen because I'd had May and Aleah's help in decorating it.

"Shall we eat?" Claire asked.

"Yeah!"

"Yes, Mother!"

And so our party began.

Ornaments made from colored paper decorated the walls—May and Aleah's handiwork. We hadn't been able to get a fir tree and instead had made our own miniature one out of colored paper and placed it in the center of the table. We'd poured our hearts into making our own inexpensive yet special Holy Night Festival.

"The meat's yummy!"

"This potage is delicious."

The children sang the food's praises as they ate. Everything but the soup was served in large communal dishes, so we each had our own small plates to transfer portions to. Little by little, we whittled the food away.

"It's all so delicious. I especially like the salad."

"Thank you, Miss Claire. Feel free to eat as much as you like."

"Of course."

I took a slice of roast beef and nibbled on it. I'd cooked it in my own brand of onion sauce, and I had to say the outcome was so-so.

May and Aleah had eaten only a small lunch in anticipation for tonight, and they were now stuffing their faces enthusiastically.

With their help, all the food was soon cleaned away. We finished the whole cake as well, sharing it two slices per person.

At last, I carried the empty plates to the sink with a satisfied smile.

"Rae, can you do the washing later? I don't think the kids can wait for their presents any longer."

"Oh, all right! I'll go get the presents, then." I went to and from the bedroom, returning with wrapped presents in my arms.

"Here you are, May, Aleah. Happy Holy Night Festival."

"Thank you!"

"Thank you very much!"

Claire and I had chosen their presents. Inside the wrapping, they found—

"Shoes!"

"So cute!"

The shoes were on the expensive side, cobbled and sold by Frater. Made from water python leather, they resisted water and stains. They were also quite cute, being meant for children.

"They're so light!"

"Yeah!"

Most leather products were heavy, but water python leather was light—perfect for children who liked running around.

"Thank you, Mama Claire and Mama Rae!"

"Thank you, Mothers!"

The twins hugged us. Claire and I happily hugged them back.

"This is for you, Rae," Claire said as she handed me a present.

I didn't know what I'd find in the wrapping, as we'd agreed to keep our presents for each other a surprise.

"And this one is for you, Miss Claire." I handed Claire a present.

We opened our presents at the same time.

"A comb? Such delicate fretwork..."

I gave Claire a brushing comb made from boxwood crafted by the guildmaster of the woodworking guild. Astute readers might notice the significance of gifting a boxwood comb. (In Japan, boxwood combs symbolized an eternal bond and were well known for being used to propose during the Edo period.)

"Looks like my present is a scarf. Wait, did you make this?"

"It's nothing special, but yes, I did make it." Claire blushed.

"Nothing special? The pattern is so beautiful, you'd think it was made by the tailor's guild." It had an argyle pattern, for goodness' sake! That wasn't something an amateur could pull off. "Can I put it on?"

"Of course."

"Hmm... Wow, it's warm."

"I knitted it from snow rabbit wool." Snow rabbits had soft, bushy fur, and they didn't hibernate in winter. No wonder the scarf was so warm.

"Thank you, Miss Claire. I'll treasure it."

"Thank you for the comb as well, Rae."

We moved closer and kissed.

Such happy times.

"Look, Aleah! It's snowing outside!"

"It is!"

Prompted by the children's voices, I looked outside the window to see heavy white snow falling from the sky.

"It looks like it's a pure-white Holy Night," Claire said.

"Is that something like a white Christmas?"

"Sorry?"

"Ah, nothing. Just talking to myself."

The four of us just stood there, watching it snow for some time. No words needed to be shared, each of us comforted by the presence of our family.

"It's been a busy year, Rae. I look forward to spending the next with you."

"As do I, Miss Claire."

We shared a kiss before pulling away and smiling at one another.

That night was a passionate one, but that will be a story for another time.

Your Pain Is Not Punishment

I
T WAS LATE EVENING when I knocked on the door. The dim twilight allowed me to make out the shape of a feather on the wood, the symbol of the Spiritual Church. I'd arrived at a branch of the Spiritual Church located in Sousse, known as the Northern Sousse Convent.

"Yes? Who is it?" An elderly nun peered out from within.

"H-hello, my name is Lilly," I stammered. "I-I'm a nun of the Spiritual Church and am currently on a pilgrimage of sorts. Would you be willing to share some food with me?"

The nun took a long, scrutinizing look at me before saying, "Why, only the truly devout go on pilgrimages these days. I'm Sister Rellette, and I'd be more than happy to share what we have with you. Please, come inside."

She smiled, deepening the many creases around her eyes.

"Th-thank you very much." I brushed some dust off my habit before entering.

The Northern Sousse Convent was far smaller than the Bauer Cathedral. That wasn't a fair comparison, as any convent was small in comparison to the cathedral, but this one struck me as particularly tiny. The building was old, too. Old enough that it might have been better off being demolished and rebuilt.

I followed Sister Rellette as I continued to observe the interior.

"You're no doubt shocked at the state of this place."

"Y-yes... I mean, n-no!"

She was so nonchalant about the matter that I inadvertently spoke the truth. I tried to cover for my mistake, but words really weren't my strong suit.

The elderly nun laughed heartily. "It's okay. It's true, after all. This convent and I are both old grannies now."

"Wh-why not have it rebuilt?"

"I've thought about it, but it's already been decided that this convent will end with me. A bigger, newer one was built nearby, you see."

"O-oh..."

"That's why I'm keeping it as is. It'd be a waste of funds to repair it, so instead, we use it knowing full well it'll be torn down someday."

Convents were often not monetarily well-off institutions. Funds were provided to them by the Spiritual Church, but an old convent like this one, situated close to a newer one, was not likely to be high on the priority list. There was even a good chance the newer convent had been specifically commissioned by the Sousse Spiritual Church to replace this old one.

"Oh, dear, I'm sorry. Not many people come by here, you see, so I just started jabbering away about unimportant things."

"N-no, it's quite all right. U-um, do you live here alone?"

"No, I live here with two younger nuns. They're about your age, I'd say."

Just as she said that—two nuns, slightly taller than me, appeared.

"A guest, Sister Rellette?"

I couldn't believe my eyes. "Rae?!"

The taller of the two nuns looked identical to Rae. She looked quizzically at my outburst while the other nun hid behind her back.

"Um, no. My name is Elie..."

"Not...Rae."

Their words brought me back to my senses. Of course Rae wouldn't be here. She was off enjoying her newlywed life with Claire.

That was right... Newlywed...

"Uunh..." I sniffed.

"Wha—hey, are you all right?" asked the nun who looked like Rae.

"I'm okay," I said between tears. "Just remembered something sad all of a sudden."

"This person seems...emotionally unstable." The other nun just seemed exasperated.

"Oh, my, what should we do? I was going to ask you to eat with us, but perhaps it's best you stayed the night as well?" Sister Rellette asked upon observing my state.

"N-no! I couldn't possibly impose."

"Oh, you're not imposing at all. Elie, Marie, could you prepare Lilly a room?"

"Yes, ma'am." The taller one seemed to be Elie.

"Yes...ma'am." Which meant the quiet one was Marie.

"N-no, really, I'm fine!"

"Hey, don't worry about it, just accept her kindness. And, with all due respect, I don't think you're in any shape to decline."

Elie put a hand on my back and urged me toward the room with surprising force. I looked down at myself, realizing my habit was torn here and there and covered in grime.

"Do you know how to mend clothes?" Elie asked.

"N-not really," I said, faltering.

"Figures." She smiled wryly and passed me some casual clothing once we reached the room. "Wear this in your room for now. I'll mend your habit."

"S-sorry..."

"It's fine, we nuns have to look out for each other, you know? All right, let me know when you've changed."

"Dinner...soon."

They left the room, leaving me behind.

I guess I'm staying, then. I've stayed the night at many a convent over my journey, but this was the first time I'd been so openly welcomed. It made me feel warm and fuzzy inside.

"We thank thee, Almighty Great Spirit, for the nourishment we shall now receive."

"Amen."

The four of us ate dinner together in the refectory. Well, I say refectory, but it wasn't as big of a room as the word might suggest.

I started with my bread after saying grace. The meal consisted of bread, fava bean potage soup, and a boiled egg—a standard meal for clergy. Apparently, Elie made the food.

You know who else could cook? Rae. My heart ached once again.

"Are you feeling better now?" Sister Rellette inquired as I finished my bread.

"Y-yes, sorry about earlier..."

"Ha ha, not at all. Did you remember something painful?"

"Y-yes... Heartbreak..." I reluctantly confessed.

"Oh, my." Sister Rellette smiled kindly.

"How could they turn down someone as pretty as you?"

"They have...no taste."

The other two nuns chimed in sympathetically. I couldn't bear it. I was about to change the subject when—

"What kind of person were they?"

"Yeah... What kind?"

The topic seemed to have caught the two young nuns' attention. Living out at this convent, I imagined they were starved for entertainment, and my love troubles were just the thing to satiate that hunger.

"Sh-she's wonderful. Very wonderful. But she already had her heart set on someone..." I mumbled.

"Oh..."

"That's...too bad."

They sympathized with me further. I had yet to realize my careless blunder.

"She?" Sister Rellette didn't appear taken aback but was clearly eliciting further information out of me.

"Ah... Um..." I floundered. *Should I say it?*

"Did you perhaps have feelings for a woman?"

"Y-yes..." I couldn't lie in the face of Sister Rellette's calm but clear voice. The Spiritual Church disapproved of same-sex relationships. They didn't go so far as to openly persecute people, but it was clear they believed love should only exist between a man and a woman.

I braced myself for a scolding.

"I...see."

But it never came.

Sister Rellette said no further than that, quietly returning to her meal.

The atmosphere after that was hard to describe. It was awkward, yes, but there was something else in the air. I ate my meal silently, not understanding the meaning of that strange tension.

"Lilly, are you awake?"

I heard a knock on my door just as it was time to sleep.

"Y-yes, I'm still awake." I rose off the bed and fixed my clothing.

"May I come in?"

"G-go ahead."

It was Elie who had knocked.

"Sorry to bother you so late at night."

"I-It's fine. Did you need something?"

"Yes... I was hoping I could have your advice on something." She looked serious. Her face looked so much like Rae's—so much so that it felt like Rae herself was before me, eliciting my help, making my heart ache yet again.

"O-of course, anything." As a cardinal, I'd been trained in giving effective counsel. Unfortunately, I couldn't often make use of this skill at the Bauer Cathedral, as they didn't offer such a service. But now, I finally had a chance.

"Thank you. I wanted to ask you about... Well..." Elie hesitated. It had to be something difficult to talk about.

"Please, sit down, Elie." I slid over and opened a spot on my bed, inviting her to sit with me. She hesitated but eventually did so.

"Some worries are hard to talk about," I began.

"Yeah..."

"The person I like, Rae—the one I talked about at dinner— she helped me with my own worries." I started by talking about myself. I told her how I'd met Rae and how she had shown me my love wasn't something to be ashamed of. I told her of how we had helped Claire expose corrupt nobles, and finally, I told her of my betrayal.

I left out the fact that I was technically a cardinal, as well as some details about the people involved, but I gave her the gist of everything that had occurred before my journey.

"I never would've thought you'd lived such a rough life. I mean...you seem to not have a care in the world."

"Th-that's mean!"

"Ha ha, sorry." Elie laughed for a moment before growing grim again. "I need some advice about me and Marie."

"The other young girl? You seem to get along well to me..." I recalled seeing Marie hide behind Elie. She seemed to put a lot of trust in her.

"Yes, we do get along. We do, but I think the feelings she has for me...aren't the same as the feelings I have for her."

"Ah..." I understood where this was going.

"Hah. I think I might be homosexual, too." Elie spoke jokingly, but her smile was pained. "I've been with Marie ever since I was young, you see. We were both abandoned by our parents, but Sister Rellette took us in and raised us as a family. From the outside, I bet I look like Marie's older sister. And I'm sure Marie and Sister Rellette think the same. But I don't. I can't anymore."

The guilt of having romantic feelings for your foster sister. The fear of being found out. And the teachings of a church that so clearly labeled such feelings impure. It was as if the world itself was rejecting her, Elie explained to me.

"What am I supposed to do, Lilly? Why am I like this? I...I wish I wasn't." No longer able to fake a smile, Elie hung her head and cried.

Unable to do nothing, I hugged her as she did. I stroked her hair and tried to think of a way to comfort her scarred heart.

"Elie, I want you to know that the pain you feel is not punishment," I said as Elie raised her head. "Love is not bound by logic; it is out of our hands. Therefore, your love cannot be sin."

"But the church—"

"Do you remember the most important of all the church's teachings?" I interrupted.

Elie looked at me doubtfully yet racked her brain regardless. "All are equal in the eyes of the Great Spirit?"

"That's right. All other teachings were merely added over the course of history."

"But what does that matter?"

"If we are all equal, then why should we alone have to deny our feelings?"

"Ah!"

That must have been unthinkable to her. I saw my past self reflected in her.

"I think Rae explained it more logically back when we met, but I'm not as wonderful as she is. Even so, there's one thing I can confidently say." I chose my next words carefully. "God would never create a world where you alone were a sinner."

This was the answer my faith had led me to. Such words might be meaningless to those without faith, but to those who believed, it was an undeniable truth. "The world may seem unfair because of our sexual orientation. But know this—that unfairness isn't willed by God but humankind."

Faith was built upon trust in God. To the faithful, to believe yourself rejected by God was to have the very core of your being invalidated. All that you could hope for after that was to be rejected by your faith and rejected by the world, and this ultimately culminated in an attempt to escape one's self. In other words—death.

"You first need to understand that your feelings are not wrong. Then you can take the next step."

Elie fell silent, deep in thought. Night in the convent was still, the two of us seemingly removed from the world. But we of faith knew: God was always by our side, watching over us.

"But...Marie might not return my feelings."

"That's just how love is. It's the same for straight people. That part, you'll just have to accept."

There was some truth in Elie's words. Our feelings often didn't bear fruit *because* of the prevailing social norm being heterosexuality. But that wasn't the fault of those we loved, just the fault of those social norms themselves. I believed we had a duty to fight to change those norms for the better. At the very least, I knew the person I respected more than anyone had always been fighting against something.

"I...still need some time to think this through, but I think I understand now. Thank you. For telling me my pain wasn't God's punishment," Elie whispered as she rubbed her eyes and smiled. "I don't know if Marie will return these feelings, but... that's all right. From now on, at least I won't deny I have them. Thank you."

Seeing her break through her own doubts, I couldn't help but think she truly reminded me of somebody else I knew.

"And then?! And then?! What happened after that?!"

"U-um, well..."

"Ease up a bit, Miss Claire. You're scaring Miss Lilly."

I had since returned from my journey and was visiting Rae and Claire at their house, recounting the events of my travels. Claire seemed utterly fascinated by this one story in particular, not giving me time to so much as drink the tea I was served. Seeing this, Rae tried to reel Claire in a bit.

"U-unfortunately, I don't know what followed. I embarked for my next destination the next morning."

"Let's write a letter to her!" Claire suggested.

"U-uh, I don't know... That seems a bit much."

"Not at all! She looked just like Rae, right? I absolutely must meet with her, then!"

Claire really did love Rae. Not that my love would lose out to hers.

"I can't believe it! Miss Claire's trying to cheat on me?!" Rae lamented as she poured me a new cup of tea.

"Of course not. You know my heart's only for you."

"Miss Claire..."

"There's no need for formalities between us!"

"Claire!"

"Rae!"

"Should I leave?" I gazed blankly off into space as I took a sip.

In truth, I was curious about what had happened to Elie. But I was also afraid. I'd done my best to help, but human emotion was an unpredictable thing. There was no knowing if her love would bear fruit, nor knowing how she would fare after.

Yet, in my heart, I believed—no matter how much pain one might suffer, God never forsook those who had faith.

The Lady Who Leapt Through Time

"O H, ISN'T TODAY the first day of the fourth month?" Rae asked me out of the blue.

The arrival of spring brought with it kinder weather, allowing us to comfortably spend the night chatting over tea in the living room. May and Aleah were already asleep in their room.

"It is—why?"

"Well, it's a bit of a strange day in my old world, you see."

"How so?"

"It was a day where it was okay to lie."

Rae brought up some nonsense I couldn't quite wrap my head around. Then again, most of what she said was nonsense I couldn't wrap my head around.

"Your world must have been pretty strange to have a day like that."

"I suppose. Although I guess it wasn't a custom from the country I lived in but one adopted from somewhere overseas."

"Is that right? That happens everywhere, it seems." Even Bauer had customs adopted from the Alpes and Sousse. I even heard that the Alpes were starting to adopt the Amour Festival. As long as countries interacted in some form with one another, there would be cultural diffusion.

"But the tradition of lying on this particular date gained a lot of traction in recent times," Rae explained. "Even commercial businesses, ah—they're kind of like the trading companies in my world—would pull pranks and such."

"Trading companies would pull pranks?"

"Yeah. Like making a weird announcement or changing the name of their business for the day, for instance."

"What's the point of that?"

"People simply liked doing those kinds of things."

Rae talked about her world every now and then, but my image of it remained that of a strange and peculiar place. All I understood for sure was that she'd lived in a peaceful country with values far different than Bauer's.

"I don't understand. Wouldn't it cost money and labor for a trading company to do that? How could a silly prank be worthwhile?"

"You're right about it just being a silly prank, but if people found it amusing, the company's popularity would soar. There were even some that became famous overnight."

"Tr-truly?"

"Truly. My world was advanced in fields other than magic. It was possible for such companies to send information across the world in the blink of an eye." Rae often claimed magic was convenient, but it seemed to me her world was far and away more convenient to live in despite the lack of magic.

It was hard to believe... So much so in fact, I had to wonder if it was true.

"What you said just now wouldn't happen to be one of those lies, would it?" I asked.

"Wow, you got the point of the day rather quickly. Lies were frequently exchanged in conversations like this in my world. But no. What I said was all true."

"Really?"

"Yep!"

It was difficult to accept that a prank could so easily change the success of a business. But while Rae did sometimes lie, she never did so maliciously. She was probably being truthful.

"Who knows? You might even have a strange dream tonight."

"Is that a thing?"

"It is. On April Fool's Day—oh, that's what the day was called—you're supposed to see a strange dream. And for a main character such as yourself, I'm sure quite the terrifying nightmare awaits."

"Oh, stop it. If I'm going to dream, I'd rather it be a good one." Besides, the main character here was Rae. I was more like the heroi... No, I was being overly self-conscious.

"If you're worried about sleep, we can do some 'exercise' before bed."

"Quit it. I'm not in the mood today. Let's just go to sleep."

"Aww." Rae gave up with ease.

That was one of her virtues. Despite having a higher-than-average sex drive, she never once pressured me into anything. I appreciated that about her, but sometimes, I wanted her to be more aggressive. Just imagining the look of rapture that might appear on Rae's face as I tried to resist her sent tingles down my spine.

But what was said was said; I couldn't eat my words now. I just needed to go to sleep without making a fuss.

"I'll be retiring for the night first. Good night, Rae."

"Okay. Good night, Miss Claire."

I kissed her once before retiring to the bedroom alone.

Our bedroom was plain, containing only the most basic of furniture and a slightly wide bed. In truth, I wanted to add more furnishings, but money was tight, and we had to be careful about making impractical purchases. Besides, if we had excess money, I'd want to use it on clothes for May and Aleah first.

The old me would never have thought like this. I could tell deep down that I had changed greatly since my time as a noble.

Part of that change had been caused by my meeting with Rae. According to her, in her book of prophecies, I was swept away by the great wave of revolution. If it weren't for her, I wouldn't be here, alive. I wouldn't have met May and Aleah, and my name would be forever besmirched as a wicked symbol of an old era. I owed the peaceful life I could now lead to Rae.

A strange thought came to mind. *What would have happened if Rae and I met under different circumstances?*

What kind of life would I have led without her, whose presence I took for granted? It was impossible to envision.

The past won't change, so what's the point of thinking about this now? I was being meaninglessly sentimental. I slipped under the bed sheets and came to yet another realization. The bed was far too wide and cold for one person. I longed for Rae's warmth.

If I called for her, she would surely come running. That was simply how she was. But I felt particularly stubborn that night. I suppressed my feelings and closed my eyes.

I better not see any strange dreams...

The Sandman visited sooner than I anticipated. I relaxed my body and soon found myself drifting into a deep slumber.

"Is something the matter, Miss Claire?"

"Hm?" When I came to, I wasn't on my bed anymore but a different place entirely. I recognized the face before me; a small, oval one with chestnut-brown hair and hazel eyes.

"Pepi?" I asked.

"Yes, Pepi Barlier. Thank goodness. I was worried something was wrong—you've had this blank look on your face for some time." By her side, a round girl with black hair and dark-brown eyes nodded in agreement. "It's quite unusual for you to be like that."

The two girls in front of me were Pepi and Loretta, my close friends from my time at the Academy, the very same who had attended my wedding. In fact, I noticed we were all wearing the Academy uniform.

"We're at...the Academy?"

"Um...maybe you aren't so well after all. Do you feel sick?" Loretta asked worriedly, but I felt perfectly fine. I appeared to be in a Royal Academy lecture hall. Looking around, I saw many familiar faces from before the revolution but not a single one I'd met since becoming a teacher.

"Loretta, what's the date?"

"Huh? What do you mean?"

"Just answer me, quickly!"

"B-by the royal calendar, it's the second day of the fourth month, 2015!"

The color drained from my face. That was the day I'd met Rae.

"Is this...a dream?" Rae *had* mentioned I might see a strange dream. In that case, this was a nightmare.

"What are you doing, Miss Claire?!" Pepi exclaimed in shock as I pinched my cheek.

"This is a dream. I have to wake up."

"What are you saying, Miss Claire?! Get a hold of yourself!" Loretta tried to pull my hand away, but I wouldn't stop. My cheek hurt from my pinching, yet no matter how much pain I felt, I wouldn't wake up.

"Why...?" I was dumbfounded.

That was when a most dreadful thought surfaced to mind: *What if that turbulent year itself was the dream?*

Could this be reality, and the days I'd spent with Rae were the dream? The word *despair* didn't even begin to describe what I felt.

"Um... You don't seem too well. Maybe you should go to the infirmary?" A female student spoke to me, noticing my sudden pallor. My head went blank the moment I looked at her.

"Rae!"

"Huh—whoa!"

I hugged her, released from the depths of my despair. Thank goodness she was here. As long as she was with me, I could bear something like being sent back in time.

"Um... Is something the matter?" Rae looked at me, bewildered, regarding me as if I were a stranger. My heart sank as I slipped back into the depths of despair.

"You're...Rae Taylor, are you not?"

"I am. And who might you be?" She regarded me with suspicion as she asked.

Did this Rae not know me?

"Excuse me! Who do you think you are to address Miss Claire so impolitely? Do you not see these curls?! Do you not see how clearly charming, albeit tiresome, she is?!"

"Yeah! I haven't seen your face before; you must be a commoner. Know your place! I especially don't approve of girls prettier than me!"

I wasn't sure if Pepi and Loretta were trying to support or embarrass me. They weren't bad girls, but they could be a bit absentminded at times, frightfully so.

"Is that right? Pardon me, then." Rae began to briskly walk away.

"W-wait!" I yelled.

"What?" she said, a little sterner this time.

"Uh, well, umm..." I floundered, not knowing what to say.

"I'll be off then, seeing as you have no business with me." Rae left for good this time, rejecting me flatly with a turn of her heels.

"Rae Taylor...isn't that the name of the top student in the incoming class?"

I already knew that.

"How awful. I bet her house is some old clothing store."

I already knew that.

"What was she thinking? She should know we nobles live in a different world."

I knew it all, more keenly than anyone else. And despite all that, Rae had found a way to surmount those obstacles and find a place in my heart.

"Excuse me, I'll be taking my leave for the day," I announced.

"Huh? Miss Claire?!"

"G-good day!"

Pepi and Loretta called after me as I ran off, but I didn't listen. I had my hands full holding back my tears.

I couldn't believe Rae could look at me with such indifference. She'd always openly displayed her affection for me, ever since the very moment we first met. Not once had she looked at me as coldly as she had just then. I'd toyed with the idea of what it might be like if I hadn't been the object of her love, but I could never have imagined it would be this painful.

Out of shock, I holed up in my bed for two days. The first time I slept, I hoped I would awake back in my world, but no such luck. Pepi and Loretta paid me a visit, worried, but I wasn't in the mood to see them. My heart hurt, the memory of Rae's cold, piercing gaze still fresh in my mind.

"Good day, Rae."

"Hm?"

On my first day back to the Academy, I worked up the courage to talk to Rae. Even if my year with her had been a dream, I could at least try to make my current reality similar to what I remembered.

"M-Miss Claire?!"

"Wh-why is Miss Claire bothering to greet an inferior like her?!"

Pepi and Loretta were spouting off something or another, but I paid them no mind. I wore my best smile and continued to talk to Rae.

"Are you not going to greet me back?" I asked.

"Forgive me... Good day, Miss Claire," she responded impassively, eyes regarding me with suspicion.

I felt hurt but continued, nonetheless. "Have you grown accustomed to the Academy? Let me know if you need any help with anything, okay?"

"Right... Thank you very much." Rae responded flatly, without so much as a smile.

The conversation petered out immediately. I never would have imagined talking to Rae when she had no interest in me would be so difficult.

"Th-the weather is nice, isn't it?"

"I guess."

"How about we go for a walk?"

"No, thank you."

She curtly denied my attempts. Each time she did so, motivation drained from my body.

"Why, you! Who do you think you are, taking that attitude when Miss Claire is so kind as to talk to you?! Although I must say, I'm absolutely delighted at how depressed she looks! Well done!"

"Yeah! You think you're special for a commoner just because you're a little smart?! You should be tutoring me!"

Pepi and Loretta snapped at Rae. Once again, it wasn't clear if they were supporting me or not. They likely thought they were helping me but were in truth hurting my chances at getting closer to Rae. Even if I couldn't have the relationship we'd had before, I wanted to be her friend, at the very least.

"Pardon my impoliteness, then. I'll be off."

But such a wish seemed impossible to realize. Rae kept me at arm's length as she returned to her seat to study.

"Honestly... This is why commoners are no good."

"Don't waste your breath on her, Miss Claire. She doesn't know her place."

Pepi and Loretta's words made my head hurt. But I didn't blame them; their values were the same as the ones I'd once held, after all. Just how hard had Rae worked to change those values of mine? Just how spoiled was I to have her?

"Hey, let's make it so she can't bear to stay at the Academy anymore. Either she leaves or I get to see Miss Claire grieve—it's a win-win for me!"

"That sounds great—let's do that, Miss Claire. After she quits the school, I'll be kind and hire her as a maid."

Pepi and Loretta grinned sinisterly. Really, what was going on with them? Regardless, they seemed to be suggesting we bully her. I was about to object when an idea came to mind.

"Yes... Why not?" I agreed, though for a different reason. You see, I'd suddenly remembered how Rae had been back when we were students—particularly how she'd taken joy in being bullied.

Wouldn't she enjoy this then? I thought. I was getting desperate.

I pushed Rae down in the hallway. "Oh, I beg your pardon. You were standing there staring into space, so I thought you were a statue."

She fell, catching herself. Previously, this was where she said: *"You have minions that could do your bidding, but you do your own dirty work and don't rely on others! I would expect nothing less from you, Miss Claire."*

I prayed in my heart she would say those words again, but—

"Is that right? I'll be more careful." That was all she said before standing up and entering the classroom.

"You did it, Miss Claire! I just love how uncouth you are, deigning to dirty your own hands!"

"That was perfect! That unhappy look on Rae's face was just... Ehe... Eh he he."

Ignorant of my true intent, Pepi and Loretta took innocent pleasure in my actions... Actually, maybe innocent wasn't the word. Regardless, I felt miserable.

But I couldn't stop here. Next time, it would work for sure.

"Ohhh, beg your pardon. I thought you were an insect," I said as I stepped on her foot.

Rae looked at me doubtfully.

Th-this feels terrible, I thought. *How could my past self bear to do such an awful thing?*

"I apologize if I've done something to displease you. Now, if you'll excuse me." She brushed me off curtly before leaving to who-knew-where.

"She's a stubborn one. Miss Claire, if you're to beat her, then tomorrow you must put an extra ringlet in your hair to increase your curl power!"

"Don't give up yet, Miss Claire. I still haven't seen Rae suffer enough. For my sake, you mustn't give up!"

Pepi and Loretta were all worked up. In contrast, I just wanted to curl up into a ball and cry.

Next time, surely.

"What's wrong with you? Is the peasant too poor to even buy textbooks?" I hid Rae's textbooks. I felt terrible. This was going too far. How could I have done such a thing?

Rae just sighed; she knew exactly what I'd done.

"It's true, my family is poor. But I've already memorized the contents of my textbooks, so you don't need to worry about me." Unfazed, she took class as she was.

"She thinks she can be cheeky just because she's a little smart?! How dare she! Doesn't she know being cheeky is Miss Claire's job?!"

"Good...good... We're making progress, eh he he he..."

Pepi and Loretta were getting progressively more twisted, while I simply wanted to stop all of this nonsense.

"Oh, you don't have a partner? That's what happens when you're a pathetic peasant." I tried excluding Rae from my assignment group. It was childish. I wished I could slap my past self for coming up with such a pathetic idea.

"It's fine. I'll partner with the teacher," Rae said as she went to explain the situation to the teacher.

"Miss Claire, please remember this is a place of learning."

"I'm sorry..."

I got scolded by the teacher. I felt so pathetic, I wanted to cry.

"Oh, dear. You're just so dirty that I thought you were mud." I doused Rae with water.

She didn't say a word, just stared daggers at me as water dripped down her face.

"Wh-what?"

Silence.

"If you have something to say, then say it!"

"Nothing," Rae said plainly before stripping off her uniform— despite the boys present in the room.

"What are you doing?!"

"Taking my clothes off so I can dry them with my water magic."

"But do you really need to undress here?!"

"Why do you care?"

Not wanting others to see Rae's bare skin, I scowled at everyone around us, causing the boys ogling her to turn away.

Good.

"Give me that." I snatched away Rae's uniform and began drying it with my fire magic.

"Trying to make yourself look good now?"

"Did you say something?"

"No, nothing."

I didn't understand the point of what I was doing anymore, but seeing as I'd come this far, I might as well see it through to the end.

I placed a flower vase atop Rae's desk. This would be the end.

"Oh ho ho ho! Serves you right!"

Personally, I thought this kind of bullying was in particular bad taste—it implied the victim's own funeral. But Rae simply looked at the vase. Thinking this would have no effect on her either, I figured I could finally bring an end to the bullying. But then—

"Unh..." Rae fell to the floor on her hands and knees and started crying. "Aaah..."

I wanted to run away.

This wasn't how it was supposed to be. I'd just wanted her to see her smile again. That was all I'd ever wanted.

But now that I looked back, I knew all I'd done was pure, unbridled bullying. To this Rae, who knew nothing of our time together, I was just some powerful noble whose eye she'd had the misfortune to catch. How painful it must have been.

I watched Rae cry and wondered how I could be so terrible.

"Unh... Unh..." I sat down next to Rae and began to cry as well. The two of us cried together, surrounded by Pepi and Loretta and all the other students who watched, confused. But I didn't care about any of them. The Rae of this world and I would never reconcile, and knowing that broke my heart.

I cried ceaselessly for some time, until—

"—aire... Miss Claire."

I awoke, someone shaking my shoulder.

I opened my eyes to a loving smile waiting for me. Her eyes weren't cold, nor distant, nor full of rejection. They simply held sincere love—for me.

I had returned.

"Are you okay, Miss Claire? You sounded like you were having a nightma—oh?"

Without waiting for her to finish talking, I hugged her tight, burrowing my face into her chest and crying my heart out.

"Thank goodness... Thank goodness..."

Our year together hadn't been a dream. Rae's cold eyes, which had turned on me—they weren't real.

Overwhelmed with relief, I cried on her without a care—it didn't matter if it was embarrassing. Rae said nothing and just stroked my back.

"I'm sorry," I sniffed once I'd calmed down a bit.

"Not at all. Did you have a nightmare?" Rae wore a warm and reassuring smile as she kissed me on the cheek.

Yes...

This was how Rae should be.

My beloved Rae.

"I was scared... So scared... I've never had a dream so frightening."

"That bad? Do you mind telling me what your dream was about?"

I told Rae what had happened, everything from how I'd returned to the day we met, to how I met a Rae who didn't know me and coldly rejected me, to how my attempts to elicit her affection backfired, and finally, how we cried together.

"That must have been terrifying." Rae spoke tenderly as she wrapped her arms around me again, hugging me tight as if to reassure me this was reality, here and now.

"It was, terribly so. I never want to have a dream like that again." I wiped the tears from my eyes.

"It's probably my fault. I shouldn't have said those weird things before bed. I'm sorry, Miss Claire."

"Not at all. I've learned an important lesson from this dream. You are irreplaceable to me." I wasn't about to cling to her and ask her to pamper me, but life without Rae was impossible to imagine. Rae was just that vital to my life.

"It's an honor. I feel a little embarrassed you'd go that far...and a little guilty."

"Guilty?"

"Nothing, just thinking to myself. Shall we get up? I'll get breakfast, so can you go wake May and Aleah up?"

"Of course."

Everything was okay now. I was where I truly belonged. This world was my reality, and while I had endured its challenges in the past, I was sure today would be the start of many peaceful days to come. Now it was time to wake up my beloved twin daughters.

"By the way, Rae..."

"Yes, Miss Claire?"

"Did *you* have any weird dreams last night?" I asked only in passing curiosity. No real motives laid behind my question—yet her answer surprised me all the same.

"Oh, I suppose I did have a dream."

"Oh, really? What happened in it?"

"Well... I was back at the day we first met. I pretended to be a meek and quiet girl, and that somehow made Miss Claire cry."

Interesting. That was quite a strange dream, too... Hmm?

Wait a minute.

"Sit down, Rae."

"Huh? But I need to get breakfast—"

"Do I need to say it twice?"

"No, ma'am."

What followed was a scolding that lasted well over an hour. Goodness! What was with this girl?

And yet, despite her flaws, I really did love her for who she was. Truly, from the bottom of my heart.

But she could still be really vexing at times!

Afterword

THANK YOU SO MUCH for purchasing the third volume of *I'm in Love with the Villainess*.

I'm the author, Inori. I ended the last afterword sounding uncertain about whether there'd be another book, but here we are—Volume 3. This book contains Chapters 9 through 11, marking the beginning of Act 2 of the story, as well as six bonus stories and an end-of-volume special. Chronologically, the stories take place as follows:

Vol. 2, Final Chapter: "Revolution"

Vol. 3, Bonus Story 1: "Things Gained, Things Lost"

Vol. 2, Bonus Chapter: "Curses and Good Luck Charms"

Vol. 3, Bonus Story 2: "Wedding"

Vol. 2: "Epilogue" (Volume 2)

Vol. 3, Bonus Story 3: "Sweet, Sweet Alcohol"

Vol. 3, Bonus Story 6: "Your Pain Is Not Punishment"

Vol. 3, Bonus Chapter: "The Lady Who Leapt Through Time"

Vol. 3, Bonus Story 4: "Birthdays"

Vol. 3, Bonus Story 5: "Holy Night Festival"

Vol. 3, Chapters 9–11

In all, there was a bit less content than the second volume, but I hope you enjoyed it nonetheless.

I'm honored to announce that the Japanese second volume made it to second place on the Amazon Bestseller rankings. There's even a Korean translation on sale now and an English translation scheduled for November. This was all made possible by you, my readers, who've supported me all this way. If you liked the third volume, please recommend it to your friends as well. (Pretty please!)

This book marks the beginning of Act 2 of *I'm in Love with the Villainess*. There will be more fantasy elements in Act 2, so look forward to that. Rae and Claire will also have to experience many more bitter moments, so I hope you'll be there to support them through it. At the time of writing this afterword, Chapter 14—the middle of Act 2—will already be posted on the *Let's Be Novelists* website. Please look forward to the series as things start to ramp up.

A manga adaptation of *I'm in Love with the Villainess* has been confirmed and will run in Ichijinsha's *Comic Yuri Hime* magazine. Maybe some readers have seen it already? The artist will be AONOSHIMO, known for their work on *Welcome to Japan, Miss Elf!* (HJ Comics) and *Fate/Grand Order: Medb, Medb, Medb!* (Kadokawa Comics Ace). AONOSHIMO's depictions of Rae, Claire, and the rest all look *amaaaazing*. Of course, Hanagata's illustrations since the first volume have been splendid as well, but I think Aonoesu's manga is not one to miss. On the off chance the manga doesn't do well, it'll one hundred percent be the fault of the original author, me. That's how good AONOSHIMO's manga is. I hope you'll give the manga a read as well.

All right, time for a probably-not-so-interesting status update. I'm living in extreme poverty—per usual—but thanks to all those who've purchased *I'm in Love with the Villainess* and subscribed to my PixivFANBOX, I've become able to upgrade my protein source from breast meat to the occasional thigh meat as well. I'd literally be nothing if not for my readers' kindness. My PixivFANBOX has early releases of the web novel, a special adult-only chapter, and more, so please consider supporting me and my food situation there.

And lastly, I'd like to make some acknowledgments.

Nakamura of the GL Bunko editorial department, thank you for listening to my selfishness and allowing me to write a continuation. I'm sure I'll be relying on you again throughout Act 2 and hope to have your support.

Hanagata, I can't thank you enough for all the illustrations you made for this book. The upcoming manga adaptation wouldn't have been possible without your character designs either.

And to my partner, Aki, who is the spitting image of Rae: I did it! Volume 3 is finished. While neither of us are drinkers, I think it's only appropriate we go celebrate with a nonalcoholic cocktail again when the book is out.

And to all the readers who picked up this book, I offer you deepest of deep gratitude. Thank you so much.

The manuscript for the next volume is almost finished, so let's meet again in the fourth volume of *I'm in Love with the Villainess*. Let's hope it doesn't get axed!

With that, I bid you all a good day.

—INORI, AUGUST 4, 2020

TWITTER:

https://twitter.com/inori_narou

PIXIVFANBOX:

https://www.pixiv.net/fanbox/creator/32244225